Dying to Sell

Dying to Sell

Maggie Sefton

Five Star • Waterville, Maine

This novel is a work of fiction. Names, characters, places and incidents are either the product of the author's imagination, or, if real, used fictitiously.

No part of this book may be reproduced or transmitted in any form or by any electronic or mechanical means, including photocopying, recording or by any information storage and retrieval system, without the express written permission of the publisher, except where permitted by law.

First Edition
First Printing: October 2005

Published in 2005 in conjunction with Tekno Books and Ed Gorman.

Set in 11 pt. Plantin by Liana M. Walker.

Printed in the United States on permanent paper.

Library of Congress Cataloging-in-Publication Data

Sefton, Maggie.
    Dying to sell / by Maggie Sefton.—1st ed.
        p. cm.
    ISBN 1-59414-310-2 (hc : alk. paper)
    1. Women real estate agents—Fiction. 2. Lawyers—
Crimes against—Fiction. 3. Real estate development—
Fiction. 4. Divorced women—Fiction. 5. Colorado—Fiction.
I. Title.
PS3619.E37D95 2005
813'.6—dc22   2005015988

Dying to Sell

Acknowledgements

I wish to thank all of the real estate professionals in Northern Colorado who helped me over the years—agents, brokers, appraisers, consultants, lawyers, teachers, and countless others. Their professional expertise and sense of humor enabled me to get my bearings in this fascinating-yet-frustrating business.

Most especially, I want to thank all of the brokers and agents of *Keller Williams Realty* in Colorado who took me under their collective wings as a rookie real estate agent and gave me a safe place to learn.

Chapter One

Divorce is not a pleasant experience. Psychologists rate it right up there on the stress scale, next to the death of a spouse. Also right up there is selling a home. Unfortunately for some people, the two experiences are often combined—the breakup of a marriage and the subsequent sale of the family home. That's where I come in. As a real estate broker, I sell the houses of feuding husbands and wives. Not that they're my only clients. Oh, no. My favorites are the fresh-faced young couples just starting out with their first home. They sort of renew my faith in marriage. They also provide a balance to negotiating the minefields of broken relationships.

Having survived a fractured relationship that ended in divorce, I can sympathize with these folks. But that doesn't make it easier. I usually enter their lives at the worst possible time—dividing up the assets. By then, lawyers have been consulted, lines drawn, and an adversarial climate firmly entrenched. My job? To tiptoe around all that barbed wire of mutual distrust and get signatures on contracts. Lots of contracts. Since I practice in Colorado, a leader in consumer protection, there are contracts for everything. The public is protected, by damn, but we're up to our necks in paper.

This time, my job was harder than usual. The divorcing couple, and my clients, were old friends of mine. Our kids had grown up together, we'd shared vacations, partied together, confided in each other—and now, after thirty years, their marriage was ending. I certainly wasn't about to point a finger, having ended my own long marriage two years before. Still, Amanda and Mark Schuster had been the Lucy and Desi for many of our friends. Despite all the loud arguments, the shouting and accusations, most of us figured if *they* could stay together, others could. But just like the originals, it was not to be.

I waited for Mark to sign the listing contract, not wanting to interrupt his lawyer-focused perusal of the document. At fifty-three, there was only a sprinkling of silver in his hair, just along the temples. Slim, fit, with a remnant of summer's tan, Mark Schuster was still a very handsome man, and he knew it. But more than that, he had a certain magnetism about him. People were attracted to him. Unfortunately for his marriage, that was the quality which had caused the most trouble with his volatile and jealous wife. Over the years, I'd listened to countless diatribes from a furious Amanda whenever she discovered a new indiscretion. Listened to what she was going to tell him, what she was going to do. And always in the end, she did nothing, except scream at him in helpless fury. She stayed.

Now, their tempestuous marriage was finally over. I never thought Mark would actually leave his still-beautiful and elegant wife, his showpiece for so long. And after all those affairs, the countless women—rich and gorgeous, professional and not—he leaves for an Ally McBeal look-alike from Denver. Go figure.

Mark dutifully initialed each page and signed, adding, "I want this in the multi-list right away, Kate. I'd like to have a buyer before I move to Denver."

"It'll go in today. Don't worry. Buyers are clamoring for homes in this area of Fort Collins. Custom-built with spectacular views. We won't have a problem, Mark," I assured him while I placed another sheaf of papers on his polished walnut desk. Glancing out the library window, I drank in the gorgeous view of the foothills. A sliver of distant Rocky Mountain peaks jutted from behind the lower hills, awaiting the first snowfall of winter to set them shimmering. I used to have a view like that.

Mark scowled at the papers. "How much more, Kate? I've got a conference call in five minutes."

"Property disclosure and other fun stuff. You can fill it out, and I'll pick it up later. Will you be here or at the office?"

He bent his wrist and checked a watch whose price would have paid my mortgage for several months. "After this call, I'll be at the office for the rest of this morning; then I'll be back here after lunch. I have to go through the upstairs closets." He feigned a shudder.

"Well, better you than me," I said, and shoved the listing contract in my briefcase. "I'll go over now and get Amanda's signature; then I've got a showing. I'll be back in the late afternoon, okay?" I started backing toward the doorway, recognizing Mark's slight but distinct dismissal signals.

"That'll be fine," Mark said as he opened a file folder beside his elbow and slipped on his reading glasses. Glancing up over the rims, he added, "And Kate, I want you to entertain all offers, understand?"

I paused, half-in and half-out the library door, while I chose my words. "I understand, Mark. But I have to consult Amanda, as well."

"Amanda will want top dollar, you know that. And it's

September. Things might slow down, and I don't *want* to be slowed down, Kate."

Seeing his slight scowl, I decided to opt for a lighter tone. Placing my hand over my heart, I backed out of the room and said solemnly, "Never fear. I will always do as my principals direct. The weight of thousands of years of English Common Law leaves me no choice."

Mark gave a derisive snort. "God, Kate, you're the only real estate agent I know who quotes Common Law. Get out of here and leave me alone." He crumbled a piece of paper and tossed it my way.

"I live to serve," I said with a deep bow, then headed for the front door before Mark could throw anything heavier.

"Bastard," Amanda swore under her breath as she scrawled her name in bold strokes across the bottom of the listing contract.

I had just told her of Mark's instructions to entertain all offers. "He said you'd want top dollar."

"You're damn right I do," she snapped. "I have to get as much as I can. He knows that, damn him." The familiar hate-filled expression twisted Amanda's lovely features into an ugly mask.

It was awful to watch what had happened to her these last six months. My beautiful, light-hearted friend with the ringing laugh had turned into a scowling shrew. Each week, her lawyer, Jonathan Bassett, brought another discovery of assets that Mark had tried to hide. Bank accounts in different countries, commodities, precious metals stashed away. Some, Bassett said, could be frozen. Others were tied up in legal knots. And with each discovery, Amanda's fury grew. She smoldered with resentment. Not only because of the money Mark was trying to hide from her, but also because he left her for a younger woman. That had been her oldest and deepest fear.

"You know I'll do my very best to satisfy both of you," I said as I retrieved the contract. "And frankly, I don't think there'll be a problem. That house will sell in a matter of days and for a good price. So, you'll both be happy." I flashed her a bright smile.

She didn't respond. "It better. He's screwed me with those foreign accounts, but I'll be damned if he'll screw me on the house." She tossed a letter across the coffee table. "Read that. It's from Jonathan. He's found another investment account in that German bank."

I picked up the letter and read while Amanda paced back and forth through her townhouse living room, cursing none-too-softly. Head bent forward, wealth of auburn hair surrounding her face, she stalked the spacious living room like a caged jungle cat.

While it wasn't as luxurious as her gorgeous home south of town, at 2,000 square feet, the townhouse was hardly shabby and afforded a beautiful view of the foothills. Once she discovered that Mark had brought his Denver girlfriend to their home while she was out of town, Amanda refused to set foot in the house again. Instead, she leased the most expensive townhouse she could find facing the mountains and went on a gigantic furniture-shopping spree. Since Amanda had expensive tastes, the final bill must have been astronomical. I didn't even want to know.

"Listen," I said in an attempt to soothe, "Jonathan is the best divorce lawyer in town. He'll make sure you get every penny that's yours. Now, stop tying yourself in knots. I hate to see you like this."

Amanda sent me a sharp look. "Don't start, Kate. You don't know what I'm going through. Your divorce was different. Andy wasn't trying to cheat you. And he didn't leave you for another woman, either. You left him."

She had me there. My divorce may have been tense, but it was quiet. No offshore accounts. No cheating. No hidden assets. It was kind of sad, really. We simply buried the body. The marriage had died years ago.

"Okay, okay," I said with a sigh. "You got me. I don't understand what you're going through. But I do care about you and what all this resentment is doing to you. You're consumed with it, and it's consuming *you*."

Amanda took a few more anxious turns around the marble coffee table and the three-sided glass fireplace, then finally sank into an armchair beside the matching sofa. I slid my hand over the creamy leather, soft as butter, and waited for her to speak. I could tell she'd calmed down.

"I wish I didn't hate him, Kate. But, so help me, I do. After all these years, how could he leave me for some little tart? Damn him! I'll bet she won't put up with his screwing around."

Not wanting to go down that path again, I kept quiet and let Amanda fume, while I traced small designs in the forgiving leather. Finally, the pauses between eruptions lengthened and I sensed it was safe to venture to neutral ground.

"Next week I'd like to take you to see some of those new homes they're building just north of Fort Collins. All custom designed. The views of the lake and foothills are fabulous. Each house is set on the hillside. Every style imaginable so far. You'll love some of the wraparound decks—"

"Don't you miss it, Kate? Those views, the house, all that? Be honest." Amanda peered at me skeptically, but at least the anger was gone.

I let out a sigh and sank back into the leather's voluptuous embrace. "No, actually, I really don't. It was wonderful living out there, and I loved it. I truly did. Especially sitting on the deck at sunset, watching the sky change color behind the mountains." I deliberately let myself remember the picture framed in my mind.

"And you say you don't miss it," Amanda said with an undisguised smirk. "Liar."

"I know you won't believe me, but I really don't. I had it once. I enjoyed it. And now I have a new home. It's smaller, of course, but then so is my mortgage," I said with an evil grin. "I live in a great neighborhood, with families and kids and students and old people. And we actually care about each other. We watch over each other's homes when someone's on vacation."

"How refreshing."

"Well, it is. In my old neighborhood, we never saw each other much, except to wave hello. We were all hermetically sealed in our luxurious homes."

"I'll stay sealed, if you don't mind." She reached across the table for her cigarettes and lit one, then rose to resume her pacing.

Amanda's fashionable black silk pants and ivory blouse accentuated her tall, slender figure. Keeping her weight in check had been a lifetime struggle for Amanda, who loved to eat, but loved even more watching men's heads turn when she entered a room. She still could catch a man's eye, and that was worth living on tiny portions, handfuls of vitamins, and two-hour daily workouts at the gym. Some of us practiced less extreme vigilance. I figured whatever was still there after my daily 6:00 a.m. hour-long workout could stay.

I glanced at my watch and reluctantly left the leather. "I have to go, Amanda. Got to check the multi-list before I take a young couple out this afternoon." I scooped up the signed contract, stuffed it in my briefcase, and headed toward the door, careful to skirt the gorgeous Oriental rug that covered the oaken floor. Hated to step on art. It just wasn't right.

Amanda ran her hand through her layered auburn curls. "I'll let you know when I feel like looking at those homes, Kate. Jonathan and I are meeting again this week. He should have a good idea of where all the accounts are hidden by then. We have to discuss our strategy."

Mention of hidden accounts was my cue to leave. "Okay, let me know," I said as I opened the door, ready to escape before another eruption. I almost made it.

Amanda's voice hardened. "I told Jonathan I'd be glad to handle it for him. I'll just go over there and tell the bastard to hand over the accounts or I'll rip his throat out."

I murmured a goodbye and silently closed the door as I hurried down the steps. Despite the balmy fall temperatures, I felt a distinct shiver ripple over me.

Chapter Two

I clicked the computer mouse. The printer hummed, then printed out my selections. Pages drifted into the tray, complete with color pictures and descriptions of each property. Four ought to be enough for this afternoon, I decided, and another four if they're super-eager.

A cold nose touched my ankle as I exited the program back to desktop icons. "Hey, Sam, how're ya doing, guy?" I rubbed the smooth, black dog head that appeared from under the desk in my snug little downstairs study. Sam, my Lab/Rottie mix, liked to keep me company whenever I was on the computer. He'd lie down beside one of the bookcases that lined the walls, gnaw an old bone for a few minutes, then drift off into an old dog's slumber.

"C'mon, boy, you've got to go outside. I have to go back to work," I said, and headed up the stairs. Sam bolted past me like always. Cataracts might be clouding his vision and winter's cold harder on him than before, but there was still a lot of puppy left in Sam. He was also company and kept me from coming home to an empty house at night.

After all those years of raising a family and lots of noise, I was surprised how quickly I adjusted to living alone. I liked it.

I soon learned that being alone wasn't the same thing as being lonely.

"Okay, big guy. Go chase that sassy squirrel," I teased, and slid open the patio door. Sam raced out and headed for the maple tree in the corner of my small back yard, which was surrounded on all sides by thick bushes, lilacs, and tall maples. Sam put both paws on the tree trunk and stared above, obviously looking for the squirrel that lived to torment him, as well as the neighbor's dog.

"Forget it, Sam. He's faster than you'll ever be, and remember, he just pretends to fall," I said, then left to meet my young clients. First-time home buyers, married only a couple of years and expecting their first child in a few months. God bless 'em.

The petite young woman circled the upstairs bedroom slowly. Her razor-cut red hair brushed back and forth across her cheeks as she scanned the room. Barely showing her pregnancy at five months, she paused and fingered the lacy window curtain. Her husband, tall and lean with a runner's build, peered up at the ceiling. "How old is this house again?" he asked.

"Twenty-four years. It was built in nineteen eighty, when the subdivision was started," I replied from my spot in the doorway, out of their way.

That was my job. To stay out of the buyers' way. Let them look at each house and form their own opinions—without a running stream of real estate commentary. Stay out of their way, answer questions when asked, do not distract their attention with real estate agent-speak, and—most important of all—listen. Listen and watch for buying signals. Most of the time they were verbal. Other times, body language indicated this house was different. *This* house, they could picture themselves living in.

Little comments, spoken so softly you had to be quiet to hear: "We could put the headboard against this wall. That way the dresser would fit." Or, simply lingering a while in certain rooms, eyes mentally rearranging furniture. *Their* furniture.

The mistake most real estate agents made when showing buyers a home was exactly that: showing the home, as if people didn't have eyes of their own. It was my experience that most buyers knew within a few seconds from opening the front door if the house was a possibility or not. No amount of babbling about room sizes and new furnaces could change their immediate first impression. It was sort of like dating. You knew within the first few moments whether the evening would be enjoyable or excruciating.

Of course, I'm not one of the real estate superstars in our community, who've been selling homes for years and make megabucks. I'm sure they see their jobs differently. But this is my second career, and one which I'm entering at what the French fondly refer to as *une certaine age*. So, I feel that I'm entitled to look at the business with fresh eyes and do things my way. The megabucks guys and gals can continue cutting their swath. I'll just stay on my own little path.

"Let's go see the kitchen again," the wife said, and I stepped away from the door. "Again." A signal word. Good thing, because this was the eighth house we'd seen this afternoon. Talk about supercharged. These folks wasted no time. Some houses we were in and out in less than five minutes. Others took more time. But none of them had held their mutual attention this long.

I followed behind them and listened, hoping for the magic words: "We'd like to make an offer on this one."

The young couple paused in the midst of the dining area

and watched the late afternoon sunlight slant through the patio door. Their gazes locked for a second, then the husband turned toward me. "We like this one best of all. But, we'd like to think about it some more. We don't want to rush."

"Not a problem," I replied, not totally surprised. It was a natural response, and I don't believe in pushing. "You've seen a lot today. You need time to sort through it all. Give me a call tomorrow and let me know what you're thinking. If you want to make an offer, just let me know, and I'll write it up."

Looking down and shuffling his feet a bit, the young man asked, "If we waited till the weekend, do you think the house will still be available?"

"I really wish I could tell you yes, but there are no guarantees. The house has been on the market fourteen days. It shows well. And there are still buyers out there trying to find something they can move into before the holidays." I watched anxiety claim their faces, so I added, "But you need to do what's right for you. If you need more time to think about it, go ahead. But I wouldn't be doing my job, if I let you think you have forever. Most of the houses we saw today will be gone in the next two weeks." There. I'd done my job. Now, the choice was theirs.

They glanced at each other and nodded. "Okay," they promised and headed for the door.

Glancing at my watch, I hoped I'd still catch Mark at home. He probably went out to eat each evening. His kitchen never looked used.

The sun hovered right above the mountaintop, blinding in its brilliance. Living a mile up in altitude made you more aware of the sun. You were closer. You tanned faster, and driving westward in the late afternoon could be hazardous. I shaded my eyes as I walked up the curving sidewalk to the

Schusters' multi-level front porch.

Amanda had used a local landscape architect to design all the plantings several years ago, when they built the house. Now, the bushes were lush and more vibrant, having passed through the adolescent growth stage.

I rang the door chimes and waited. Nothing. I rang them again. Still no answer from inside. *Strange,* I thought, glancing toward Mark's black Mercedes parked in the driveway.

Deciding Mark might still be upstairs going through closets, I dug into my briefcase for my electronic keypad. All the listed houses in Fort Collins were on electronic lock boxes. More expensive, but they provided the seller with better security than the old mechanical combination locks. I inserted the keypad into the gray, rectangular box dangling from the front door handle, punched in my code, then pressed a key-shaped button. A few seconds later, a familiar metallic rattle sounded. The key container dropped from inside the lock box. I retrieved the key, then opened the heavy door, its center a beautiful oval of etched and beveled glass.

Stepping into the open foyer, I glanced about the sunken great room, which commanded one whole side of the house. The sun's last rays danced above in the vaulted ceilings, red and orange beams bouncing off glass and mirrors, then downward to warm, polished, oak floors that stretched forever.

"Mark?" I called as I closed the door. "Mark, it's Kate. I've come to pick up the last of the paperwork."

No response. I walked over to the stairway and called again. "Mark! It's Kate. Are you up there?"

No answer. Maybe he was in the shower. If so, I wasn't about to go upstairs and surprise him. I would wait.

On the far side of the great room, I saw the open door to

Mark's library. Maybe he had left the papers on his desk. If so, then I could grab them and go home. No need to wait around for Mark to finish his shower—or whatever. The thought that Mark might be indulging in one last local dalliance had crossed my mind. I definitely didn't want to interrupt that.

Heading for the library, I paused at the door and peered inside. To my surprise, there was Mark sitting behind the desk, his leather chair turned sideways, its back to the door.

I laughed as I entered the room. "Mark, are you getting deaf in your old age? I've been calling you? Didn't you hear me?"

He didn't respond. The chair stayed turned away from me. A prickle ran up my spine. "Mark? Is there something wrong?"

No response. More than a prickle ran over me this time. Something was definitely wrong. I slowly edged around the desk, until I could see Mark seated in the chair; then I stopped—and stared.

Mark had been stabbed. A slender, gold letter-opener jutted out of his throat. Blood soaked his clothes, the chair, and the expensive Oriental carpet beneath his feet.

The briefcase dropped from my hand, and I backed away in horror.

Chapter Three

"Would you like some water, Ms. Doyle?" the earnest young police officer asked.

I shook my head. I didn't feel like swallowing anything for quite a while. The sight in the Schusters' library was still with me. And the smell. The sickly-sweet smell of blood.

"No, thanks, Officer Sanchez. I'll just sit here until Detective Levitz wants me."

Sanchez nodded solicitously and backed away, giving me space which I appreciated. I glanced across the great room toward the library door. Investigators kept coming and going from the once elegantly appointed room. My brother-in-law, Detective Bill Levitz, was in charge of the investigation. Not because he was related—by marriage to my sister, who died two years ago—but because he was Chief of Detectives for the Fort Collins investigative unit. This was his show.

I watched him directing his men, who were wearing surgical gloves. Another flash went off inside the library. So many pictures. How could people stare at pictures like that for a living? I shuddered. I just hoped I'd be able to forget the images.

Reaching across the end table, I flipped on a table lamp. It was long past dusk, and the great room, where I sat alone, felt chill as well as dark. I needed light. Lots of it. Jumping up from the sofa, I proceeded to turn on every light in the entire room, even the spotlights for the artwork. Somehow I felt better. Bill approached just as I sat down again.

"So, Kate," his deep voice rumbled, familiar and reassuring. "I've read Sanchez's notes, but what do you say we go over all this again. Start at the beginning." He sank into an adjoining sofa.

I stared at my big, shambling brother-in-law, with unkempt, gray hair, suit always wrinkled, tie barely covering a protruding belly—despite my sister's years of trying to help him diet. Perhaps his new wife would be successful.

I exhaled a sigh. "Whatever you say, Bill. I saw Mark this morning, when I brought him the listing contract to sign. He didn't have time to sign the rest of the documents then, because he had a conference call. So I left them and told him I'd stop by late this afternoon and pick them up."

"What time was that?"

"About nine or so. I wasn't here long. I was gone before ten and drove straight to Amanda's."

"Amanda Schuster, his wife. Who's divorcing him, right?" Bill didn't look up, just kept scribbling in his little spiral notepad. It was small, the size that would fit in a shirt pocket. For years, I remember seeing that notepad in Bill's shirt pocket. He always put it carefully on his desk every night when he'd come home. A poignant memory of happier times when my sister was alive flashed through my mind, and I forced it away. Had to stay focused on what Bill was asking.

"Yes, that's right. Amanda lives in the west part of town now. I went there, got her to sign the contract, then left to go home. I had some work on the computer."

"Did she sign the contract willingly?"

"Of course. She wants the house to sell. They're dividing up the assets . . ." I paused. "*Were* dividing up the assets."

Bill glanced at me then around the room, taking in all the tasteful display. "Lots of assets, from what I can see," he observed, a shaggy, gray eyebrow arching.

"This is only what you can see. There were lots of assets squirreled away. Cash, stocks. You name it."

"Where'd you learn that, Kate? You been talking to their lawyer?" That eyebrow arched again, in what I recognized as his skeptical observation. One raise, curiosity. Two raises, skepticism.

I hesitated for a moment. "From Amanda. She's been giving me daily updates. This divorce has really hit her hard, Bill."

"I can imagine," he said, surveying the room again. "Giving all this up would be hard."

A prickle ran up my neck. Something in Bill's tone concerned me.

He scribbled, then eyed me again. "Okay. Tell me what you did when you left your home and came here."

"Well, I didn't come directly here. I showed a young couple several houses. That occupied the entire afternoon. It was after four-thirty when I got here."

"So tell me everything you did. Don't leave out any detail. It might be important."

I took a deep breath. "I parked my car out front and walked up to the house. I noticed Mark's Mercedes in the driveway, so I knew he was home. That's why I was surprised when I rang the chimes and there was no answer."

"What'd you do?"

"I let myself in with the keypad and lock box."

"Then what?"

"I called out his name several times as I walked around the

foyer. I even called up the stairs. I . . . I didn't want to go up-stairs, in case he was showering. So, I went to the library, thinking he might have left the papers there, and I could just take them and not disturb him. In case he was . . . uh, show-ering. You know." I glanced away.

"Or otherwise involved, right?" Bill shot me a knowing look. "It's no secret, Kate. He's been tomcatting around town for years. For all you knew, he might have had someone upstairs."

"The thought did cross my mind."

"So, you went to the library and what?"

"I glanced inside first, and saw him sitting in his chair be-hind the desk. Well, at least I assumed it was him. The chair was turned away from the door. But I saw the back of his head."

"And?"

I took another deep breath. I really didn't want to picture this again. "I called out his name and asked him why he didn't answer. And when he didn't answer again, I got scared."

"Scared?"

"I don't know, Bill. I felt a chill go over me, or something. I can't remember. But I knew I had to find out why he wasn't answering me. So, I walked around the desk . . . and . . ." I closed my eyes. "That's when I saw him. Sitting there in his chair with . . . with that knife-thing sticking out of his throat." I shuddered involuntarily. "Good Lord, Bill. It was awful. I've never seen anything like that before. And I hope I never do again."

"That's okay, Kate. It's a normal response to seeing a murder victim. Not a pretty sight. I wish you hadn't been the one to find him."

"So do I."

Bill tapped the end of his pen against the notepad. "That's

when you called nine-one-one?"

"Yes. I flew out of that room. Then I sat here and waited for you."

He sank a little lower into the soft sofa cushions. "So, this has been a pretty bitter divorce, hasn't it?"

I hesitated, feeling disloyal somehow to Amanda. "Yes, it has been."

The tapping began again. "Amanda Schuster was pretty angry, you think?"

Narrowing my gaze, I peered at my brother-in-law. "What are you getting at, Bill? You can't seriously suspect Amanda of committing murder, can you?"

"I can't rule out any possibility, Kate. You know that." He flipped the notepad shut with one movement, then shoved it in his shirt pocket. "We have to notify her. Do you think she'll be home now?"

I glanced at my watch: 7:00 p.m. "Probably. Should I go over there with you?"

"Naw. That's not necessary. Besides, I want you to go to your office with Sanchez and give him copies of all the contracts Mark and Amanda Schuster signed with you. And any other documents you may have relating to this sale. Everything. Okay?" Slowly, he pulled himself out of the soft sofa.

I nodded, then rose and grabbed my briefcase, eager to be allowed to leave this scene of death.

Bill motioned Sanchez over and spoke, while I drifted toward the front door, anxious. Men were still milling around inside the library. What more could they find?

"Okay, Kate, go on. Sanchez will follow you there." Bill ran his hand through his already-mussed hair. "Afterwards, he'll escort you home, if you want."

"That won't be necessary, but thanks anyway."

Sanchez held the door open and I headed for it, then

paused. Turning back to Bill I called, "Go easy on Amanda, Bill. She's been through a lot already, and this will hit her pretty hard."

Both brows shot up this time. "Not as hard as Schuster," he said dryly.

Luckily there were others still working, so I didn't have to unlock a darkened office. Shamrock Realty's modest building was located in a central area of Fort Collins, right on the main north-south thoroughfare, College Avenue, the same street that ran past the university a few blocks north.

Waving at an associate who was bent over his computer, I hastened to my office. Sanchez followed right behind. I closed the door; otherwise someone might stroll by and notice a uniformed officer. I did not feel like making explanations tonight. I simply wanted to go home and unwind, Sam at my feet.

"Sit down, Officer Sanchez; it'll only take a minute to make copies of those files for you." I tossed my purse and briefcase on the paper-strewn desk. As I plopped in my chair, I noticed the blinking red light on my phone. Messages. Out of habit, I punched the button and pushed speakerphone, so I could listen while I searched the files. "Mind if I check my messages while I'm getting this?" I glanced up at Sanchez.

"No, ma'am. Not at all," he said as he lowered himself to a nearby cushioned chair.

The messages whirred backwards and began to recite. First, the young couple from that afternoon. They'd already thought about it enough. Please come over tomorrow and write the offer on the last house they saw. I felt a little flutter of pleasure waking up inside. Life's routines were a salvation.

Another message was a cancellation of a broker's appointment, and a change of time for another. I made notes in my

Day-Timer, then retrieved the Schuster file from my desk drawer. I was about to head for the copier, when Amanda Schuster's voice came on the phone—tight and full of fury. The sound of it stopped me cold.

"Kate? This is Amanda. You'll never believe what the bastard has done now. He's sold the house in Rist Canyon. He waited until we closed it up, then he put it on the market without telling me. Damn his soul to hell! He knew how much I loved that place. It was my sanctuary." Her voice sank to a harsh whisper. "He's stolen everything from me, Kate. I can't take any more of it. I didn't think I could get any angrier, but I'm so mad now I could kill the son-of-a-bitch!"

The abrupt sound of the phone being slammed down ended the message. I stood frozen on the spot.

Officer Sanchez slowly rose from the chair and drew closer. "Ma'am, was that message from Mrs. Schuster? Mrs. Amanda Schuster?" He peered at me expectantly.

I swallowed to make sure I could speak. "Yes," I whispered. "Yes, it was." And I sank back into my chair. Now I really felt sick to my stomach.

Chapter Four

Hiding in my littered little office, I leaned over the computer keyboard and pretended to be engrossed in what appeared on the screen. The truth was, I had stared at the same property description for ten minutes. I'd even resorted to turning off the continual-motion screensaver—a breathtaking view of sparkling glaciers and mountain lakes—otherwise, anyone who passed my office door would know I was watching test patterns. I wanted to appear busy. Perhaps that would dissuade more sympathetic comments and the myriad questions.

My associates and fellow real estate agents at Shamrock Realty had been shocked that I'd walked in on a murder scene. Suicides were one thing, but murder? They all offered their sympathies, along with their questions. People couldn't help it. They were curious. Murder was not a common occurrence in Fort Collins. Sixty miles north of Denver, we had a gorgeous climate that spoiled us rotten, recreational opportunities for the rugged or the retired, more cultural amenities than we could ever take advantage of, and few of the big city problems. Folks just didn't go around stabbing each other in the throat.

I rubbed between my eyes, trying to make the memory go away. A woman's voice interrupted. "Why don't you go home, Kate. You look tired."

Spinning my chair around, I watched Veronica Kelly settle into the comfy client chair before my desk. Slender, sixtyish, and silver-haired, Ronnie started Shamrock Realty twenty-five years ago, right before the recession hit Colorado. Somehow, she had survived while other agencies, far larger and richer, had gone under. She was my mentor and could be counted on for calm, considered advice, no matter what the problem. And in real estate, there always seemed to be a problem. We regularly put out fires. Ronnie, as owner and managing broker, was the voice of experience. She'd seen everything, and she was tough as nails.

I leaned back in my chair and exhaled a deep breath. "I can't, Ronnie. I have to write an offer for the Kerchoffs, then take it over to the other agent. After that, I had planned to go to Amanda's."

Ronnie peered at me. "Have you heard from Amanda yet?"

"No, not yet. She's probably still in shock."

"You will. Especially since you were the one to find Mark. She's going to want you to tell her all about it. I don't care if they were divorcing, she's his wife."

"I know. I'm dreading her call." Meeting Ronnie's direct, blue gaze, I said, "She still loves him . . . or loved him. You know that, don't you? Despite everything, Amanda never stopped loving Mark. That's why she stayed all those years."

Ronnie pursed her lips and tapped a sculptured nail against the chair arm. "That may be, Kate. But the message she left on your voice-mail was damning. The police don't have the benefit of years of friendship to color their perception of Amanda's behavior. You said yourself that Bill was acting suspicious, even before he knew about the message."

I sank my elbows on the desk and rubbed my temples. "I know, I know. I can't believe she left that message. It's one thing to say in private, but—"

"But that's Amanda. Tempestuous, headstrong, and willful. She's always been that way, Kate. Like it or not, she's going to be Murder Suspect Number One."

"I don't even want to think—"

"Well, well, well! If it isn't Nancy Drew," an unwelcome voice sounded at the doorway.

I shut my eyes, not wanting to look. The most obnoxious real estate agent in all of Northern Colorado had suddenly appeared in my doorway. I recognized the voice from his annoying television commercials. At least his bus stop signs were silent. Just Larry Banks' blinding capped-tooth smile grinning out at you. And I thought the day had started off badly.

"What brings you over to our shop, Larry?" Ronnie asked, slanting a smile at the tall, impeccably-tailored man leaning against the doorframe. "What deal are you working?"

"I've got a buyer for Diane's Sunstone listing," he said, flashing his expensive smile. "And since I was here, I thought I'd drop by and see Kate. I didn't know she moonlighted for the cops."

Surprised that Fort Collins' mega-real estate agent even knew my name, I made an effort to smile. "You've got me confused with someone else, Larry. I'm just a hardworking broker who had the bad luck to walk into something awful."

Larry crossed his arms and slouched into a more relaxed position, as if he planned to stay a while. "Who was it, Kate? Any idea?"

I didn't have to feign amazement. "How would I know? That's for the police to find out."

"Aw, c'mon, your brother-in-law's the chief detective.

30

You can't tell me he didn't give you a hint."

"The only thing Bill told me was to go home. That's all."

Larry's smile turned sly. "I bet Amanda did it. They've been fighting for years, and now he's divorcing her for some Denver chick."

The cold spot returned to my stomach. Ronnie was right. People were speculating already, and Amanda was Suspect Number One. Fortunately, I didn't have to respond.

Ronnie rose from her chair and observed, "Oh, that's like saying the butler did it, Larry." She took his arm, nudging him away from the doorway. "Can't you be more creative than that? Mark had been involved in a lot of deals over the years. Some of them went sour. You and I both know he'd made enemies."

"More than a few," Larry said, no longer smiling. Since Ronnie was directing him down the hall, he gave me a parting wave. "See you around, Kate."

Not if I see you first, I vowed. Relieved to be able to return to my computer search, I bent over the keyboard once more.

"Hey, Kate," another voice cut in. "I just heard. Man, that must have been gross! I mean, really."

"Yeah, it sure was, Ben." I nodded solemnly to our newest associate. Bright-eyed and bushy-tailed, Ben Babbitt was fresh out of college and full of energy. He cut a broad swath on campus. Students loved him, and so did parents. He had made a killing in kiddie condos last year.

He raked his shaggy blond hair from his eyes. "Geez, was there blood everywhere or what? Did you touch the knife? Who do you think finished him?"

That was it. I was out of there. I sprang from my chair. "Yes, no, and I don't know. And don't ask anything else, Ben. I'm trying to forget." Snatching the Kerchoffs' offer from my desk, I shoved all four copies into my briefcase and headed for the door. The back door.

It was late afternoon before I'd obtained both Kerchoff signatures on the offer and delivered it to the listing broker's office. Once again, the sun was fast approaching the mountaintops as I drove to Amanda's. I involuntarily shivered. Just like yesterday. This was the same time I drove to the Schusters' house and found Mark.

My cell phone jangled its musical little sound. Amanda. It had to be. I hadn't heard from her all day. My daughter's voice sounded, instead.

"Mom? How are you? Uncle Bill just told me what happened. How awful for you. I'm so sorry you had to see that." Jeannie's voice radiated concern.

"I am too, Jeannie. I'm trying to forget I ever saw it."

She paused. "Who do you think killed Mark, Mom? He was so . . . well, so respected by everybody. Who do you think?"

Suppressing my annoyance that everyone seemed to think I had an inside track on the investigation, I sighed loudly. "I have no idea. Everybody's asked me that today, like I know something. I'm just as clueless as everyone else."

"You don't think Amanda did it, do you?"

Appalled that my own flesh and blood could so easily suspect my old friend, I snapped, "Of course not! That's crazy. She loved Mark. She really did. Divorce or no divorce. She couldn't have done it. I know everybody suspects her. Damn, that's so unfair!"

"Okay, Mom, okay. It was just a question. Don't get mad."

I exhaled a loud and purposeful breath. "I'm not mad. It's just that everybody's been asking, and I'm worried the police will think that, too." I deliberately refrained from mentioning the voice-mail message. That was privileged information and Bill had warned me not to tell anyone. I'd already slipped with Ronnie, but I knew I could trust her.

"Well, I just wanted to know how you were doing. Do you want to come over and have dinner with me tonight?"

I pictured my daughter, the graduate student, living on a tight budget and student loans. Her idea of dinner would be tofu. Yummy. Oh, the sacrifices of motherhood.

"Gee, sweetie, that would be great. I'll be over a little later, though. I've got to go see Amanda first. She's still in shock, I think. She hasn't called."

"Okay, see you later. Love you."

"Love you too, Jeannie. Bye."

Somehow, the few moments of hearing her voice had chased away the chilly apprehension that had crept up all afternoon. What was I scared of, I wondered? That Amanda would appear dry-eyed and elated that her cheating husband would humiliate her no more? Had a whole day of other people's suspicions caused me to create my own?

A brilliant orange sunbeam reflected off the townhouse door knocker. I had to step aside or be blinded. Amanda opened the door. Unable to stop myself, I scrutinized her face for signs of grief. No makeup could disguise her eyes, bloodshot and deeply-shadowed beneath. Lack of sleep, probably. But no red puffiness which would indicate crying.

"Amanda, I'm so, so sorry," I offered. It was the only thing that came to mind at the moment. I reached out and hugged her. She hugged me back tightly for a long moment before breaking away.

"Come in, Kate," she said in a weary voice, stepping inside. "I was hoping you'd come. I called last night after Bill came, but your phone just rang, so I couldn't leave a message."

Feeling guilty, I said, "I'm sorry, Amanda. I just couldn't deal with anything more last night. And today I've been busy with clients until now. Otherwise, you know I'd have been here sooner. You haven't been alone, have you?"

She waved her hand as she sank heavily into the living room sofa. "Friends have been coming over all morning, nonstop. Marilyn brought me lunch, but I couldn't eat it." Amanda closed her eyes and rubbed her forehead, as if trying to remember. Lines that I'd never noticed before seemed to have sprouted overnight. "Some of Mark's friends from the club were here till three. And then Jonathan and Sharon. They just left a little while ago."

Suddenly I felt enormous pity for Amanda, who had no children to come to her side at such a heartbreaking time. She and Mark had never had the time or the desire to have kids. Or so she'd said. I often wondered if it was really a shared decision or mostly Mark's. He had a certain lifestyle established. Kids definitely slowed you down.

I sat beside her on the sofa, sinking into the leather's embrace. Placing my hand over hers, I whispered, "Amanda, I can't believe this happened. Who would want to kill Mark?"

"You'd be surprised, Kate," she said in a husky voice, her eyes still closed. "Mark's done a lot of things over the years. A lot of deals. Not everyone in Fort Collins was in his fan club." A shudder seemed to run over her, and she sat up quickly. Fixing me with a piercing stare, her voice gained an edge. "I need to know what happened, Kate. What did you see? Was there a sign of anyone else over there?"

"No, Amanda, no one. But I did hear the officers talking about finding clothes spread all over the bedroom upstairs."

She peered at me. "Women's clothes?"

"I don't know, Amanda. Honest. I just overheard a comment Bill obviously wished I hadn't."

Amanda sank back into the sofa. "Start at the beginning, Kate. And don't leave anything out. No matter how awful. I want to hear everything."

I swallowed down the uncomfortable feeling that rose in my throat, took a deep breath, and did as my friend requested.

Chapter Five

Saint Luke's Episcopal Church sat nestled in the midst of its comfortable neighborhood embrace. Like the houses surrounding it, Saint Luke's was established, tree-shaded, and gracious. I always liked driving through older neighborhoods. They were reassuring, somehow.

This morning, however, I didn't feel reassured at all as I pulled into a parking space behind Saint Luke's. It had been five days since Mark's murder, and the coroner had finally released Mark's body for the funeral. Amanda's numbness had also worn off. Yesterday she'd locked herself in her bedroom and sobbed all day and into the evening. She didn't eat. She didn't sleep. She just waved away anyone who offered sympathy. Those of us who came to comfort her wound up clustered in her living room, worrying.

How would she hold up under the strain of a funeral, and with such a crowd, I wondered? Especially since the young Denver lawyer who'd been Mark's bride-to-be had announced she was planning to attend. In fact, several of the attorneys from her firm, the same one Mark planned to join, also would be coming. Judging from the stream of mourners arriving, Saint Luke's would have to put chairs in the vestibule.

I slowly walked around to the front of the church, enjoying the early scent of fall in the air. Crisp and clean. Leaves hadn't fallen yet, but still, the aroma was detectable. The sky was overcast instead of its usual brilliant Colorado blue, another hint of the season to come. I'd used the weather's change as an excuse to wear a black knit skirt and long sweater. Suitably somber, but since I usually wear bright colors, I added a white silk scarf at my throat, so I wouldn't scare myself when I passed a mirror.

Just as I reached the canopied front entrance, a black limousine pulled up in front. I hesitated, thinking it might be Amanda. Jonathan Bassett stepped out, followed by his always-stunning wife, Sharon. Sharon glanced about the entrance, spotted me, and nodded. Next, Jonathan helped Amanda from the car. I sighed in relief to see that she had shrouded herself in black. Long-sleeved elegant black dress and a shoulder-length black veil concealed all but a hint of her features. Whether it was vanity or self-protection, I was glad. Amanda did not deserve to be stared at mercilessly for two hours, while her husband was eulogized.

Jonathan guided Amanda by the elbow toward the church door, until she turned my way and gestured for me to join her. I obliged, although reluctant to be sharing the spotlight during this service.

Amanda grasped my hand and held it tightly as we entered the church. The tension in her grasp startled me. The ushers settled us into the front pew, Amanda seated between Jonathan and me. I heard the slight rise in the hum of voices, indicating everyone knew the widow had arrived. I tried to peer across the aisle as discreetly as possible, to see if I could spot the Denver entourage, but spied no one who fit the description. However, the other front pew was conspicuously vacant so far.

Suddenly, Amanda leaned over. "Kate," she said, her voice low and still hoarse from all the tears. "Kate, I'm so scared! A detective came over last night and asked me all sorts of questions about Mark and me and our divorce. Then he told me not to plan any trips anytime soon. That I shouldn't leave town. They may want to ask me more questions. My Lord, Kate, do you think they suspect *me* of killing Mark?"

This close, I could see the panicked look in her big brown eyes. "I don't know, Amanda. They're just doing their job," I whispered beside her veil, then glanced away.

Almost as if she read my mind, Amanda's voice quavered as she said, "Kate . . . did the police hear that message I left on your voice-mail?"

I met her horrified gaze and nodded. Amanda's mouth dropped open. "Oh my God, Kate. They *do* think I killed Mark! What am I going to do?" I reached over and took both her hands in mine as I bent beside her, hunching my shoulders so no one could observe our conversation. Jonathan kept glancing our way but said nothing.

"Let's not jump to conclusions, Amanda." I tried to reassure her as the strains of subdued organ music began to float through the sanctuary.

"Kate, I swear I didn't kill Mark. Please tell me you don't think I did!" Her bottom lip trembled.

I held her frightened gaze. "Of course not. Everyone who knows you knows you couldn't kill Mark. You loved him." I squeezed her hand beneath mine.

Amanda's eyes began to glisten behind the veil, and she bit her lip. "Help me, Kate, please," she begged, then sank back into the cushioned pew, her hand clutching mine.

Jonathan glanced over, patted her other hand, and whispered something in Amanda's ear. She slowly turned in the pew and discreetly scanned the packed church. Settling back, she leaned over once more and rasped, "Jonathan just said that this large turnout was a fitting tribute to Mark. All I see is a church filled with women, most of whom have bedded my husband."

Her comment startled me, but when I searched for a familiar expression of anger, I saw nothing. She simply gazed back sadly. I squeezed her hand, not knowing what to say. Grief must have quenched the last of Amanda's anger.

Just then, a rustle stirred through the sanctuary, audible even over the Bach cantata. I didn't have to turn. I sensed the Denver group had arrived. Anxiously peeking at Amanda, I worried how she would handle this added tension of seeing the woman her husband left her for.

I shouldn't have worried. Amanda didn't even stir as a tall, thin young woman, suitably adorned in stylish black silk, led a procession of four dour-looking gentlemen to the other front pew and noisily sat. Amanda continued to stare ahead as if transfixed. She didn't even turn her head. I wondered if she'd even noticed.

The other mourners noticed and commented accordingly, the swell and fall of subdued conversation competing with the organist's considerable skills. I concentrated on the music, recognizing it as a piece we had sung in Chorale several years ago. Finally the minister began the service, and I occupied the following hour alternately peering at Amanda and trying to stifle my annoyance at the young woman lawyer's noticeable crying. Her sobs rose and fell, dependent upon the eloquence of the individual eulogy. Several acquaintances had volunteered to speak their remembrances of Mark. Oftentimes, the memories brought a lump to my own throat. Then I would hear Weepy across the aisle and my tears dried up. If only she would.

Somehow, her audible grief seemed intrusive in this setting. She had only known Mark for a year. The rest of us assembled in this lovely sanctuary had known him a lifetime. She and her consorts were intruders, and I sensed I wasn't the only one in church who felt it.

Suddenly, I felt something else. A prickle along the back of my neck. A sense of something disturbing passed over me. Unable to stop myself, I glanced over my shoulder and scanned the mourners. My gaze quickly honed in on the source. An icy brunette seated only three rows behind me was staring daggers at the conspicuously-grieving young woman lawyer. The brunette's hate-filled gaze was a laser beam, and the red light danced on the back of Weepy's head.

As if she sensed my attention, the brunette swiftly glanced my way, then down to her lap. Just then, I noticed the man seated to her right. He was a tenor from my singing group, the Larimer Chorale. He sent a concerned glance toward the brunette, then fixed his attention back to the speaker, who was waxing eloquent.

Thankfully, the people behind me were watching the speaker as well. I would have turned away, except I suddenly saw a transformation before my eyes. As the speaker effusively praised Mark Schuster's virtues, a purple-faced rage seemed to consume the normally mild-mannered tenor. It was palpable. The intensity of that anger made me catch my breath.

Why have these people brought so much enmity here today? I didn't recognize the woman seated next to the tenor, but observed she was lovely in a delicate porcelain-featured way. Her jet black hair was razor-cut at the jaw line, thick and luxuriant. Her suit, conservatively tailored. Perhaps another lawyer, I mused, as I settled back into the cushions.

Amanda still stared ahead, seemingly oblivious to the proceedings. Maybe that was better. There would be the graveside service later, and then friends would be dropping in the rest of the afternoon.

I took a deep breath while the speaker droned and let myself drift away—watching the stained glass windows catch an occasional sunbeam and send it dancing in shards of colored light across the floor.

Grabbing a clean mug from our tiny office kitchen tucked behind the copy room, I poured it full of black coffee, then headed toward Ronnie's corner office. "Hey, got a minute?" I leaned inside.

Ronnie peered over the rims of her glasses and looked up from the file on her desk. "Sure, what's on your mind?"

I chose my favorite stuffed chair, pulled it to just the right spot, so I could enjoy the gorgeous view of the foothills while I talked. "I need the name of the very best appraiser in town. I've only had to work with a couple and they're okay, but not for this job. I want the most reputable, the most experienced one in town. The one whose word is unquestioned," I said as I leaned back.

"No one's word is unquestioned, Kate. You know that," she decreed with a smile. Always teaching.

"Okay, okay. So, the very best of the best. I just want someone who's so good at appraisals that when he or she says a house is worth so and so, then there won't be any problem."

Ronnie narrowed her gaze. "And which property are we talking about, pray tell?"

"Amanda's."

"Ah."

I swallowed a large gulp of coffee. "The vultures are circling, Ronnie. I can tell. I've already had a couple of calls from real estate agents, feeling me out about the price. Everybody expects Amanda to dump the property, since Mark was killed there."

"Not an unreasonable assumption. What does Amanda want?"

I stared out over Ronnie's shoulder, into the mountains, wishing I could take an afternoon off and go hike. Forget all about murders and accused friends and circling vultures. "She hasn't said yet. But I'm afraid she'll panic and want to dump it."

Ronnie shook her head. "That would be a shame."

"I'm not going to let that happen, Ronnie. I'll be damned if I let those vultures steal that house."

"What's your plan?" She arched a silvery brow.

"Now that the police are finished, I can have the cleaning lady in. Once she's done, I'll pack up the entire library. But leave the rest of the house furnished and show it that way."

"You're going to have an open house?" she asked, incredulous.

"You bet," I said, defiant.

"You're going to get a lot of ghouls."

"Well, maybe there will be a few real buyers," I said, trying to convince myself as much as her. "And I'm going to work every web contact I have. If folks in town aren't interested, maybe someone moving in will be."

Ronnie gave me an encouraging grin. "Go get 'em, Kate. I wish you luck. It would be a shame for that house to go for below value. And if you want support for that, then Jake Chekov is your man. He's been in business for as long as I've been in real estate. He's the best and the most respected. His appraisal will help you out. Ask Jennifer for his number."

Sensing she needed to get back to the work I'd interrupted, I rose from the chair. "Thanks, Ronnie," I said as I headed out the door.

Her wish of "good luck" floated down the hall after me. I snatched it and held it close. I would need all the luck I could get.

Chapter Six

Skirting a parked car, I checked oncoming traffic, then jay-walked across the street, heading for the sidewalk café ahead. I held my face to the noontime sun for a second, enjoying the glorious fall weather. No wonder people kept moving here in droves. As a real estate broker, I should be happy about the influx of new business. Instead I, like many other Fort Collins citizens, worried about losing all the things that made our small city special. The signs were already there—increase in traffic, congestion, sprawl. It was scary.

I stood for one more precious second in the sun before approaching the café's wrought iron entrance, knowing that once I found my friend, Marilyn Renfrow, she'd be in the shade. Not a sunflower, Marilyn. More of a shade plant. An exotic shade plant.

Marilyn and I had been friends for two decades. We'd met at our kids' school and became fast friends. We understood each other and had shared most of life's vicissitudes—marital and otherwise. She was also my opposite in many things. Where I was restrained, Marilyn was outgoing, often outrageous. She delighted in raising eyebrows. Flirtatious, outspoken, and the only woman my age who managed to be voluptuous while slightly plump. Men loved Marilyn. Old, young, and in-between. She was always surrounded at parties. The attraction was decidedly mutual. Whereas I had refrained from becoming involved with anyone after my divorce, Marilyn approached life differently. Twice divorced and with more past lovers than even she could remember, Marilyn was the definition of a free spirit. In fact, she may have been the original.

She was also the best source of gossip in town. Marilyn had been in Fort Collins since dirt. Having grown up here when it was still a sleepy little undiscovered college town, she knew every prominent family—and their secrets. She also took delight in keeping track of who was sleeping with whom and why. I knew the best way to discover who was on Mark Schuster's scorecard was to probe my best friend and confidante.

I spied Marilyn seated at a shady table. "Hey, there. How're you doing?" I asked as I sat. "Like your outfit."

Marilyn patted the rainbow-colored silk print and smiled. "Don't you just? I loved it the moment I saw it." Her caramel brown hair was its usual tousle of curls that fell about her face and neck. All natural curls, too. She never had to stand over a curling iron. Last year I'd opted for a shaggy pixie. Goodbye hot rollers and curling iron. Just fluff, spray, and go.

"Let's order now, so we can talk," Marilyn said, beckoning the waiter.

I ordered a chicken Caesar salad with iced tea, while Marilyn chose a gooey lasagna. If I ate that, it would take weeks of workouts to remove. Marilyn didn't mind if it stayed or not.

Watching the white-aproned young waiter leave with our orders, Marilyn leaned over the table. "How's Amanda today?"

"As good as can be expected. She sounded exhausted over

the phone. I told her to go to bed and sleep."

Marilyn traced a pattern on the white tablecloth before speaking. "You know that everyone in town has the same unspoken thought, don't you?"

I sighed loudly. "Yes, darn it, I do. Everyone thinks Amanda killed Mark. But you know she couldn't do that! At least you and I know. She still loved Mark. I don't care how angry she became, she still loved him."

"All of Amanda's friends know that. But lots of people like to think the worst of someone, when they get the chance. And with Amanda, it's easy. She's thrown her money around and kind of got in people's faces."

Tracing a pattern of my own now, I glumly agreed. Amanda had often flaunted her wealth over the years. That doesn't set well with Old Money. Of course, out here in the West, nothing was really old, including money. Not like Back East, as I still referred to it, where money went back centuries.

"Listen," I said, changing the subject, "yesterday at the funeral I saw a woman who caught my attention. When I pointed her out to Amanda later, she mumbled the name Cheryl Krane. Then a funny expression crossed her face, and she didn't want to say more." I eyed Marilyn knowingly. "I figured if she was someone from Mark's past, you would know."

Marilyn started to answer, then opted to lean out of the waiter's way so he could serve our lunch. Afterwards, she once again leaned forward. "Cheryl was Mark's longest affair. You know how he operated, right? He'd love 'em, then drop 'em. But he always came back to Cheryl. And Amanda, of course," she said wryly. "And Cheryl always kept herself available. She never married. Even though poor little Stanley Blackstone carries his heart on his sleeve for her. For years.

Such devotion is amazing." She shook her curls. "Anyway, they're both workaholics over at Hoffman Associates. Personally, I think that Cheryl secretly harbored a fantasy Mark would one day divorce Amanda and marry her. That's why she's stayed single and at his beck and call." Marilyn gave a curt nod, her disapproval at curtailing one's options in life clearly evident.

I stared off into the traffic flowing past, remembering Cheryl Krane's murderous look in church. "That makes sense, then. Yesterday at the funeral, I caught her staring daggers at Mark's almost-bride-to-be. Boy, if looks could kill, Weepy would be dead now."

Marilyn chuckled. "Yeah, she was something, wasn't she? I got a kick out of her."

"I figured you would. She annoyed the hell out of everyone else, though. I almost expected her to throw herself across the casket."

Marilyn laughed. "That would give the gossip mavens fodder for months."

I arched a brow. "Are you including yourself in that group?"

Feigning offense, she drew herself up. "Don't be snide. I don't gossip. I volunteer useful information when asked, that's all. And be nice, or I won't tell you all I know about Cheryl."

"Oh, many pardons, Most Gracious One," I said. "Do speak. Thusly."

Marilyn shot me a wicked smile. "Before I grant your request, you have to grant mine. I have someone I want you to meet. How about dinner this Thursday night, just the four of us?"

I groaned and sank my forehead in my hand. I sensed this conversation would cost me. "Not again, Marilyn. The last one kept putting his hand on my thigh all through dinner."

She grinned. "What's wrong with that?"

I scowled. "I didn't like him to begin with. He annoyed me with all his bragging. So the hand was more than I wanted to deal with."

"Oh, I think you dealt with it pretty well, if somewhat vigorously." She leaned back and crossed her arms under her ample bosom. "Spilling hot coffee all over his lap was a bit much, some would say."

I glanced around innocently. "I didn't try to spill it, honest. He just startled me, that's all. Reflex action, I guess."

"Some reflexes. A guy will have to have a black belt to date you."

I exhaled in exasperation. How long were we going to have this conversation? "I've told you. I'm not ready to 'get back into circulation,' as you so charmingly phrase it. Dating is something I did in college. I can't even imagine it now." I forced a scowl, before I sipped my iced tea.

Marilyn was undaunted. "This one will be different. He's a lawyer with—"

"Oh, God, another lawyer," I whined, hoping to be as difficult as possible. "Please, no. How about a nice teacher? Got any of those in your queue?"

A decidedly evil grin danced across her face. "There's still that professor of civil engineering. He's asked about you several times."

A wince of remembered pain shot through me. "You are heartless, truly heartless. I'll take the lawyer," I said dejectedly. Marilyn just laughed.

"You won't regret it. He's nice, actually."

"A nice lawyer? Isn't that an oxymoron?"

She gave me a warning look. "Promise to be good, all right? No coffee spills, okay?"

"Depends on how he behaves. No promises."

Marilyn glanced upward, for heavenly guidance, no doubt. "Why do I try with you? Oh, well. I guess it's the challenge. I love challenges."

She finished off the rest of the lasagna, while I moped through my salad. Shoving her plate aside, she leaned over the table once more. "Anyway, back to Cheryl and Mark. My humble take on her reaction at the funeral was simple. She felt betrayed. She'd always been there for Mark to go to between girlfriends. And, as I said, I think she actually believed he'd marry her one day. And yet he never did. Over ten years, she was there if he snapped his fingers. And what happens? After all those years of service and devotion?" Marilyn made a face as she said the words. "Mark finally leaves Amanda. But does he turn to Cheryl? Hell, no. He runs off with Little Miss Weepy in Denver. And to add more injury, he plans to move to Denver. She may never see him again. Assuming, of course, she wants to."

I forked my way through the rest of my salad as I listened. In light of what Marilyn was saying, Cheryl Krane's intense look of hatred was understandable. But could her hate have turned murderous? Truly, she must have felt betrayed. Did that drive her to take revenge upon her former lover?

Another memory returned to tease. Stanley Blackstone's glare while Mark was being eulogized. "What do you know about Stanley? I've only seen him at Chorale. What's he like?"

Marilyn arched a brow. "Quiet, nondescript, totally devoted to Cheryl and always has been, ever since I can remember."

"I guess that accounts for his glare of undisguised hatred yesterday, when Mark was being praised to the heavens. I caught one of his looks and, frankly, it took my breath away."

"My read is that he resents everything Mark has stolen from him over the years," Marilyn said, pouring a heavy dollop of cream into her coffee.

"Stolen from him?"

"Sure. Stanley wanted to marry Cheryl. He asked her over and over. She always refused, even though she was fond of him. She didn't really love him, or so she once admitted to me. But, to Stanley's way of thinking, if it weren't for Mark Schuster, he and Cheryl could be sharing a life of wedded bliss. If such a thing exists," she added with a sly wink.

I considered that explanation. It made sense. But did Stanley hate Mark enough to kill him? And why now, when Mark would be moving to Denver? Cheryl would still be in Fort Collins. Stanley would have the inside track at last. Unless he had already broached the possibility to Cheryl, and she'd refused him yet again. Perhaps poor Stanley believed Mark was the cause of his lack of a life partner, when in reality, Cheryl simply didn't want him. Had Stanley become so deluded that his frustration turned to revenge?

"Hmmmmmmm," I pondered aloud. "Do you think—"

Marilyn shushed me quiet, waving a warning finger as she glanced over her shoulder to the café's interior. I peered through the plate glass and saw Cheryl Krane being seated at a table with a luncheon companion of her own. None other than Sharon Bassett, wife of Amanda's divorce attorney.

"Now, there's an odd pairing," Marilyn said.

"What could those two be sharing?"

"It does make one wonder," Marilyn said quietly.

I tried not to stare, but the look of discomfort on Cheryl's face was visible all the way through the glass. Sharon, however, seemed oblivious. She was steadily talking, while Cheryl sat mute.

"Cheryl doesn't look too happy," I observed.

"Yes, you're right, and there's more."

I glanced toward Marilyn, whose face had the open, impassive look that came over her whenever she "sensed" something. Over the years, I'd learned to respect Marilyn's special abilities. She was a little bit psychic and could see more than the rest of us.

"What do you sense?" I probed.

"Sharon's baring her soul, so to speak. She's sharing secrets with Cheryl. I can't tell what, though. But they're disturbing Cheryl greatly. Look, see how tense she is." Sure enough, Cheryl Krane sat rigid as a fence pole.

"Sharon share secrets? You've got to be kidding. The only thing I've ever heard that woman share is the name of her personal trainer."

Marilyn closed her eyes, and I waited, hoping for more. "I can't tell what it is, except that it's very disturbing news to Cheryl."

I watched Cheryl and Sharon for another moment, until the waiter brought our check. Digging out my credit card, I glanced at Marilyn. She'd returned to normal and was finishing her coffee. "What do you think?" I probed again.

"I don't know for sure." She paused. "But let's think about it. What could Cheryl Krane and Sharon Bassett possibly have in common? They don't share the same social affiliations, the same church group, the same tastes even. What else is left but . . ." She left the sentence hanging.

I pondered for a moment, then suddenly understood what she'd left unsaid. "Oh, my word," I whispered, incredulous. "Not Mark!"

Marilyn nodded knowingly. "It's possible. And now her news makes more sense."

"What news?"

"Sharon told me last week that she plans to divorce Jonathan." She glanced once more through the window before she grabbed her purse and rose to leave.

I picked my chin up off the table and followed her from the restaurant.

Switching on the blinker, I guided my elderly Explorer into another lane. Meanwhile my mind was clicking faster than the blinker. The image of arrogant, elegant, and wealthy Sharon Bassett joining the list of Mark Schuster's too-numerous-to-count conquests tried to come into focus. It took some doing. I searched my memory for some hint in the past: a gesture, a subtle glance, something that would have drawn my attention. Nothing. Sharon had never paid Mark much attention at any of the gatherings I could recall. Not like some women who delighted in his practiced flattery. Cool and aloof, Sharon always hid behind her inscrutable mask and stayed above it all. Apparently she was too inscrutable for even the best divorce lawyer in town—her own husband—to fathom. I remembered the fond, worshipful looks Jonathan always cast his stunning wife's way. How was he handling this? He'd looked his usual adoring self at the funeral.

My cell phone jingled and I reached for it while I eased around a corner, pleased that I hadn't taken my eyes from the road. I'd promised my daughters I would be "good" and not use it while driving. I'd lied through my teeth. But I had vowed to myself to stop the death-wish bad habits real estate agents are prone to—like steering with their elbows while talking on the phone and digging through their briefcases at the same time. Being good was relative.

"This is Kate."

"Kate, this is Mary Baxter. I thought you'd like to tell your young couple the good news. My sellers just accepted their offer."

A surge of much-needed elation shot right through me—a mixture of happiness for the young couple and for me. They get a house and I get paid. Cool. I don't know if the "money surge" is akin to this Kundalini energy my Yoga-teacher neighbor keeps telling me about, but it must be close.

"Hey, that's great!" I said. "They'll be so excited. I'll call them right away and get them started with the inspector."

"Thanks, Kate. My folks are pretty anxious to move things along. Keep me posted. Uh, oh. Gotta go. Another call coming in. Talk to ya later." She clicked off.

I tossed the little phone back onto the seat. Cell phones had become indispensable. We'd only been using them a few years, yet they'd become another appendage. Had it really only been a few years ago when we'd walked around without these things stuck in our ears? However had we managed? And how come we were so dependent now?

Suddenly I remembered why. I had to call the appraiser and schedule him for Amanda's house. I could be good—change direction and go all the way back to my office to use the phone there. But I'd promised to join Amanda for dinner, and I was already two blocks from her condo. My office was halfway across town. Of course, I could always use a public pay phone—with half the world eavesdropping. No contest. Being good was just too inconvenient.

I used a stop light to check the appraiser's number and punched it in. A baritone voice introduced itself as belonging to "Jake Chekov" and left instructions for voice-mail. I obediently left my number and a brief message. Appraisers rarely answered their cell phones. They were usually out in the field, crawling through houses, apartment buildings, or other structures. Plus, they weren't selling anything. Unlike real estate agents, who're so afraid they'll miss a call, they take the phones into the bathroom with them.

Pulling into the condo parking lot, I noticed Jonathan Bassett's silver Acura next to Amanda's jet-black baby Jag. As I approached the door, I decided I'd better stay on the balcony and make calls, so I wouldn't hear any attorney-client discussions.

Much to my surprise, Jonathan opened the door before I even knocked. He was still talking to Amanda over his shoulder. "Amanda, I've told you that will never happen. But even if it did, Bob Carruthers would take care of you. He's the best in town." He started through the door, so I stepped aside. Amanda spotted me.

"Kate! Thank goodness, you're here," she exclaimed. "Some investigator called me today and asked all these questions. He scared me to death! He kept asking about the divorce and what properties had Mark sold and where was the money—"

Jonathan swiveled around just in time to avoid colliding with me as I slipped through the doorway. "Oh, hello, Kate. Sorry, didn't see you there," he said before turning his attention back to an obviously distraught Amanda.

One glance at the coffee table told me how bad it was. Three ashtrays were overflowing with cigarette stubs. Totally out of character for fastidious Amanda.

"Amanda, do not worry." Jonathan's tone scolded. "The police are only gathering information as part of their investigation. Don't get paranoid."

"How can I help it, Jonathan?" Amanda's voice went up the scale. "You didn't hear that detective. It was—"

She broke off as her cell phone rang. Her face paled for a moment until she obviously recognized the caller's number. She waved Jonathan goodbye as she headed for the balcony and privacy.

Deciding to take advantage of her absence, I positioned

myself between Jonathan and the door, blocking his retreat. "Jonathan, I'm really concerned about Amanda," I said. "She's Prime Suspect Number One in everybody's eyes. The police have already questioned her once, and today they're after her again. Frankly, I'm worried."

Jonathan's lawyerly skepticism softened just enough to bring a slight smile. "Now, Kate. Not you, too? It's bad enough that Amanda's getting paranoid." He shook his head, admonishing. "The police couldn't possibly suspect Amanda. She's just not the criminal type. They're simply gathering information, that's all. You're letting your imagination get the better of you."

Surprised, I countered, "Jonathan, you don't know Bill Levitz. I do. And I know when he's 'locked on' someone and when he's not. I've watched him work for years. And he definitely suspects Amanda. And he's the chief of detectives."

"I'm sure he's just doing his job, Kate. In Amanda's present state, she cannot tell the difference between probing questions and interrogation."

His patronizing tone annoyed me, so I decided to do a little admonishing of my own. "Jonathan, you're missing the picture here. Trust me. I know Bill Levitz. You do not ignore him. He's like a pit bull, once he's latched onto someone. Now, you're Amanda's lawyer. You've got to convince her to protect herself before this goes any further. Maybe she needs to hire a detective of her own."

"A detective?" he echoed, not even bothering to hide his amusement. "What on earth for, Kate?"

"Mark had enemies, Jonathan. He had his fingers in a lot of deals around town, you know that. Amanda's mentioned some of the ones that went bad. Plus, he ran roughshod over a lot of people. Not just in business either. I'd say that's reason enough to investigate."

Jonathan chuckled and fixed me with a patronizing grin, as he verbally patted me on the head. "There, there, now, Kate. You need to relax. You will not help Amanda with all these wild imaginings. Obviously, this whole ordeal of walking in and finding the body has been too much for you. I suggest you go home and rest. Better yet, call your doctor and get something to relax you first. Then go home and rest." He stepped around me and aimed for the door.

That did it. His patronizing manner I could handle. I'd been patronized by the best and survived. But his cavalier dismissal of the very real threats to a dear friend was too much. Obviously he wasn't going to protect Amanda, so I cut him loose.

"Forgive me, Jonathan. I shouldn't be burdening you with this anyway. You've got too much on your mind right now. I was very sorry to hear about you and Sharon." I headed into the living room, and watched Jonathan's reflection in the mirror as he turned to stare at me, all trace of amusement wiped clean.

"What are you talking about, Kate? What about Sharon and me?"

I sat on the sofa's soft arm and said with genuine sincerity, "Marilyn said you and Sharon are divorcing. I know how painful that can be, Jonathan. You have my deepest sympathies." I meant it.

A quick flash of anger swept across his face, then was gone. The cool arrogance that had been his hallmark for years returned. "Marilyn is mistaken. Sharon and I are not divorcing. Not at all. We're simply working out a few problems right now." His lips curled. "That gossiping shrew ought to know better than to spread rumors." He turned and stalked out, slamming the door behind him.

Surprised, I stared after him, wondering if Marilyn's impeccable instincts had slipped this time. Just then, Amanda returned from the balcony. "Jonathan's left?" she asked wearily and collapsed into the buttery soft sofa.

"Yeah. Did you need to talk with him again?"

"Heavens, no. I'm exhausted." She laid her head back on the leather. "Kate, can we just order in? I don't think I want to go out to eat. I'm afraid people will stare at me. And I just don't think I can deal with that right now." She closed her eyes.

Amanda always preferred going out. Seeing her cowering in her condo made my heart ache. "Sure. We'll order ethnic."

I headed for the kitchen and the directory, when her tired voice spoke up. "Kate. I want you to take care of whatever needs to be done with the house, then sell the damn thing and take what you can get."

"Amanda, I will not let you dump that property. It's too good."

She sighed loudly. "I know, Kate. But I just cannot handle any of it right now. You'll have to do it."

"I will. Don't worry about a thing," I reassured her as I reached for a notepad in my purse. "I need your cleaning girl's number. You trust Rachel to go in there and take care of everything, don't you?"

Her eyes flicked open. "Of course. She'll do it for me. And her son helps her out. You may need to . . . uh . . . ."

"Don't worry. We'll get everything clean and polished, and strip the library down to the wood. I'm leaving that empty. Next, we'll have the appraiser in, and then I'm having an open house."

Her tired face paled beneath her makeup. The lines and wrinkles that had suddenly appeared the other day were still there, aging her quickly. "Good Lord, Kate, you've got brass.

Go ahead. I don't care. Let the ghouls come."

I grinned. "That's okay. Buyers are out there, too. We'll just pretend it's Halloween. Now, what's Rachel's phone number?" I scribbled down the number, then rifled through the yellow pages for the restaurants.

Chapter Seven

The morning air held the early fragrance of fall. It was unmistakable, especially this early in the morning. I wheeled around the corner leading into the Schusters' neighborhood. Elementary students were walking to school, laden down with backpacks large and small. Some packs looked huge on the small bodies. I wondered if we were raising a generation of future hunchbacks. How'd we carry all that stuff to school?

Turning into the Schusters' triple-wide driveway, I deliberately parked on the far side. Rachel and her son would be arriving any minute. I grabbed the empty boxes in my back seat and headed for the door, then stopped. I couldn't help it. The last time I'd walked up this beautifully landscaped path, I was blissfully unaware of what horror awaited me inside. Now, I'd never forget it. The image of Mark's death-pale face still popped into my head at unnerving moments, almost like Marley's ghost. But there was no warning with this vision. I almost wished there was.

I dug into my jeans pocket for the keypad as I approached the door. The key dropped obediently, and I slipped it into the lock, took a deep breath, and stepped inside. The house was just as beautiful as ever. Morning sunshine poured through the windows, bathing the warm woods, dancing from mirror to crystal to mirror again. Despite that and my warm sweater, I shivered with the chill of memory. I tried to shake that away as well, but it didn't leave easily.

"Okay, stop it, you're getting weird," I said out loud. Just then, I heard the sound of a car door slamming, and exhaled a grateful sigh. Rachel.

"There you are, Kate," Rachel called as she entered, arms laden with cleaning supplies. "I was hoping you'd be here, because I wasn't about to come in all by myself." She brushed away a wisp of pale blonde hair that had escaped its bun. Her face had that careworn, sad look that settles on some women's faces later in life.

"Yeah, I know how you feel," I said. "It spooks me, too. I just hope it doesn't spook away the buyers."

"Well, let's see what we can do about that. Jerry will bring his truck later and help us when we have to clear out that room." She pointed to the library.

From where we stood, I could see the furnishings were still there, which meant the bloodstained carpet would be there as well. Hopefully, that cleaner in Denver would be able to salvage it. At least he wouldn't be able to gossip.

"I can help all day, Rachel, so maybe we can finish. I want to schedule that appraiser, and I can't until we've got this place immaculate."

"Don't worry. I've cleared all day and rescheduled my other people. Amanda needs our help. We'll get it done." She glanced around the vaulted great room. "I still remember all the parties. Amanda would have everything just perfect," she said wistfully before she headed toward the kitchen.

I remembered those parties too and the many dinners—all filled with laughter, joyous good fun, fine wines, and delectable food. They were good memories, and they were real. In time, they'd replace these awful scenes.

"C'mon, Kate. Let's start in here." Rachel's voice beckoned.

I willingly obeyed. Amanda was counting on us.

The sun was edging toward the foothills by the time I stepped outside again. Lacing my fingers together, I indulged in a long stretch. We were almost finished. We'd worked steadily since early morning, with only a few breaks, and the end was in sight. I took a long drink from my water bottle. We'd sent Jerry for a pizza so we could keep working. This close, we didn't want to stop.

Thank goodness for Jerry. Quiet and methodical, he hadn't flinched at the odious job he'd been given—clearing out the library with its all-too-fresh reminders of death. Bless him, he simply went into the room and took it apart, piece by bloody piece. Then he piled the desk and carpet into his truck and hauled them to Denver—the carpet to the cleaners and the desk to be refinished. Amanda would decide later if she wanted to keep them.

With the grim reminders of murder removed, Rachel and I were actually able to enter the room and finish the job. I packed up everything in boxes—books, computer, pictures, files, whatever was left—labeled and stacked them all in the garage. Amanda could go through them later, if and when she felt up to it. Meanwhile, Rachel scrubbed and scrubbed and scrubbed some more. Even though there was no trace of blood on the floor or walls, a telltale odor permeated the room. It made us both shiver. Rachel scrubbed until our shivers stopped.

The metallic clatter of skateboard wheels rattled the late afternoon quiet. I watched as three young boys careened past, one wiping out as he attempted to jump the sidewalk, the others veering off into the grass, and laughter. Instinct prompted me down the steps and across the wide expanse of lawn, heading for the boys before they boarded up once more and rode off around the corner into the approaching sunset. I skirted the For Sale sign at the lawn's edge and sped across the street. They were still trading mutual insults on each other's riding abilities.

"Hey, guys, you got a minute?" I called as I neared them. All three heads turned and gave me a cursory glance. "You guys live here, in this neighborhood?"

No response at first, then some nods. A wariness registered on a couple of faces, so I broke out my friendliest smile. "My name's Kate Doyle, and I'm the real estate agent who's selling the Schusters' house over there." I pointed toward Shamrock Realty's bright green sign. "I'm going to have an open house this weekend. So there'll probably be a lot of cars parked all over. You might want to tell your parents, so they won't wonder what's happening."

All three stared at me with that expression which appears on pre-teen faces somewhere between sixth and seventh grade. A shade comes down over the eyes and guilelessness is gone forever. Guardedness is the order of the day, especially when communicating with adults.

"Yeah, we saw you hauling stuff out," the blond boy said laconically, twirling his board on its edge.

"Was that all the bloody stuff?" The short dark-haired one spoke up, a hint of childish curiosity in his voice.

I hesitated to go into details, but the piercing gazes fixed on me told me this was a test. They knew what happened there and wondered if I would lie to them or not. I didn't. Children have unerring antennae, when it comes to adults trying to hide things deemed unsuitable.

"Yeah," I replied and watched my candor be rewarded.

They regarded me differently, imperceptible but real.

"Looked like a rug and a desk," the third, a freckle-faced redhead, observed. "Was it all covered in blood and all?"

"Pretty much."

The blond hopped on his skateboard and methodically rocked backed and forth as he addressed his friends. "My mom said he was stabbed in the throat. So it must have splashed all over."

"Gross. Why don't you just pitch that stuff out? Why'd you want to keep it?" Freckles said as he balanced on the edge of his board.

Good question. "Well, first of all, it's not mine, so I can't make the decision. It belongs to Mrs. Schuster and it's a pretty expensive Oriental rug, so we're trying to salvage it, if we can."

"Yeah, those rugs cost a lot," Blondie added. "My mom bought a new one for the dining room last year, and my dad just about split a gut yelling about it."

The smaller, dark-haired one spoke up with an honesty that brought back my hidden fears. "Jeez . . . who'd wanta buy a house that had a dead guy in it? His ghost's probably walking around at night." He gave an exaggerated shiver.

I tried to eliminate that picture from my own mind. That's all I needed—Mark's ghost to keep me company at the open house.

It was time to broach the real reason I had sought them out. "Guys, I was wondering if you could think back to last week and see if you remember seeing anything unusual that afternoon. Did you notice anyone leaving the house? Or any cars parked outside? Anything different at all?"

Blondie shrugged and started revving up his skateboard, clearly anxious to return to his activity. Freckles, however, scrunched up his face. "Hey, was that the day we got out early?" he asked his friends.

"Uh, that was a Monday. Teacher service something."

"Yeah, that was it," Freckles continued. "I remember that afternoon we were all set to practice jumps 'cause we had extra time, then some jerk parked in our lane."

"Yeah! You're right. That *was* the day," Blondie said with sudden interest. "There was some junky old car sitting right in our lane. Remember? We couldn't set up the ramp."

My heart speeded up. Mark had been killed Monday before last, and it was a teacher service day. I remembered, because several real estate agents in the office had to find sitters because their kids were off from school.

"It was a white car, too," the smaller dark-haired boy said, eyes bright with excitement.

"It was a Rabbit," said Freckles.

I couldn't believe my good fortune. I hadn't really expected the boys to remember anything. After all, who remembers cars parked in their neighborhood? But thankfully, this car had been an intruder and had caught their attention as well as spoiled their plans. "Are you sure?" I probed gently.

"Yeah, I'm sure," he said. "My sister used to have a Rabbit before she bought her Toyota. I know what it looks like." He turned to his friends. "Hey, man. Maybe that was the killer's car. Way cool."

I decided to push my luck. "Did you guys see anybody get into the car while you were out here riding? Or anybody walking around near the house? Anyone at all?"

Blondie and Freckles shrugged "no," but I noticed the smaller boy stared at the ground and shifted his board from one hand to another. My instinct prodded me to ask again.

"Anything at all would be helpful. Maybe you boys can help the police catch the person who did this."

Almost as if he could feel my gaze, he glanced up at me,

chewed his lip, then stared at the ground again. I waited, hoping something would prompt him to tell what he knew.

"I saw a funny, fat guy running around the block. But I can't remember when. Sometime that afternoon was all," he ventured in a soft voice.

This time my heart skipped a beat. I had hoped I'd be able to glean a few morsels. I hadn't dreamed I'd hit pay dirt. "A funny, fat guy? What made him funny?"

"Because he was wearing a hat and gloves, and it was sunny out. And he was wearing regular shoes, not sneakers. He looked weird."

I deliberately held my excitement in check. "Did you actually see him come out of the Schuster house or come down the sidewalk?"

The dark-haired boy didn't get to answer. His companions, obviously older than he was, broke out into peals of derisive laughter at that point.

"Oh, yeah, Greg! Right! Sure, you did."

"You liar!" accused Freckles. "There wasn't anybody like that on the street, and you know it. You're just tryin' to show off. Pretend to know somethin' when you don't."

Greg, who'd gone mute as well as turned a bright red with the sound of his friends' laughter, seemed to draw himself taller. "I'm *not* lying!" he said hotly. "I remember seeing that guy. I wiped out right in front of the Schuster house when he was coming down the walk. I couldn't miss him!"

"You wipe out in your own driveway," Freckles said, then jumped on his skateboard and pushed off.

"Bogus, Greg, totally bogus," yelled Blondie as he shoved off.

Greg scowled after them for a second, then hopped on his board and pushed off. He moved so quickly I was caught totally by surprise. "Wait, Greg!" I called helplessly, watching my little gold mine speed away. "Where do you live? What's your last name? What—"

I stopped, realizing it was futile. They had tired of the questioning. I'd been lucky to learn what I did. Finally I had some real information to give to Bill. "A funny, fat jogger." My heart beat even faster at the thought. Now, *that* sounded suspicious. Even Bill would have to admit that, wouldn't he?

Just then, Jerry's old, blue pickup truck turned into the Schusters' driveway behind me. Dinner had arrived. I waved to Jerry as he exited the car with two large pizza boxes in hand and some soft drinks under his arm. I hastened back to the house, my mind racing.

I had to find the right way to present this information to Bill Levitz. He might be family, but that didn't mean he'd pay attention. I'd have to have more than the funny, fat jogger story, as told by neighborhood children.

Rachel beckoned to me from the front door, and I sped up. Somehow, I would have to gather more information. Then, even hard-nosed Bill Levitz would pay attention.

Chapter Eight

Braking for the red light, I slowed into the intersection while I waited for the appraiser's voice-mail greeting to finish. We were still playing phone tag. I really wanted to schedule him for the Schusters' property before the weekend and my planned open house.

"Mr. Chekov, Kate Doyle again," I said after the beep faded. "Is there any way you could squeeze the Schuster home onto your appraisal schedule this week? I was hoping to have an open house either Saturday or Sunday. Please let me know. Thank you." Thanks in advance never hurt.

The red light switched to green, and I headed toward the Schusters' upscale subdivision, Burgundy Acres. Small lots and huge houses. They were all the rage. Burgundy Acres had been the first to build the mini-estates. Now, they practically encircled Fort Collins.

Wheeling around a corner, I took a large sip of my coffee and punched in another phone number. This one answered. "Freddy, this is Kate. Have you scheduled the Kerchoffs' inspection yet? I didn't see it on our calendar. I thought they talked with you last week."

"Had to reschedule, Kate. I just called your office. I've got it on for this morning." Freddy's voice sounded whiskey-rough. He was outside in the wind, judging from the static.

"Great. Don't forget, they're paying to have Ted check the heat exchanger. This is the original furnace and it's prime age. We want to know if there's anything waiting to jump out at us."

"Will do. I'll have a report to you tomorrow, Kate. Gotta go." He clicked off.

While waiting for a yellow school bus to lumber along the Schusters' street, I finished my coffee; 7:30 in the morning was the best time to check the house. Rachel and I had stayed late to finish, and night was not a good time to judge a home. You needed the naked light of day to reveal any flaws, especially the unforgiving morning light. I wanted to see if it looked as good as we thought before we staggered home, bone-tired.

The school bus picked up speed and I aimed for the Schusters' driveway, only to see another car already parked there. A bright red sports car, no less. *Who else would be here at this hour,* I wondered. Maybe the appraiser had a cancellation. I pulled up and parked, delighted that this Jake Chekov had been so cooperative, even if his choice of vehicles was out of character. Admiring the sexy Viper as I scooted past, I hoped the guy had a four-by-four for the mountain properties.

Once inside, I paused in the foyer for just a minute and looked around, letting my gaze travel slowly from the vaulted ceilings to the linen-papered walls to the muted sheen of the oak floors. I felt my insides relax. The house was beautiful. I closed the door and was about to call out "hello" when something stopped me. I didn't know what. Instead, ambling slowly past the great room and heading for the kitchen, I listened for the sound of another person.

I heard it. The sound of movement came from . . . where? The garage? That was it. Bumps and paper rattling. Whatever is he doing out there, I wondered, and pushed open the partially-closed door to the garage.

An impeccably-tailored, silver-haired gentleman jerked his head around to stare at me. I blinked. Henry Ackerman, Mark Schuster's law partner. What was *he* doing here? And why was he rifling through the boxes that I'd carefully packed yesterday? Boxes that contained the contents of Mark Schuster's office.

"Henry Ackerman," I said. "What the heck are you doing here?"

The brief look of surprise that claimed Ackerman's face disappeared, and a smooth, lawyerly demeanor slipped into place. "Oh, hello, Kate. I just needed to get some office files Mark kept at home. He gave me a key years ago." Ackerman flashed me a bright smile.

I wasn't having any of it. The only box he was rummaging through was the one that contained Mark's computer. There were no other files in that box. I packed it myself. Besides, this house was the scene of a murder. Unauthorized persons didn't go mucking around a murder scene whenever they felt like it. I'd learned that much from Bill over the years.

"Henry, you'll have to hand that key over to me," I said as authoritatively as I could. "The police informed me only authorized persons were allowed in the house. I even had to get permission to hold an open house this weekend, and the garage is strictly off-limits." I advanced toward him, palm outstretched, hoping he would cooperate.

His eyes narrowed, and anger registered there briefly. Then the lawyer returned. "No need to get all huffy, Kate," he said in a silky voice, as he reached into his pocket. "I just need a couple of files. After all, our partnership was ending."

He dropped the key into my hand.

Huffy? I couldn't remember the last time I'd huffed at anything. This was plain old-fashioned indignation he was witnessing. I resisted his oily reasoning. "That may be the case, Henry. But everything from Mark's office is still classified as evidence. So the police would frown on anything being removed. I'm sure Amanda will see that you receive any files you need, after this ordeal is over. After all, she's heir to her husband's estate. And your partnership is still intact, am I not correct?" I deliberately locked my steady gaze on his.

Ackerman didn't even bother to respond. He shot me a glare which sent a chill up my spine; then he turned on his heel and stalked from the garage. I followed behind him.

"I do not need an escort," he declared icily as he strode through the kitchen.

"Just doing my duty," I said.

A slammed front door was Ackerman's last comment. I stood and breathed deeply for a moment, wondering what had just happened. Had I thwarted the murderer's plan to steal evidence, or had I just annoyed a social acquaintance? Probably the latter. Ackerman didn't look like enough passion flowed through his veins to commit such a crime. Then I remembered that glare of hostility he'd sent me, and thought again. What could be on Mark's computer that Ackerman wanted so badly he'd lie about it?

I wandered back to the garage. The computer poked from its box. Ackerman must have been in the process of lifting it out. Pretty sneaky, showing up so early on a weekday morning. I'm sure he thought no one would ever see him, even if he sat at the kitchen table, plugged the sucker in, and fired it up. He hadn't figured on a real estate agent. We're liable to turn up anywhere, anytime.

Curiosity prodded. Maybe I should take a look. After all, I

was an "authorized" person. The familiar Voice of Caution whispered in the back of my mind that I was "getting into trouble," but I ignored it. Besides, I'd vowed to help Amanda, hadn't I? Well, this was helping.

Before I could think about it too much, I grabbed the box and carried it into the kitchen. Lifting the computer onto the glass-topped kitchen table, I attached the cables and plugs and fired it up myself. I only hoped my brother-in-law didn't walk in on me.

Desktop icons flashed into place, and I was surprised there were only a few. Maybe Mark kept most of his files on his office computer. But Ackerman certainly would have checked that one first. Obviously, whatever he was looking for wasn't on the office computer. Otherwise, he wouldn't risk sneaking in here.

I methodically started opening files and perusing the contents, wishing I had another coffee at my elbow. This was office work, so it called for accompanying support. Strong coffee. Even though I knew where the coffee was in the cabinets, I resisted the urge to get up and make some. Instead, I opted for speedy efficiency, just in case someone walked in on *me*.

It took just over a half-hour to open and scan every file Mark had. There was nothing suspicious at all, or even very interesting. They were mostly short briefs or correspondence with other attorneys. There was nothing about himself, or Ackerman for that matter. I had to confess, I was disappointed. Part of me expected to find some detailed document that mentioned Ackerman or the partnership. Nothing like that could be found.

I glanced at my watch and realized I had fifteen minutes to get back to the office in time for the weekly sales meeting. Muttering under my breath, I disconnected the computer cables and quickly transferred everything back to its box in the garage. I checked to make sure all doors were secure, then raced to my car. Ten minutes and counting, and I didn't have a prayer of making it on time.

As I wheeled out of the driveway and sped down the street, a tiny thought came out of nowhere. For someone who worked at home a lot, Mark certainly didn't have many files. Maybe he'd deleted some.

Another thought teased its way forward. Wasn't there a way to retrieve deleted files? Maybe someone at the university could help me out. They'd have computer jocks there who could make any machine give up its secrets.

"How does the house look, Kate?" Ronnie asked, scooping a sheaf of listings off the conference room table as she headed toward the door. Everyone else had already left the room, racing to meetings with clients, other real estate agents, lenders, appraisers, inspectors, lawyers. Our jobs were a never-ending stream of meetings—talking, talking, talking. It was draining, even for us life-long communicators.

I pushed the upholstered chair under the table and followed Ronnie through the door. "Well, thanks to Rachel and me, it looks beautiful. I mean, it wasn't messy before the, uh . . . the murder, but the police crew left dirty footprints and dust-stuff over everything. Even the yellow police tape left a gummy residue on the doors and railings outside."

"How long did you stay last night?" She peered at me.

"Till ten."

Ronnie shook her head as she stopped in our small kitchen. "Well, Kate, I really hope all this work pays off. You've certainly done more than your part, for sure." She poured a stream of coffee into her mug.

The aroma wafted up and teased. I followed suit, grabbing

one of the multitude of monogrammed mugs that sat beside the coffee station. Lender mugs, builder mugs, title company mugs, and, of course, real estate agent mugs. Everyone knew the way to our hearts and into our memories was to feed us and give us free stuff that we'd use. "Keep your fingers crossed, Ronnie. I've gotten some emails from out-of-town folks who're looking for a home like this. They said they'd try to schedule a quick trip." I took a sip and almost gagged. Lisa must have made the coffee. Someone had to take that girl in hand. How Ronnie could drink that weak brew was beyond me.

She grinned at my reaction. "Has Jake Chekov been there yet?"

"He's going this afternoon. Got another message from him. Haven't talked to the guy in person yet."

"Well, Jake will do a good job. He'll also give advice, if he thinks it necessary. Pay attention." She glanced at her watch. "See you later, Kate, and good luck. Keep me in the loop, okay?" she said as she headed toward her office.

"You got it."

Ronnie paused at her door and gave me an appraising glance. "And when you have a spare moment, let's sit and talk. I can tell you're up to something. Maybe something you shouldn't be. We need to talk."

"I . . . uh, I . . ."

"Don't deny it, Kate. You've got that look in your eye. Talk to me later. Meanwhile, stay out of trouble. And if you can't, for heaven's sake, be careful." She was gone.

How did she do that, I wondered. It was as if she could read my mind. Good thing she couldn't tell everything. Otherwise she'd hit the ceiling. I glanced at my watch, then headed back to my own office and grabbed my briefcase. There was just enough time to talk to that computer guy at the university.

My daughter Jeannie had recommended him. A fellow class-mate and computer genius. According to her, Chester Yosarian could make a computer give up any secret it ever knew.

I headed for the back door. Rounding a corner at my usual fast pace, I nearly ran right into Lisa. She jumped back with a squeak, hands up in the air. "Whoa, Kate! You gotta signal around those curves," she joked.

"Sorry, Lisa," I said. "I'm always in such a hurry that I forget to look." Pointing to the walls, I added, "Maybe we can invest in truck mirrors up there. It would help."

"I was just coming down the hall to introduce Ted Sandowski. He's joining the agency." She gestured to the smartly-dressed, balding man standing behind her, wisely out of the way of traffic. "Ted, this is Kate Doyle, one of our ju-nior brokers. Kate, meet Ted Sandowski."

Somehow I'd never gotten used to being referred to as a "junior," but I guessed it was better than "newbie." With only three years under my belt, I was still gaining experience. But I knew enough to recognize the guy who'd recently snagged Fort Collins Real Estate Agent of the Year. Turn 'Em Ted Sandowski. If it was investment real estate you were after, Ted was your man.

"Welcome aboard, Ted," I said, extending my hand. "I'm really impressed that Ronnie was able to lure you away from all those high rollers at the big shop across town."

"She made me an offer I couldn't refuse, Kate, and it's great to meet you, too." He grabbed my hand and pumped enthusiastically, watery blue eyes alight. "Wow, Lisa, are all your junior agents this good-looking?"

"Just the women, Ted," Lisa said with a laugh.

"Hurrying to a hot deal, I hope," Ted said, when I pried my hand loose.

"I wish. No, I'm just going to, uh, make some new contacts." *Every word of it is true,* I told myself.

"Atta, girl," he encouraged, fist pumping for emphasis. "That's where the business is. Outside. Not sitting behind a computer in the office."

We've got a live one with Ted, I thought. That was okay. Every office needed a cheerleader. Ted looked as if he had lots of experience egging on others and himself.

"Ted's the king of rental real estate in town," Lisa said with a sly grin. "In addition to being Real Estate Agent of the Year."

"Yes, I know. I was there for the coronation at last spring's banquet," I put in for good measure.

Ted seemed to grow an inch as he smiled under her praise. "Well, I don't know about being the 'king' but I do a fair share," he said in a slight nod to modesty.

"How about the grand duke?" I offered with a smile, hoping the extra flattery would allow me to continue on my path to the door.

Ted just laughed and checked the knot in his tie. "Ahhh, you ladies sure know how to flatter a man."

I took that as my cue. "Glad to meet you, Ted," I said, backing away. "I know how Ronnie's been looking to increase our share of that market. Sounds like you're perfect for the job. I've got to run now."

"Go get 'em, Kate!" Ted called, as I escaped into the parking lot.

If traffic cooperated, I could make it to the university, see this guru, get his advice, then make it back to the south of town and the Schusters' home, in time to meet with the appraiser. I checked my watch again. Obviously, food would be out of the question, so lunch—once again—would be coffee. Wishing I'd remembered to throw some walnuts into my briefcase, I turned my Explorer into the heavy flow of

College Avenue and headed north.

Despite the time crunch, I deliberately slowed down as I drove around the University Oval. Green and gracious, ringed with towering cottonwoods that had already turned golden, the Oval was the very heart of the old campus. Surrounded by some of the original university buildings, it was crisscrossed with pathways and filled with students. I angled down a side lane and began the odious task of trying to find a meter in the guest parking lot. Not easy. Thankfully, a woman backed out, and I grabbed her space.

I double-timed it across the Oval and aimed for the Engineering wings, which held most of the Computer Science labs. This Chester guru holed up there, Jeannie had said, then added, "He's a little weird, Mom, but he's definitely the one to help you. If he can't find your files, no one can."

I'd told her I accidentally deleted some of my own files, to cover my need for this guy's services. As for weird, well, real estate attracted the weirdest assortment of people I'd ever met in my life. So, I was definitely comfortable with weird.

Racing up a second long flight of stairs to the Computer Sciences department, I grabbed the banister and paused to catch my breath. I slowed and walked down the long and empty hallway. In this department, people didn't seem to stand in the hallways and talk, as in other buildings. I spotted Chester Yosarian's door before I even reached it.

It was covered in a chaotic collage of old movie posters, newspaper clippings, advertisements, and political slogans, all glued or laminated on top of each other in haphazard fashion. *Young Frankenstein*'s Gene Wilder looked as if he were screaming in horror at the UFO that hovered over the "X-Files" ' Scully and Mulder, who scowled at an angry Nixon, who shoved a newspaper in the Dell dude's grinning face. I admired Yosarian's creativity and knocked on the door.

"Enter if you dare," a deep voice advised from the other side.

I dared, so I did. The door display was neat, compared to the chaotic disarray I walked into. Computers and peripherals covered a desk and two tables; shelves crammed with books and boxes lined the walls, papers hanging out of each. Boxes filled practically every inch of floor space, except a narrow path from the doorway to the desk. A young man, sandy-brown hair pulled back in a long ponytail, was seated with his back to the door. On the desk in front of him, three different computer monitors simultaneously ran different streams of data, interrupted occasionally by beeps and cryptic message boxes.

"Chester Yosarian?" I said to the young man's back, when he didn't turn.

"Guilty."

"I'm Kate Doyle. Jeannie's mom."

At that, he spun his chair around and stood up, hand outstretched. He was so tall I had to look up, and I'm pretty tall. "Glad to meet you, Ms. Doyle. Jeannie said you needed some help." He smiled down at me. Nice face, nice smile. He didn't look overly weird on the outside.

"Yeah, I shouldn't have deleted those files without checking." I shrugged, feigning a casual and careless air. "And I really, really need to get that data back, so I can update it." Better stop now, before the lie got too convoluted. "Jeannie said you would have some software I could use to retrieve those files. If you do, I'd really appreciate using it, if I could. I'll bring it right back." I strove to look earnest and honest.

Yosarian grinned. "You don't have to bring anything

back. It'll be yours to keep." He motioned toward a small chair. "Sit down and tell me what you've got, and I'll know what to give you." He sank his lanky frame into his upholstered chair, while I gingerly sat on the wobbly-looking folding chair beside him.

"Hold on just a sec," he said as he moved around the semicircle and three keyboards, inputting data into each computer. The screens' output changed accordingly.

"Okaaaay, tell me what you've got," he said as he leaned back, hands behind his head. "Standard PC with Windows, I take it?"

"Uh, yeah. That's about it. Nothing special," I said, remembering Mark's setup.

"Figured." He reached into his second drawer and pulled out a black plastic box, filled with CDs. He flipped through several, then withdrew one, slipped it into a plastic case, and handed it to me.

"Thank you, uh, Mr. Yosarian."

He let out a loud laugh. "You sound like my landlord. Chester's fine. Or Yosh. Whichever."

I grinned back. "Okay, Chester. Thanks a lot. What do I owe you?"

He scowled at the idea. "Nothing. It's free."

"Shareware?" I said.

"Naw. Yoshware. I developed it."

"And you give it away. That's pretty generous."

"I guess." He grinned, then cocked his head. "You know, Jeannie told me you were the one that walked in on the murder a couple weeks ago. That right?"

My grin faded. More curious questions. Well, he'd done me a favor, so I owed him. "Yes, that's right. It was pretty gruesome, and I hope I never experience anything like that again." I deliberately shivered, so he'd get the message not to press further.

"I'll bet. I was wondering if the police have any idea who did it," he probed, ignoring my signal.

"You know, Chester, I haven't a clue. Everybody asks me that, as if I know something. And I don't know a thing. I assume the police are working on it. I'm sure they'll find the killer." I rose from the wobbly chair, trying to signal that I was ready to move on and out at the first opening.

He eyed me for a moment, then leaned back into his comfy chair. "You'd hope so," he said enigmatically. "Tell me, did the guy—the one who died—did he have a computer?"

I stopped fidgeting with the CD case and glanced back to Chester. He was smiling just a little.

"Yes, he did. I packed it up myself when we cleaned his office. After the police had finished, of course." I added. "The house is still on the market, you know, so we had to get it ready to be shown to buyers."

"Packed it up, huh?" he said with a nod. "Well, let's hope the cops don't forget to check it, too. There may be some clues. They wouldn't want to miss anything." He sent me a lazy grin.

"Uh, yeah, you're right." I nodded, trying not to let my anxiety show. "I'm sure they've already checked that. I mean, they were all over the place for a week, looking for evidence. They must have checked the computer."

"You never know." He rocked slowly.

Uncomfortable with his close questioning, I decided it was time to leave. "Well, Chester, I can't thank you enough for your help. I really appreciate it. Thanks again." I yanked open the door, ready to escape.

"Anytime, Ms. D. And let me know if you need any more *help*," he said, emphasizing the last word. I waved thanks as I left, convinced I needed serious work on my transparency. Two people in one morning saw right through me. Not good.

Glancing at my watch, I ran down the stairs and out of the building. Somehow the time had run faster than I had, and now I was behind schedule. It didn't seem right to race through the Oval without taking time to drink in its beauty, but I had no choice. The appraiser was probably pulling up in the Schusters' driveway that very minute. As short and succinct as his messages had been, I was worried that he might finish his appraisal before I even got there. I was thirty minutes away in slow traffic. Lucky for me, the coffeehouse owner knew my order by heart and practically poured it for me the moment he saw me walk in the door.

Chapter Nine

The appraiser was still parked in the Schusters' driveway, so I pulled in and gave the big, black truck plenty of room. J. CHEKOV, LICENSED APPRAISER was written in white block letters on the side. Saying a brief prayer of thanks, I grabbed my briefcase, balanced my coffee, and hurried up the walk. Checking the door, I found it unlocked, so I stepped inside and took a deep breath to slow down. The espresso rush had hit me fifteen minutes ago on South College Avenue. An empty stomach just heightened the effects.

"Mr. Chekov?" I called out. "It's Kate Doyle." Hopefully, a muffled voice would reply from upstairs.

Nothing. I scanned the side and back yards to make sure he wasn't finishing up outside and heading for his truck. There was no sign of him. I strolled through the house.

"Mr. Chekov? Kate Doyle, here. Where are you?"

Again, nothing. Maybe he was upstairs in a bathroom and couldn't hear. I started up the stairs. Then I heard a bump, then another, above my head.

What the hey? There it was again, unmistakable this time. He was in the attic, walking around. Brother, talk about thorough. Ronnie was right. A lot of appraisers wouldn't bother crawling around the attic, especially with a newer custom home like this one. They'd assume everything was okay. But the really, really good ones never assumed. They'd check everything.

The footsteps headed across the ceiling toward the kitchen. I followed, figuring he must be finished and headed for the garage. Sure enough, the long pull-down ladder angled out of the attic entrance in the garage ceiling. Slowly, a man began to emerge. I set my briefcase down on a nearby shelf, sipped my coffee, and waited for him to safely descend.

Jake Chekov sped down the sloped ladder and jumped the last two steps. Tall, with a close-cropped beard, dressed in jeans and a khaki shirt, he spotted me watching. "You the real estate agent, Kate Doyle?" he asked as he approached.

"That's right," I replied, watching him brush his hands across his shirt and pants. Hard to believe the immaculate Schuster home would have a dusty attic, but I noticed cobwebs in his dark hair. "I'm glad you're still here, Mr. Chekov. I wanted to show you the comps I used when I priced the home. I really make an effort to use appraiser techniques when I adjust for different properties. I took all my GRI classes last year, and one of them was an appraisal class. And ever since then, I've made sure to use those techniques when I have to adjust between properties. For comparables, that is. Of course, in this case, we had several strong comps already. Three sales in the last six months. Almost the exact square footage. Slight differences, of course. I wanted to show you how I adjusted for those differences. If you'll step into the kitchen, I'll—"

"Whoa, easy, easy," Chekov said, hands up signaling me to stop. Still no smile. "I'm not finished here yet. When I am, you can show me what you've done."

"Sure, sorry. Didn't mean to hurry you." I wondered if

this guy was as hard-nosed as he was thorough. If so, I'd dazzle him with numbers. I was good with those. Real good.

"Believe me, I won't let you hurry me. It takes as long as it takes." With that, Chekov turned and headed out the side door into the back yard.

Well, alrighty then. Heading back into the kitchen, I decided this Chekov was definitely no-nonsense. I'd really have to give him the evidence for the high-end price I'd put on the home. Murder or no, this house was worth every cent. So I rifled my briefcase for the file, and spread out the market analysis I'd used in determining price, complete with accompanying comparable sales worksheet with adjustments.

Meanwhile, I kept track of Chekov's outside maneuvers, paced the kitchen, and finished my coffee. When an antsy fifteen minutes passed and Chekov was still outside examining the exterior, I called my office to re-schedule an appointment with a colleague. Annoyance flirted with impatience, all mixed with the caffeine buzz, as I continued to pace.

Brother, was this guy thorough. Either that or he was deliberately testing my patience. Better not. He didn't know what kind of day I'd had. My pacing quickened, so that I completed a sweep of kitchen, dining room, and great room in just under two minutes.

After another five minutes, I was about to go outside and start on him there, when Chekov entered the kitchen, clipboard in hand. I practically raced toward him.

"Hey, how'd it go?" I asked.

He glanced up from the clipboard, gave me a quizzical look, then went back to his scribbling. "Still wired, huh?"

I blinked. Did he mean me or the house? "What?"

He reached into his shirt pocket, withdrew a small package of peanuts, and handed them to me. "Eat these, then we'll talk. Meanwhile, I've got to check one more thing." And before I could reply, he turned and disappeared through the basement door.

I stood holding the peanuts and stared after him. It was like trying to have a conversation with the White Rabbit. Every time I'd ask a question, all I got was a cryptic reply before he'd disappear down another hole. I looked at the peanuts, debating whether to toss them blatantly on the counter in rebellion. Then I thought better of it. The purpose of this visit was to "support" the appraisal, not aggravate the appraiser. That was part of my job. Besides, I was hungry. I consumed the peanuts in less than a minute.

I was chasing them down with water when I heard Chekov climbing the stairs. This time, I deliberately waited for him to speak, rather than accosting him with questions. Instead, I waved the empty package at him before I tossed it in the trash.

Something that resembled a smile made a fleeting appearance, then was gone. "Good. Now we can start. First, let me tell you why I chose the comps I did; then you can show me yours. Plus, that'll give the peanuts a chance to catch up with the caffeine. Okay?"

Spying a genuine smile at last, I responded in kind. "Sorry. Didn't mean to scare you a moment ago."

"I work with a lot of real estate agents, so I come prepared. Now, here's what I did."

He proceeded to methodically run through every one of the same houses that I'd chosen as comps myself, how he'd adjusted them to the subject property, and so on. As I listened, I exulted, convinced we'd be on the same page for sure.

"Now, about this house. Everything is in good shape. However, I did notice a separation beginning beside the chimney flashing. Only a slight trace of water shows in the attic now, but not for long. None of the comps had any roof defects. So, I'll have to adjust for that . . . and other things." He placed his clipboard on the counter. "You can tell me what you found, if you'd like."

Suddenly my exultation was gone, like air escaping from a balloon. Leaks? Water in the attic? So much for their custom builder from Denver. And so much for pushing the top of the price envelope. I tried to disguise my reaction, but it didn't work. Chekov was watching me like a hawk. "Well, darn it," was the mildest version I could think of.

"I figured you didn't know about the roof. Otherwise, you wouldn't have shoved the price up."

"This is a gorgeous custom property. I didn't shove anything," I responded, not a little defensive. "You've seen all the designer work they've done here. Look at those shelves. An artist from Santa Fe designed them. And the chandelier. That's from France. And the wine cellar—you did see the wine cellar, didn't you? How about—"

He held up his hand. "Don't worry. I saw everything. Stop selling."

I deliberately took a deep breath. This guy was more than annoying. Appraiser or no, I'd had enough of his needling. I crossed my arms and leaned back against the counter. "Tell me, are you always this charming, or am I just lucky today?"

He grinned and imitated my pose. "Believe me, I'm being nice."

I was about to rise to the bait, then thought better of it. Whether this guy was trying to push me or not, I still needed him. So I switched tactics. "You mentioned other concerns. Such as?"

"Such as the other properties do not have a notorious history, so to speak."

"Notorious history?" I feigned ignorance. "I have no idea what—"

"You know what I'm talking about. No one's been murdered in those houses. Like it or not, I have to take that into consideration."

This time I didn't even bother to hide my frown. "You mean you're really going to mark this gorgeous house down for psychological impairment? Brother. Ronnie said you were hard-nosed. She has no idea. I want to see you explain that to her."

"Ronnie will understand. I had to do it to one of her properties years ago. Over in Old Town. That one was haunted."

I bit my tongue to ward off further argument, or the price might plummet like a stone. Instead, I turned away in obvious disgust. "Boy, this day just keeps getting better and better," I muttered.

"Sorry."

"Yeah, yeah." I began to pace the kitchen.

"Tell me, how were you planning on handling that issue anyhow?"

I shot him a skeptical look. I'd had it with this guy. "If you're trying to be cute, it's not working. You know I can't reveal those issues. It's against the law. Besides, everyone in town knows what happened here, so I don't have to say a thing. They already know."

"What about an out-of-town buyer? What would you say to them?"

"What are you, a spy for the real estate commission?" I retorted. "It doesn't matter. I cannot disclose that information. Besides, their real estate agent will have blabbed it already."

"What if they want to work with you? And they're from another state? They're clueless."

I stopped my pacing and faced him. He might have been

smiling, but it was hard to tell. "You must not have any more appointments today, Mr. Chekov, or you wouldn't be standing here asking me all these annoying questions."

"Just curious."

"Sure, you are. Okay. You're the appraiser. You've got the power. You win. In that situation, I would advise the buyers to use another real estate agent to represent them. In fact, I would recommend one personally."

A raised brow was his only reply.

Hoping I'd quieted him at last, I scooped up the market analysis and worksheet. "I chose the same comps you did, so I don't think I'll waste any more of your time. If I may ask, do you have any idea how much that roof will hurt?"

He pushed away from the counter and grabbed his clipboard. "I'll put everything into the computer and see what I come up with. I'll give you a call when I have it done."

I can hardly wait, I thought. The caffeine high had evaporated, and I was crashing. The roof and Mr. Chekov had merely hastened the descent. "Did you make sure the doors were locked when you finished outside?" I asked. He'd started across the kitchen and I was hoping for his exit.

"Yep." He nodded as he headed for the great room, then paused. I braced for more questions. This guy was positively perverse. "Tell me, are you really going to have an open house this weekend?"

Not looking up, I kept loading my briefcase. "Yes, Mr. Chekov, I really am going to have an open house this weekend."

"You're either brave or crazy."

I had to smile. Finally he'd said something I could agree with. "A little of both."

"That's what I thought," he said, and headed for the front door at last. "I'll call you when I have the report ready."

I won't be holding my breath, I thought, as I finally heard the door close with Chekov on the other side.

My office phone started ringing the moment I entered the office. Too tired to dive across the desk and grab it, I dumped my briefcase, then collapsed into my chair and let it ring. When I finally answered, Marilyn's voice was leaving a message.

"And don't think you can avoid me, either," her rich contralto scolded. "I know where you live. I'll come and get you if necessary—"

"Why would I avoid you, Marilyn? What have you done since I saw you last week? Any amusing escapades?" I needed some cheering up.

"Boy, you sound tired," she said. "That Schuster house is wearing you out, Kate. Take it easy. Amanda doesn't expect you to kill yourself. Uh . . . bad choice of words. You know what I mean."

I rubbed my eyes. The peanuts had only reminded me how hungry I was. "Yeah, well, it's been a rough day. Plus, I'm starving. Haven't eaten since breakfast, except for some peanuts."

Marilyn sounded truly horrified. "That's awful. Go get something now. That's an order."

"Can't. Too busy. Besides I'm having dinner with Jeannie tonight. But I don't think I can last. If I hadn't sworn off them, I'd send Lisa across the street for one of those delicious-but-terrible-for-you burgers."

"Now, you're talking. What happened today? I thought you and Rachel had the house all ready to show."

Not wanting to reveal Ackerman's spying or my own for that matter, I grabbed the only information I could share. "Oh, it's that appraiser Ronnie recommended. Jake Chekov.

She swears by him, but he's a jerk. Told me he's going to drop the appraisal because of the murder."

"Hmmm. Chekov. Chekov. I've met him before. Yeah, I agree with Ronnie. He's good. And good-looking too."

Only Marilyn could find a way to get back to her favorite topic. "If you like the rugged outdoor type, I guess."

"And you don't?"

"On somebody else, yeah. But not this guy. He rubbed me the wrong way the moment I got there."

"How?"

"Oh, little annoying things. Needling comments. Plus, he tells me he's going to mark the house down because of the murder. Damn." Remembered aggravation made a brief appearance.

"What kind of comments?"

I sorted through my mail as I detailed Chekov's most endearing traits. "On top of everything else, he finds a leak in the attic! I don't have the heart to tell Amanda, but I'll have to."

"I agree. He sounds very annoying. Being so thorough and all. Also, the jabs about the coffee were totally out of line. Sounds like a jerk."

I heard Marilyn's teasing tone, and I was not in the mood to be ribbed twice in one afternoon. "C'mon, it's the only vice I have."

"I know, that's the problem. I've been trying to get you to develop others, but you resist me at every turn. But, we'll talk more tomorrow night. You do remember you're joining Frank and me for dinner, don't you?"

I didn't. I squeezed my eyes shut. "Marilyn, I'm really busy right now. Can we reschedule?"

"No, we can't. Finley is really anxious to meet you. And I'm not going to let you weasel out of this. No way."

I could picture Marilyn planting her feet even as we spoke. She was right. There was no way to get out of the dinner. Besides, it would be rude. "Finley, huh?" I replied. "Interesting."

"Well, he is, in a quiet sort of way. He's very nice-looking and—"

"Why is that the first thing you notice? What about his personality?"

"That's nice too. And he's very clever. Frank says he's one of the sharpest estate lawyers in town."

"Well, if I ever earn enough to have an estate, I'll call him."

"Anyway, the poor dear lost his wife in January, and he's just started dating again."

"Please don't use that word. I'll join you folks for dinner, but it is not a date, understand?"

"Yes, yes, whatever you say. Just make sure you're at my house at six o'clock sharp. We can catch up first, before Frank and Finley arrive for drinks."

I assured her I would be there so I could get off the phone. A headache was forming right between my eyes. Okay, that's it, I decided and shoved away from my desk. One thousand calories and one hundred grams of fat, who cares? I was going for a burger.

Chapter Ten

Reaching up to adjust the small desk lamp, I suddenly noticed it was dark outside. I glanced at my watch. How could it be 11:30? I'd come straight from Jeannie's apartment and gotten to the Schuster home at 8:00. Had I been hunched over Mark's computer for three hours?

Once I paid attention, my shoulder muscles testified to the time. When I arrived, I'd carried Mark's computer upstairs to Amanda's old study, assuring privacy for my search. Now, I leaned back in the chair and stared at the screen, fascinated by what I saw.

Yosarian's software worked very well, indeed. After a few moments of whirring, beeping, and blinking, plus a strange grinding noise, Mark's nearly empty desktop popped out three more icons. I wasn't surprised.

Nothing, however, prepared me for what I found. There were letters to various off-shore investment entities transferring funds, and emails to stockbrokers, analysts, tax lawyers. *Jonathan Bassett would have a field day with this information,* I thought.

But my surprise turned to concern when I opened the last file. It consisted of accounting records involving the Schuster and Ackerman partnership and various fund transfers that had taken place over the last few years. I scanned them, thinking they were simply another form of the partnership's financial statements. Unfortunately, they were not. A cold spot developed in my stomach as I realized what they were.

Mark Schuster had been transferring funds from the partnership and depositing them in an international brokerage account for years. There was only one name on that account—his. Part of me hoped there was a reasonable and honest explanation for all those transfers, disguised as business expenses to "Gerald Moss & Associates, Consulting." It might have been easier to convince myself had Mark not done such a meticulous job of matching up each consulting expense, duly deposited in a Fort Collins bank, with its accompanying withdrawal and re-deposit in the brokerage account.

I stared at the screen, wondering who else might know of this subterfuge. Surely not Amanda. The other files contained letters that all-too-clearly revealed Mark's strategies for concealing assets from his wife. I also suspected Henry Ackerman didn't know about these transfers either. It made his early-morning garage search all the more understandable.

Remembering Ackerman's cold glare when I'd prevented him from his search, I wondered if he'd become suspicious of Mark and the expenses to Gerald Moss Consulting. Had he learned of Mark's cheating and confronted him? Had Ackerman been so enraged he'd killed Mark?

I reached into my purse for the disc I'd brought, and copied each of the incriminating files. Meanwhile, my imagination started spinning elaborate plots with Henry Ackerman cast as the villain. Suddenly a thump sounded from downstairs. My heart skipped a beat. Could that be the wind?

I stared at a nearby tree outside the upstairs study window. Its leaves and branches were perfectly still, no sign of a breeze. Deciding I was just tired and imagining things, I slipped the disc into my purse, turned off the computer and the desk lamp.

The room was pitch black. I'd forgotten to turn on any lights downstairs when I arrived. Fortunately, there was enough moonlight for me to see my way across the study to reach the hall light outside the door. My fingers had just touched the switch when I heard the thump downstairs again. It was definitely not my imagination. My heart almost leaped out of my chest this time.

I stood, pulse racing, straining my ears to hear. Nothing. *Maybe it really was my imagination,* I thought after a couple minutes of quiet. *I've been sitting up here conjuring crimes and wound up scaring myself to death.* Nobody would try to sneak into this house. My car was in the driveway. Then again, the entire house was dark. It appeared empty, parked car or not.

Okay, enough of this, I said to myself. *The house is locked. Stop being ridiculous.* I stepped into the upstairs hallway and was about to flip on the light, when suddenly something told me not to. Instead, I reached into my purse for my cell phone and punched in 911, ready to call. Then I approached the stairs and slowly went down each step.

At the bottom of the stairs was a panel with all the great room light switches. Surely a sudden burst of light would frighten any trespasser away. I reached the landing and held my breath. Moonlight poured through skylights and windows, making the downstairs look eerily foreboding. I took a deep breath and fumbled for the wall switch.

Light flooded the great room, so bright I had to squint my eyes for a second. Heart pounding in my chest, I looked around, praying I wouldn't see anyone lurking behind the sofas. I didn't. Part of me wanted to check the rest of the house to see if someone had tried a forced entry. The other part said, *Get Out Now!* I listened to the latter. Deciding to leave the lights on overnight as a deterrent, I headed past the dining room toward the entry.

A heavy French door swung out and slammed right into me. I yelped as the force of it knocked me backwards. My purse and cell phone went flying. I fell against the wall and slid to the floor, just as all the lights went out. Terrified I was about to be heinously murdered like Mark, I screamed as loud as I could and scrambled to my feet.

The sound of footsteps running away, getting fainter, then the slam of a door, was all I heard. I stumbled beside the wall, frantically sweeping my hands across the nubby wallpaper weave until I found another set of switches. Light flooded the room once more.

My heart beat double-time. I leaned against the wall and tried to catch my breath. Clearly, someone had been lurking. Who else had a key? Maybe that thump had been the sound of the keyholder breaking in.

Gulping in several deep breaths, I decided against checking doors. This time I would follow my instinct to get out. I retrieved my purse and phone and raced for the front door, slamming it securely behind me. Let the lights stay on. I'd turn them off tomorrow, when I returned with the locksmith. These locks were being changed, and there would only be one key—mine.

"You're having the locks changed?" Ronnie spoke up from the doorway. "Not a bad idea. No telling who has a key."

Startled, I wheeled my desk chair around. I hadn't known she was standing in the office doorway and listening to my phone call. Not wanting to reveal what happened last night, I replaced the phone and reached for some files. "Yeah, that's precisely what I thought. Better be safe than—"

"Sorry," she added. "Good advice, Kate."

I glanced up, but Ronnie was already down the hall. She was still reading my mind, which made me very uneasy, because there was a lot inside I didn't want her to see.

Leaning back into my comfy chair, I tried to think of who else Mark might have given a key to over the years. Ackerman, certainly, but who else? I rocked a moment, running faces and names through my mind. Finally, one face came and stayed.

Cheryl Krane. After all, she and Mark had the longest love affair of all. Perhaps he'd given her a key, so they could meet clandestinely when Amanda was out of town. I rocked rhythmically for another moment, then glanced at my watch. The locksmith wouldn't be at the house for another two hours. There was just enough time to stop by Cheryl Krane's law office in Old Town. I grabbed my briefcase and headed for the back door to the parking lot before I could talk myself out of the decision.

All during the twenty-minute drive into the northern part of town, I practiced various excuses I could offer Cheryl Krane for prying into her private life. This woman was a stranger to me. She had no idea I knew so much about her personal history. I almost felt guilty, but not enough to change my mind. Last night had scared me into taking action. Someone had tried to prowl through the Schuster house. Perhaps the killer had left something, a clue to his or her identity. Perhaps Ackerman had come back to search the computer.

If Cheryl Krane didn't have a key, then I would feel even more confident presenting the computer disc to Bill. Those incriminating financial records gave a strong case to take the spotlight off Amanda and shine it on Ackerman. I only hoped Detective Levitz saw it that way.

Grabbing a parking spot beside Cheryl's office building, I

hurried around the manicured walkway toward the front. As I rounded the corner, I nearly ran into someone. I jumped back with a startled, "Excuse me!" and stared straight at Sharon Bassett.

Clearly surprised, Sharon asked, "Why, Kate, are you rushing to a closing?"

I wish. "Ah, no. No, I'm not. I'm visiting a client," I lied. It was the best I could do. Then something pushed me to ask *her* a question. "Were you here to visit Jonathan? Has he moved his offices?" I knew he hadn't, but I needed an opening.

Sharon fiddled with her sunglasses. "Actually, Kate, I was here on business myself. I met with Rick Boyer, the second-best divorce lawyer in town. Jonathan being the first, of course."

I didn't even try to hide my surprise. Not at the news, of course, but at her blatant delivery of it. "Sharon, I . . . I don't know what to say."

She eyed me skeptically. "Come now, Kate. You don't have to pretend you didn't already know. I told Marilyn two weeks ago, precisely because I knew she'd spread the word and I wouldn't have to."

Might as well confess. "You're right, she did. And I was sorry to hear the news. Divorce is so traumatic. For everyone concerned." Remembering Jonathan's angry denial last week when I'd offered condolences, I probed Sharon. "How is Jonathan handling it?"

She stared off toward the still-green foothills edging the western part of town. "He's making progress."

"I imagine he's taking it rather hard. He's so devoted to you, Sharon. Hard to believe he could manage without you."

"Well, he'll have to. We all have to do what's best. You

know that, Kate. You did this yourself, so I'm sure you understand."

Yes, I did, and I wanted to leave it at that. So I switched into real estate agent-mode. Always an effective defense. "Well, if you're wanting to look at other areas of town, I'll be glad to show you some of the properties I've shown to Amanda. Gorgeous patio homes by the lake. Or, there are some golf-course communities south of town that are fantastic."

"Actually, Kate, I'm moving to Denver."

"Really?" I said, genuinely surprised this time.

"I need to make a fresh start. I've lived here for over twenty years, Kate. If I'm going to begin a whole new life, then I'm not going to do it halfway." She glanced away for a moment. "And, to be honest, this horrible episode with Mark's murder has made me rethink a lot of things."

Genuine emotion radiated from normally aloof Sharon Bassett, and I was amazed. "I understand." Better than she knew. "When were you thinking of moving? I can call our offices in Denver and get a referral agent to help you there, if you'd like."

"Thanks, Kate. I may take you up on that offer in a few weeks." She turned to walk away. "I'll talk to you later." She waved goodbye.

As I continued on the walkway to the building's front entry, I couldn't get over the transformation I'd just witnessed. Divorce often brings out the worst in people. But Sharon Bassett seemed to visibly thaw before my eyes.

As I reached to push open the glass entry door, who should come out but Cheryl Krane. She glanced at me briefly and continued down the walkway. I spun around. Obviously, I was meant to have important discussions outside today. I glanced up at the gorgeous shade of blue above me. Colorado blue, I called it.

"Excuse me, Ms. Krane?" I called, hurrying after her.

Cheryl whirled around, as if startled. Her jet black hair was a striking contrast against her porcelain skin. As I drew nearer, I was struck by her huge blue eyes, which seemed owlish behind her oversized glasses.

"Yes? Do we know each other? If you're looking for Hoffman and Associates, our offices are—"

"No, it's you I came to see, Ms. Krane. Let me introduce myself. I'm Kate Doyle with Shamrock Realty here in town, and I'm representing the Schuster home now that it's on the market."

Cheryl Krane's surprised expression changed to general wariness. "You're a real estate agent? Well, I'm not interested in buying another home. I already have one."

I deliberately assumed a friendly, chatty manner, designed to disarm even the most suspicious souls. "Oh, no, Ms. Krane. I'm not trying to sell you a house. Heavens, no. I, well, I just need to ask you some questions. You see, I'm handling the Schuster property and something, well, something happened at the house the other night, and it concerned me."

Curiosity flashed across her face, even though she didn't say a word. "I was upstairs arranging the rooms for this weekend's open house," I continued, "when I heard noises downstairs. It was late at night, so I admit I was frightened. But I forced myself downstairs to check." I deliberately chose a dramatic tone to relate this story, meanwhile watching Cheryl's reaction. Her wary expression hadn't changed, but I did spy a flush creeping up her slender neck and tingeing her cheek.

I let my voice move up the scale. "Well, I flipped on all the light switches and flooded the house with light. Then I heard footsteps running through the kitchen . . . and then a door slammed! Someone had gotten inside. But there was no sign of break-in. I figured they must have had a key. That house is securely locked every day, believe me."

The slight flush had reached Cheryl Krane's exquisite cheekbones by now. But her voice was anything but warm. "Ms. Doyle, this is all quite dramatic, and it's obvious you are very upset, but I cannot think why you are telling me all this. Are you looking for legal counsel?"

Okay, now came the hard part. I paused and searched for words. I was venturing into dangerous waters here and I knew it. "Well, to be perfectly honest, Ms. Krane. I'd been told you had a long-standing, uh, relationship with Mark Schuster. And quite frankly, I wondered if he had ever given you a key, and perhaps you'd mislaid it or given a copy to someone else." Better give her an out.

Cheryl Krane's flushed face paled in an instant. "Are you accusing me of being this . . . this intruder?" she snapped.

"No, no, of course not," I replied, trying to look contrite. "I was not suggesting *you* entered the home. Perhaps someone else used the key, or made a copy."

Fury radiated from Cheryl now, and she swayed on her feet. I could almost see the sparks. "Ms. Doyle," she enunci- ated the name in a menacing tone. "I will give you the benefit of the doubt and assume you are an overwrought, overzealous woman with an overactive imagination. But mention my name again to anyone in this town, and I promise you, I will charge you with slander." With that, she stalked off, heading toward the parking lot.

I was up to my neck now and treading water fast. Only one thing to do. She'd given me an out, and I took it. Playing overwrought was easy. I raced after her.

"Ms. Krane! Ms. Krane, I'm so sorry!" I cried as I caught up with her. She ignored me and headed toward the front row of parked cars. "I never meant to upset you. I was just so worried about the house! I'm responsible, you see, and . . . and . . ." The rest of my apologia died away when I saw the car Cheryl Krane was unlocking. A vintage white Rabbit. I stood there with my mouth hanging open.

"You probably surprised a would-be burglar, Ms. Doyle, that's all," she said before she revved up the loud engine. Apparently my look of abject stupidity had helped. Cheryl Krane's menacing tone was gone. I stood and watched as she drove away, my mind racing a mile a minute.

White Rabbit. Obvious embarrassment at the mention of her relationship with Mark. And an angry, threatening response, instead of answering my question about the key. That was enough to move Cheryl Krane to the top of my list, where she was neck-and-neck with Henry Ackerman.

She must have visited Mark that afternoon. But did she kill him? Could Cheryl Krane's fury at being rejected lead her to kill her ex-lover? Was she the "funny, fat jogger" the boy remembered? Clearly, there wasn't an ounce of fat on Cheryl Krane's body. Maybe she'd stuffed clothes inside the jogging suit to disguise herself. What about the men's shoes? Had she actually worn Mark's shoes to complete the disguise?

I found my own car and headed back into traffic. The locksmith would be arriving at the Schuster home shortly. My mind buzzed with questions. Should I tell Bill what I had discovered? Exactly what *had* I discovered? Evidence of possible embezzlement on Mark Schuster's part was the only solid evidence of wrongdoing I'd uncovered. And it was against Mark. But it led to Ackerman. I decided to take the disc to Bill, and let his detectives follow up. Meanwhile, I wouldn't even mention Cheryl Krane. All I had was gossip and testimony from an eight-year-old boy, who'd go silent as a stone if police came around. My own suspicions wouldn't count with Bill Levitz. And, above all, I would not mention the late-night prowler. Bill would hit the roof. Then I would really be in trouble.

Yeah, like you're not already there, the Warning Voice said, as I caught the tail of a yellow light. Checking the time, I mentally ran through my schedule. I'd be lucky to finish at the Schuster house with enough time to head home and change, before reporting in to Marilyn for dinner duty.

With everything that had happened in the last couple of days, I didn't think I had an evening of small-talk in me. Surely I would drift off in the middle of a conversation, conjuring motives and murderers. Knowing my own low threshold for arranged evenings, I was already impatient and it wasn't even dinnertime yet. I slowed the car into an intersection and stopped. Then I closed my eyes and prayed this evening would be both merciful and swift.

Chapter Eleven

It was midmorning the next day before I visited Bill at the police department. I'd planned to arrive earlier, but I'd been unable to pry myself out of bed at the usual time. Compassionate listening took a lot of energy, and I'd spent almost the entire night doing just that. It was clear that my dinner partner, Finley, hadn't had a sympathetic listener in a long time, so it was nearly midnight before I could escape. Anyone can escape, but escaping without bruising takes some doing. And energy. I was exhausted.

Sipping my coffee, I tried to look relaxed while Bill read the documents I'd printed out from Mark's secret files. Unfortunately, a police department does not tend to make anyone feel relaxed, especially someone who's concealing information like I was. Knowing my tendency toward transparency, I distracted myself by remembering every defect I'd read in an inspection report earlier that morning. My young buyers had been shocked. Their dream house had problems.

Bill turned the last page, read, and paused, then eyed me over the rim of his glasses. "What made you check Mark Schuster's computer, Kate? Did Amanda ask you?"

"Of course not," I said, shocked that he'd asked. A cold

spot settled in my stomach. His comment indicated Amanda was still Bill's Suspect Number One. "I was checking to see if I could find anything which might give a clue as to who the murderer was. I was hoping there'd be some letter or something that would point to someone—"

"Someone other than Amanda, you mean." He peered at me none-too-kindly. "Kate, you know better than to go poking your nose into a police investigation. You had permission to pack up the study, so you could sell the house. That didn't give you the right to go through evidence."

"I didn't see you folks checking out the computer, so I figured I'd help you out," I volunteered brightly.

"We know how to do our jobs, Kate. We don't need help."

"Well, you missed this, didn't you?" I couldn't resist digging him. "So, admit it. I helped."

Bill scowled. "We'll look into it," he said tersely and tossed the report on his desk.

Leaning forward so no one else could hear, I decided to push what little advantage I had. "I think you should check out Ackerman. After all, I caught him sneaking into the house early in the morning, so he could go through Mark's files. He admitted it himself when I confronted him. And if looks could kill, I'd be dead right now. Just because I'd demanded the key back. I'd say he had plenty of reason to kill Mark. Two hundred thousand dollars' worth of reason, if I read those figures right." I sat back, convinced I'd scored some points, even if Bill would never admit it.

"I said we'd look into it, Kate. Now go back to the office and stay out of trouble." He pointed a stubby finger at me. "Stop poking around. That's an order."

"Absolutely. No problem." That wasn't lying, really. I'd only promised not to poke around Mark's study anymore. No reason to now. I sprang out of my chair, eager to make a quick getaway before Bill could read my mind.

"Oh, yeah," Bill said, leaning back in his squeaky chair. "Mary and I want you to come for dinner some time next week. We've got someone we want you to meet." He grinned.

I grimaced. "Sorry, Bill. Marilyn just trotted out someone last night. I can't take this twice in one month. Call me next spring." I practically vaulted a chair in my haste to escape the office before he could strike again.

"C'mon, Kate," he wheedled. "How're you ever gonna meet someone?"

"Are you kidding?" I replied, incredulous. "I meet all kinds of people every day. The good, the bad, and the ugly."

"What was the guy last night?" Bill teased. "The latter?"

I paused, almost to the door. "No, he was one of the good."

Bill brightened. "Great!"

"Not interested," I said, dashing his hopes.

His round, care-worn face wrinkled into a frown. "Jeez, Kate, you're impossible."

"I know. It's a character defect I've been cultivating." This time I actually made it halfway out the door, when Bill's voice called me back. There was a plaintive sound to it.

"Have you heard from Katherine lately?" he asked.

I leaned on the doorframe. "Yeah, I got an email from her last week. She's so excited. They've already deployed and are heading out to sea. I'm so proud of her, Bill." My niece and namesake was like a third daughter to me. We'd grown especially close, since my sister died two years ago.

He glanced down. "Yeah, I am too. I just wish I'd hear from her. She hasn't sent me a thing."

And I knew why. Being a parent was hard. So I gave him the best advice I could. "She mentioned you chewed her out for not calling. C'mon, Bill. She's a junior officer on her first command. She's up to her neck in duties, and you expect her to check in? Get a grip," I scolded gently. Bill was as over-protective as he was gruff.

"Yeah, well, I just worry. She could at least email me too," he said, his voice petulant.

"She's probably convinced you'll yell at her electronically. Ease up and stop worrying. She's on an aircraft carrier in the middle of the Pacific, for Pete's sake. Even if they get close to action, she won't get hurt. The worst that could happen is she'd slip in the corridor on the way to chow."

"Ha! She's in Flight Operations. She could fall off the damn carrier! No one would see in the dark. I've heard those things happen."

I stared at him, amazed that this hard-nosed detective could lose his objectivity when it came to his only child. "Bill, she's up in the Command Center talking to the pilots, not standing on the Flight Deck holding the trap wire. C'mon."

Bill scowled. "Well, she could still write to me."

"She will, if you write first and tell her how proud you are of her and how you want to hear everything she's doing. That's what I tell her. But no fussing or complaining! Understand? That's an order," I mimicked.

"I'll think about it."

"Good. Now I've got to go put out some fires. Dream house, nightmare inspection. Take care." I pushed away, determined to leave this time. Once again, however, Bill's voice caught my attention.

"Amanda's hired a criminal defense attorney," was all he said.

I slowed down but didn't stop. There was nothing to say.

"Bastard," Amanda muttered softly as she read Mark's correspondence with his secret bankers, but there was no passion in her voice now, as there had been weeks before. Leaning back into Amanda's sinfully soft sofa, I sat and sipped her great coffee. She liked it the same way I did—strong and dark. I was somewhat uneasy, since I'd neglected to tell Bill I'd made two copies of the files. Amanda and Jonathan had been searching for weeks, trying to locate all of Mark's clandestine accounts. I was only helping. The file containing Mark's purloined transfers I included in a separate envelope, without explanation. Jonathan would recognize it for what it was. He and Amanda could take it from there.

"I knew he had hidden files. I just knew it," she said, peering at me. "How'd you find this stuff, Kate? I saw none of these files when I went looking a month ago."

I nearly choked on my coffee. "What do you mean? You went looking where?"

"On Mark's computer," she said. "I went over when I knew he had a long meeting, and I went through every file. I still knew his password. I was certain he was hiding stuff. But I never saw these files." She grabbed her coffee cup and leaned into the creamy leather.

Her statement took me by surprise. She'd admitted sneaking around Mark's office when he wasn't there. That didn't sound like Amanda. But then, divorce can make people do things they normally wouldn't. A very scary thought emerged from the back of my mind. *What if Amanda really had killed Mark and was simply playing me for a fool and a friend?* I almost shuddered, then shook the thought away. No. I knew her better than that.

"Amanda, I've given the same files to Bill and the police. So there may be more questions coming. Bill doesn't know I made a copy for you. So keep quiet about it, please. Tell Jonathan, too. I don't want to get in any more trouble. But I figured you ought to have this information." I was able to say this with complete sincerity.

Amanda sipped her coffee. "More questions. That should be fun," she said in a subdued voice. "I was over there for two hours on Monday. I don't think I could have done it without Bob Carruthers. He was wonderful. He told me what to say and when to say it." She closed her eyes.

I could feel her fear radiating outward. "So, you like him? You feel confident with him?"

"Yes. He's everything Jonathan said he'd be. He took over entirely and told me step-by-step what to do. And you know how hard it is for me to take orders, Kate."

Despite the circumstances, I had to laugh. "Yes, I do."

"Even so, I was terrified. I really was. The detectives may act polite and all, but you could tell they still think I'm guilty."

Hoping to distract her, I said, "Amanda, think back. You've mentioned before that Mark had made enemies in town. Was there any one of them that might have been angry enough to do this? Anyone at all?"

Amanda stared off. "I've tried, Kate. And the only one who comes to mind is that builder, Rupert McKenzie. The one who lost out in the bidding for some land Mark was dangling, playing off one developer against another. You know how he worked."

McKenzie. I'd almost forgotten. He nearly went bankrupt when he lost out on one of Mark's deals two years ago. And ever since then, he'd bad-mouth Mark at every opportunity. But, killing? "You're right. I'd forgotten about McKenzie. I'll check it out with Ronnie. She knows all those builders."

"I don't know how to thank you, Kate. Please don't get into any more trouble for my sake, okay?"

I nodded and finished my coffee. It was too late for that.

On the way back to the office, I listened to my cell phone messages and heard a typically cryptic one from Jake Chekov. He'd be at Coffee Connection at 3:00 p.m., if I wanted to discuss the Schuster appraisal. I wondered if his choice of meeting place was another dig, but let it slide. It was one of my favorites, so at least that would help the appraisal go down.

As I raced through the back door to my office, I figured I'd have just enough time to check in with my young buyers and take their pulse about the inspection results, finish some paperwork, then zoom over to meet with Mr. Chekov. Just enough time. However, I hadn't figured on Ronnie. She waylaid me as I hurried down the hall.

"Kate, step in here for a moment, please," was all she said, but it was the tone. I immediately complied.

"Hey, Ronnie. Everything's coming into place for this weekend," I said, plopping into a comfy chair. "I'm meeting with Jake Chekov in an hour to go over the appraisal, so I'll be all set."

Ronnie leaned back in her chair, a sign she was going to talk about something important. *Uh-oh,* I thought uneasily.

"Kate, you've been anxious and more rushed than usual, and that's going some. What's been happening? There's something you're not telling me, and it has to do with the Schuster house, not with Amanda. I sense it. Something has worried you over and above selling that sucker. Now, what is it?"

"Uhhhhh," I began.

"Come on, Kate. Tell me everything. That's an order."

Orders. First from Bill, now from Ronnie. I ignored Bill, but Ronnie, no way. She was my managing broker. Plus, I respected her more than anyone I knew.

"Okay, okay. It's kind of complicated."

"I figured."

I took a deep breath and recounted everything that had happened—Ackerman sneaking into the house, my pumping the neighborhood boys for clues, searching Mark's computer with special software. I detailed everything I found, including the midnight intruder and my confrontation with Cheryl. Listening to the litany myself, I had to admit it was quite a list.

Ronnie sat silently for a full minute. "Have you told Bill?"

"Only about Ackerman, and only after I'd found those incriminating files. There's nothing to tell him about Cheryl. Some young boys remembering a white Rabbit, that's all. The rest are just suspicions."

"Your suspicions, too."

"Well, she sure acted guilty when I told her about the intruder."

"Maybe. Maybe she was simply angry at being accosted in a parking lot. But Cheryl doesn't concern me. The intruder does. You did tell Bill about that, didn't you?"

I examined my manicure. "Not yet. He'd just yell. Besides, I've had all the locks changed, so whoever had a key is out of luck. It's tighter than a bank vault now. I've even got locks between the garage and kitchen. Believe me, no one's getting in there without my knowing." When I dared glance at Ronnie, she was shaking her head.

"Kate, Kate . . . you better be careful. Whoever did this awful thing is still out there. I understand your wanting to help Amanda, but don't let your feelings drag you too deep. Don't let Amanda convince you either."

That comment surprised me. "Amanda's never asked me to do anything, Ronnie. In fact, she asked me not to get into any more trouble for her sake."

"Yes, and I'm sure she looked pathetic when she asked. Don't let Amanda's neediness suck you into a situation, okay? She's a big girl, and appearances to the contrary, she can take care of herself. Incidentally, how much have you told Amanda?"

"Everything except the intruder and Cheryl Krane. I didn't want to upset her." Suddenly I remembered something else Amanda and I discussed. "Oh, yes, before I forget. What do you know about Rupert McKenzie?"

"What I know about Rupert would fill a book, Kate," Ronnie said with a wry smile. "He's been a brilliant, if erratic, businessman and builder for years. And you can take him right off your list of suspects."

She'd done it again. Read my mind. This was becoming unnerving. "But, Ronnie, Mark's double-dealing nearly drove him into bankruptcy. He had motive, for sure."

"Maybe so, but I think he was in Denver giving a speech with the Metro Council that afternoon."

"Are you sure it was that same Monday, the day Mark was killed?"

"I'm pretty sure it was that same afternoon, Kate, so you can forget about Rupert." The phone at her elbow gave a low-pitched bleat. "Now, I've got to take this call. Be careful, Kate. Promise?"

I pondered Ronnie's advice, as I grabbed my briefcase and headed for the door, "Okay, Ronnie. I promise." Maybe I meant it this time. Naw, not really. I was already thinking of whom I could call at the Denver Metro Council to check on McKenzie's whereabouts that afternoon.

I scanned the Coffee Connection's large, pleasantly-cluttered interior while waiting for one of my weaknesses, a Breve Latte. The random assortment of old worn-out furniture gave the place a certain funky charm. Almost every sprung sofa or tattered chair was filled with someone—students studying/sleeping, office workers taking a break, retirees conducting book clubs, whatever. I'd even stumbled upon a Twelve-Step program one night in my search for caffeine.

Finally, I spied Chekov seated in the corner by the front windows. Another man stood by the table and talked to Chekov. Both men laughed; then the visitor waved goodbye and left. My cue. Time to get this over with. I wasn't looking forward to bad news.

"You holding court?" I asked, as I set my coffee on the table and sat down.

Chekov looked up with a smile. "Whenever I come in here, I see people I know." Pointing to my coffee, he added, "What're you drinking? It looks different than what you had the other day."

Surprised that he noticed such small details, I took a sip before answering. "It's a Breve. A shot of espresso and half-and-half. I have it whenever I need to mellow out. And I figured I better be mellow to listen to what you're going to say."

"I have a feeling your idea of mellow is a pause between breaths."

I deliberately let that one pass, even though it was difficult. I'd promised myself I would not let this annoying man get to me. I just smiled and sipped.

Chekov grinned. "Not going to take the bait, huh?"

"Nope. It's the cream. It's already working. Go ahead. Hit me with your best shot, Chekov. Annoy away."

He laughed as he reached into a weathered briefcase on the chair beside him and withdrew a legal-sized packet. "I'm not going to hit you with anything, Kate."

"It's *Ms.* Doyle to you."

"Okay, *Ms.* Doyle. You can relax. It's not that bad. See for yourself." He handed it over.

I proceeded to read the appraisal, line item by line item, while I sipped my decadent coffee. He was certainly meticulous and accurate as hell. He'd found every fact and every flaw. Had to hand it to him, he was good. My stomach tightened as I turned the pages, afraid of the final verdict. How much lower would his price be than my ballpark? Chekov sat quietly while I read.

When I finally read his determination, I blinked, not sure I had seen the figure correctly. It was only $15,000 lower. Admittedly a lot for a modest home, but a pittance for a high-end property like the Schusters'. I looked up, unable to conceal my surprise.

"Don't look so shocked," he said. "The roof repairs aren't that expensive, and the rest is a judgment call. Some appraisers might mark it down more. But I don't shaft people. The home is in beautiful shape, and it's packed with custom extras."

I leaned back into the worn upholstery and collected my thoughts for a moment. "Thank you," I finally said.

"No thanks necessary. I do my job, Ms. Doyle. And I try to be fair, even with hyper real estate agents bouncing off the walls."

That didn't even faze me. Whether it was the good news or the cream, who cared? Nothing could bother me now. I allowed a smile at last. "Trust me, Chekov, you haven't *seen* hyper."

"I'll bet. Tell me, have you had any bites on this property yet? Those homes usually go in days, so I figure this one, with its history, might take maybe a couple of weeks."

"Just feelers, that's all. I'll have a better idea after tomorrow. I'm having an open house Saturday, ten to four."

He shook his head. "A six-hour open? Now I know you're crazy."

"I'll have some help," I said, feeling mellow at last, thanks to the cream. "A couple of our office assistants will help me out. Keep track of people. Keep them from causing a traffic jam in the library. Watch where there're going, what they're doing, see if anyone acts suspicious. Stuff like that."

"Suspicious? What do you mean?" Chekov folded his arms on the table and leaned forward.

"Oh, you know how you have to be on guard at opens. There are some light-fingered folks out there. And after Wednesday night, I'm not taking any chances." I drained my cup.

"What happened Wednesday night? Did someone steal something during a showing?"

"No, nothing like that. It was just . . . well . . ."

"Go on," he said.

I mentally kicked myself for letting that slip, so I decided to make light of the midnight episode. "I was upstairs, getting ready for Saturday, and I heard noises downstairs. I think someone was trying to get in."

"Did they?" Chekov focused on me like a laser beam.

"Uh, did they what?"

"Don't play dumb. Did they get in?"

"Yeah, but I scared them away when I turned on all the lights." I deliberately avoided the rest.

His eyes narrowed. "Back up a minute. Why weren't the lights on?"

"It's really nothing. I'm sure it was just kids trying—"

"Right. Start at the beginning and don't leave anything out. What time was it?"

I exhaled a long, painful sigh. This guy was relentless. But he'd given me the ammunition I needed to ensure Amanda got a fair deal on her house, so I complied.

"It was nearly midnight Wednesday, and I was still working at the house."

"With no lights on?"

"No, I had a small light on upstairs at the desk, but all the lights downstairs were off."

"Go on."

"Well, I heard a couple of loud thumps. I thought it was the wind, but I decided to leave anyway. I'd turned all the lights off upstairs and was heading down the hall—"

"In the dark? Do you usually do that?"

"Actually, I was about to turn them on, when something stopped me."

"What?"

"A feeling, that's all. So, instead, I crept down the stairs. I was going to throw the main switches, figuring it was probably teenagers trying to get in, when they thought no one was home. I mean, with the lights out."

"A logical assumption. Even for teenagers."

"I thought flooding the house with light would scare them off."

"Did it?"

"Yes, it did." Examining a long crack in the table, I decided I'd said enough.

"Keep going. There's more. I can tell."

Brother. He wasn't going to let go. "Okay, okay. Whoever it was that came in must have hidden in the dining room when I turned the lights on, because one of the French doors slammed right into me when I passed by. I screamed, the lights went out, and I heard him running away. That's it."

Chekov stared at me intently, then said in a low voice, "That's all you have to say? You could have been attacked, or worse, you know that?"

"But I wasn't. It was probably a vandal hoping to steal something, that's all."

"But it could also have been the killer returning. If it had been, tell me, how would you have protected yourself?"

I was feeling very uncomfortable now. "I had my cell phone dialed to nine-one-one, ready to punch in."

A pained expression crossed Chekov's face. "That's all? A lot can happen in the ten minutes it takes police to respond. You could be assaulted, even killed. Had you thought about that?"

"Not until now," I retorted, unhappy with the unpleasant turn this conversation had taken. "Thank you so much for scaring the daylights out of me."

"Maybe that's good. You need to be more aware of the dangers out there. Working alone late at night in that house was risky. The killer is still out there."

A chill crawled up my spine, so I sent a cold blast his way. "I don't need you to remind me."

"You're in a hazardous occupation, you know that?"

"I'm a real estate broker, Chekov. Get a grip."

"You regularly go off alone to meet with strangers in deserted houses, some in remote locations with no one else around. You don't think that's risky?"

That stark depiction definitely sent another chill through me. At this rate, I'd need more coffee to recover from Chekov's active imagination. "My office always knows where I am," I shot back.

"Great. They'll know where to look for the body."

"What *is* it with you? You like scaring women? You're way out of line, Chekov."

"You don't believe me, check with Ronnie. At least one real estate agent a year turns up dead or assaulted. All from being unaware and not taking precautions."

I froze. *One a year?*

"Got your attention? Good. Aside from the cell phone, what other means of protection do you have? Any martial arts training?"

I was still trying to process the startling statistic. "Uhhhh, no. No martial arts."

"Would you like a weapon? If so, I can help you choose one, then teach you how to handle it. I've taught several real estate agents over the years."

I blinked at him. Surely he hadn't said what I thought. "You mean a gun?"

He gave an aggrieved sigh. "Yes, a gun," he enunciated. "A weapon."

I stared at him, disbelieving. If the first images caused problems, the image of me waving a gun in some randy client's face was more than I could process. "Are you nuts? What am I supposed to do with a gun? Carry it around in my briefcase?"

"The purpose is not to ever have to use it. It's a deterrent."

"Deterrent?" my voice traveled up an octave. "You've got to be kidding! The only thing it would deter would be clients. I reach inside my briefcase for a property disclosure and out comes the 397 Magnum. Great!"

"357."

"Whatever."

"Just consider it, okay?" he said slowly, as if I had trouble understanding the words.

I understood all too well. Carrying a gun would be ludicrous. I'd be more of a danger to myself than to any criminal. Not to mention the harm I could accidentally inflict upon clients.

"Before you reject it out of hand," he said, voice dropping, "remember that you've already made yourself a target by asking questions all over town. You think the killer won't pay attention?"

"How do you know what I've been doing?"

"I spoke with Ronnie. She's worried about you."

That did it. Now he was pumping my boss for information. Who the hell did this guy think he was, anyway?

I pushed back my chair with a loud scrape and stood up. "Okay, Chekov, I've had it. I don't know what your problem is, and I don't care. You may be a great appraiser, but you're one sorry-assed conversationalist. I thought being nice would help you respond in kind. Obviously not. Polite is just not your strong suit."

He quirked an eyebrow and peered at me. "I take it the cream has worn off."

I hesitated for a second. "Chekov, there's not enough cream in the world to sweeten you." I watched him try to hide a smile, and I knew I'd better leave before I really insulted him. "I'll recommend you to others, but I'm afraid I have checked you off my list." At that, I turned and walked away.

"You've been thinking about that one, haven't you?"

His parting shot grazed my shoulder. I let it go.

Chapter Twelve

"Everything going okay upstairs?" I asked Lisa, one of our young office assistants.

"Yeah, busy, but no problems," she said, bending over the Schusters' refrigerator and withdrawing a cola. "Melanie and I are switching at one o'clock."

I looked behind me at the assorted couples milling about the Schuster great room. "Sounds good. Remember, direct any questions on the property to me. You just hand them the printout."

"Gotcha." She twisted off the cola cap with a hiss and headed upstairs once more.

I went back to my pacing. Kitchen, great room, foyer, dining room, wherever necessary to stay out of a visitor's way. Glancing around, I counted heads. Curiosity being what it was, I'd figured a lot of people would take advantage of the open house to gawk and gossip at the murder scene. I was sure it would be topic number one in some offices on Monday. But I hadn't anticipated such a large turnout. I just hoped there would be some real buyers in there somewhere.

Melanie had been playing discreet traffic cop for the past three hours, shepherding the cluster that hovered at the door to the library. There was nothing to see. The room was stripped bare, sparkling clean, and scented with orange. But still, people lingered at the doorway, conjuring probably. Melanie let them hover, then would gently guide them along so others could take their place. That way I was free to answer any genuine questions about the property.

So far, there had only been two couples who appeared to be serious buyers. Both were accompanied by real estate agents, and both couples were from out of town. Hopeful signs.

My cell phone rang, and I headed down the hallway and away from visitors. "This is Kate," I answered.

"Well, finally," came Marilyn's voice. "I've been trying to reach you since yesterday, but all I get is voice-mail."

"I've been swamped. In fact, I'm in the middle of the Schuster open house right now, so I can't talk long. What's up?"

"How's it going?" she asked.

"About as I expected. Lots of gawkers. Only a couple bona fide buyers so far."

"How long will you stay?"

"Till the bitter end. Four o'clock."

"Well, take it easy. Listen, I never got to hear any feedback about Finley. So, tell me? How'd it go the other night? You looked like you two were really focused on each other. Such intensity. I was amazed you had it in you, frankly."

"What you saw was me giving him my full, undivided attention all that time. Boy, was it draining. I was wiped out when I got home."

"What do you mean? He was talking to you, that's all. I swear, Kate, you find fault—"

"I'm not finding fault, Marilyn. Honest." I lowered my voice. "He's a really nice guy. Too nice, almost. But he's got a lot of problems to sort through. Plus he's searching hard for the next woman."

"Well, what's wrong with that?" she countered. "That's what we all do."

"Yes, but he's searching so hard, it's scary. I felt this wave of desperation come at me. Kind of like a tsunami. It was all I could do to stay afloat."

I heard an exasperated sigh. "Now that is a novel excuse, if ever I heard one."

"It's not an excuse. He's just too needy right now. What he should do is take some time and find out how to be comfortable with himself for a while, then go looking."

"You've been reading those empowerment books again, haven't you?"

I snickered. "Yep. Can't help myself."

"I won't be able to help you, either, if you keep finding microscopic flaws with everyone."

"Marilyn, I've got to go. Catch you later," I said, and switched off my phone.

I'd spotted a familiar face in the throng near the library. Stanley Blackstone, Cheryl Krane's devoted swain. What was he doing here? Instinct told me to watch him, so I eased down the hallway to find a less noticeable vantage point. The artistic glass-and-stone planter at the edge of the great room offered me an unobtrusive place to watch the crowd.

Stanley hovered with several others in the doorway to the library, then glanced about the great room. I watched him carefully, and concluded he was not here to look at real estate. The brief, disinterested gaze he cast about the Schusters' impressive great room was a giveaway. Why was he here, then? Idle curiosity? Perverse pleasure in viewing Mark's murder site? That wasn't out of the question, given Stanley's reaction at the funeral.

Grateful that the plants concealed my spying, I continued to watch Stanley as he meandered through the downstairs. After a cursory glance over his shoulder, he headed for the kitchen and out of sight. I left my spot and edged slowly around the great room, following him. I hovered near the dining room doorway and watched Stanley wander about the huge kitchen, casting brief glances left and right.

An exuberant couple entered the kitchen and commented loudly on the decor. Stanley didn't leave, which surprised me. He hadn't shown real interest in anything, yet he stood staring at the cabinets for a full five minutes. My instinct sent a buzz through me. Something was definitely up.

Sure enough, after the chatty couple wandered off, Stanley glanced over one shoulder, then another, then stealthily approached the door that led to the garage. Son of a gun. He was looking for something. Just like Ackerman, he had come to search the stuff from Mark's library.

I wasn't worried. The door to the garage was securely locked. Stanley wasn't going anywhere. Deciding to corner him, I slipped into the kitchen and pounced. "Can I help you, Stanley? Is there anything in particular you're looking for?"

He jumped at least a foot off the floor. I didn't mean to scare him really, but I did take perverse delight in watching him turn beet-red, mouth hanging open.

"M-m-ms. D-d-doyle," he stammered. "I was just, uh, I just wanted to . . . to . . . see the garage." His huge blue eyes bulged behind his old-fashioned, horn-rimmed glasses.

"I'm sorry, Stanley. I can call you Stanley, can't I? After all, we're in Chorale together." I deliberately chose a chatty tone. "We have to keep the garage securely locked now. Everything from Mark's office is stored in there. And someone tried to break in the other night."

All color quickly drained from Stanley's flushed face, and his gaze sought the floor. "Uh, really? That's awful," he mumbled.

"It was probably vandals, looking to steal something," I offered.

"Oh, y-yes, yes," he stammered and began to edge away from the doorway, where I had him trapped.

I stepped in front, blocking his path, and let my tone chill. "Or, it could have been someone trying to search through Mark's belongings. I caught a person pawing through the boxes just a few days ago."

Stanley's head snapped up as if on a string. "Who?"

"I cannot divulge that, Stanley. The police are looking into it now."

Sweat started to bead his forehead. Why would Stanley Blackstone be so nervous? Was he the intruder? What was he looking for? I found it hard to imagine Mark Schuster had anything in his possession that belonged to Stanley Blackstone. Except . . .

"Oh, yes, of course, I understand," he managed, then drew a deep breath, obviously preparing his next question.

Poor Stanley. He practically had a blinking neon sign over his head, saying: GUILTY. How could this guy be a lawyer? He couldn't even lie.

I gambled and decided to push him and see what happened. "Are you here searching for something, Stanley? I couldn't help noticing how distressed you looked, when you discovered the garage door was locked."

Panic darted across his face. "Me? No! Of course not! What would I be looking for?"

Following a hunch, I adopted a solicitous tone. "Oh, perhaps an item of a personal nature. Not really valuable, except to the owner."

Bingo. Stanley's huge eyes nearly popped out of his head.

He swallowed, licked his lips, then said, "Maybe."

"If that were the case, Stanley, I promise you that I'd search for the item and return it to the owner."

He stared at me in disbelief. "Really?"

The change in Stanley's countenance told me my suspicions were true. "Of course," I assured him. "There's a place for discretion, after all. Could you give me a description of the item? Everything is packed in boxes. I'd need some clue where to look."

"It's a book. A book of poetry, with a . . ." These words came harder to him. "With a personal inscription."

"All right, I'll take a look. I may not be able to search until after the weekend, though."

"That's fine." He exhaled a long breath.

Just to make sure, I said, "Oh, yes. Is this book from you, Stanley, or someone else? Someone who was a close friend of Mark's, perhaps?"

Stanley flushed crimson. "Someone else," was his terse reply.

I was about to ask another question, when a woman's voice cut into my thoughts. "Are you the broker? Could you please tell me who the architect was for this property?"

Stepping away from Stanley, I switched back into real estate agent-mode and focused my attention on the tall, stylishly-dressed young woman in front of me. While we talked, Stanley slipped quietly from the kitchen and out the door.

I felt immense relief. Stanley must have been the intruder. Chekov's fears were groundless. Stanley simply came searching for a book. A book that would have caused great embarrassment, if the police found it. And I didn't have to wonder too hard who the book's owner was. My money was on Cheryl Krane.

One of the sad facts of life for a real estate agent is that there are no weekends free. We work 24/7, all the time. Of course, top-selling real estate agents have assistants and buyers' agents to run open houses for them, handle the office, and oversee transactions. They were the big dogs, so they could lie on the porch and rest in the sun. But I was still a puppy, and waaaaay out in the back yard. I couldn't even see the porch. So I worked all the time. Whenever a client called, I was there.

Consequently, this Sunday I was previewing properties in one of our nearby canyons. Some out-of-town buyers had emailed me their wish list and I was trying to find it. As I steered my Explorer around the familiar, curving mountain roads, I punched in another number before the hills would steal my signal.

My young buyers, the Kerchoffs, were deciding exactly what to ask for in the Notice to Correct. Three days had helped calm them down a little, I'd noticed. Just as I was about to connect, my cell rang with an incoming call.

"This is Kate," I answered.

A smooth voice slid over the airwaves. "Kate, this is Henry Ackerman. I hope I didn't disturb you on this beautiful morn?"

I was so surprised I couldn't respond at first. Ackerman was calling *me?* Why? Our last meeting had been icy. And why was he sounding so friendly? "Hello, Henry," I managed at last. "You're not disturbing me. I'm out previewing property."

"That's great!" he enthused.

I almost lost the curve on that one, his voice boomed so loud into my ear. *Got to remember to turn off the cell before I enter the canyon,* I thought. I really could use two hands on the wheel about now.

"My wife and I just drove by a home we are dying to see," he continued. "Over here in Devonshire Estates. We wondered if you could take us through it later today?"

It was fortunate there were no curves on this stretch of mountain road, because I would have gone off for sure. Henry Ackerman was asking me to show him property? What could possibly have inspired this change in behavior? "Devonshire Estates? I didn't think they'd finished any models yet," I said.

"Yes, two are up. And the one Ruth and I want to see is the large two-story, with tiered decks in the back. You can't miss it. It's at the edge of the subdivision. Looks absolutely fabulous. We can't wait to see it. What time works for you, Kate?"

There was something wrong in this conversation, but I couldn't pin it down. Part of me wanted to say no, but the hungry real estate agent replied, "How about three o'clock?"

"Perfect. See you there. Thanks, Kate." And he clicked off.

This time I did turn the cell phone off and tossed it onto the passenger seat, while I concentrated on the tighter turns as the road climbed higher and higher to the top of the ridge. Meanwhile, I continued my inner wrangling. There was something about Ackerman I didn't trust. And that oh-so-friendly tone didn't sway me either.

My practical side spoke up then. There could be a very simple explanation for his sudden change. Perhaps Jonathan Bassett had mentioned my role in finding the secret financial records. Clearly, that's what Ackerman had been searching for the morning I walked in on him. Maybe he was grateful and had decided to throw a little business my way.

I considered that possibility as I edged toward the high point of the canyon road. At the top, however, I forgot about Ackerman entirely. The view was as breathtaking as always. I pulled onto the shoulder to stare and enjoy, before I headed down into the valley below.

The Rocky Mountains glistened with the early snows September had brought them. The high country always got snow earlier than the rest of us in the foothills. I watched the sun glint off a sequestered glacier nestled beside Long's Peak. Feeling the peace this serene view always invoked in me, I just sat and stared for several minutes before I reluctantly nosed my Explorer onto the downward slope of the road.

I'd made a decision. There was enough time to check out all six houses I had on the list before 1:00 p.m. Since the last house was located in another beautiful canyon, I would be able to indulge myself in one of my favorite pleasures—a short hike to a cherished view. Then I could sit on a rock and stare at the mountains for an hour. I was in serious need of some quiet time. These last two weeks had been nonstop chaos. Peace and serenity were what I needed right now. I could worry about Ackerman later.

Spying a parking spot in front of one of my favorite coffee haunts, I quickly grabbed it, hopped out, and raced inside the small shop. A huge version of Van Gogh's *Starry Night* adorned one wall and gave the shop its name. But there was no time for sitting and sipping, so I grabbed my usual from the accommodating barista and zipped outside.

I'd only been out of the canyon and into cell range five minutes before the messages started beeping. Normal stuff until I got to Ronnie's. Her message was short. I was to meet Jake Chekov tomorrow at 4:00 p.m. at the county firing range south of town. No arguments, she added. It was an order.

Order or no, I was going to register a protest. This whole idea was ludicrous. So I fortified myself with a dose of caffeine and punched in her number. To my surprise, she answered on the first ring.

"Ronnie, it's Kate."

"I knew you'd call after you heard my message. I figured five minutes. It took fifteen."

"I was in the canyon previewing. Listen, Ronnie, that idea is crazy. This guy Chekov is a gun nut. He wants me to carry a briefcase full of weapons. Can you picture that? I mean—"

"Jake is no nut. He's trained several agents. And none of them had anything to worry about. You do."

Her words took me aback. Not her, too? "Ronnie, you're exaggerating."

"I'm not exaggerating, Kate. You've been taking entirely too many chances lately. That litany of yours took my breath away the other day. I'm concerned for you. I know you want to help Amanda, but you cannot jeopardize your own safety in doing so."

Hearing her concern voiced with such feeling loosed all those nagging anxieties I'd tried to keep at bay. They raced up and nipped at my heels. Partly to assuage Ronnie's fears and my own, I began to bargain. "Okay . . . okay . . . I promise I'll be careful. Really."

"Not good enough, Kate."

I thought fast. Guns, with or without Jake Chekov, were scary. I didn't need any more anxiety in my life right now. "Okay, I've got an idea. How about martial arts training? Self-protection. I can learn Kung Fu or whatever. Even Chekov the jerk mentioned that as an alternative."

"Chekov the jerk?" I heard a smile in her voice, and I knew I was in the home stretch. All I had to do was convince her of my sincerity.

"Yeah. He's impossible. He goes out of his way to annoy me. I've met a lot of jerks, but this guy is in a class by him-self."

"I see."

"No, you'd have to hear. He deliberately scared the bejeezus out of me."

"In your case, that's good."

"Listen, I'll sign up for classes tomorrow or the next day. Whenever they start. I swear."

Ronnie paused. I held my breath until I heard a long sigh, then exulted. She'd bought it. Now, all I had to do was find some nice neighborhood Jackie Chan to teach me the moves. Or, some of them at least. Climbing up the side of buildings I didn't need.

"Okay, Kate, but you'd better register this week. And I want to see the course description. Tai Chi in City Park won't cut it. Understand?"

Rats. I'd already put that on the top of my list because it fascinated me. Guess I'd actually have to find Jackie Chan. "You got it, Ronnie. I promise."

Chapter Thirteen

As I drove through the entrance to Devonshire Estates, I was struck once again by the incongruous view. Ten miles down the interstate, east another three miles, out in the middle of what used to be nowhere. Like it or not, the small nowheres of Northern Colorado were becoming somewheres faster than we could say "development." Sprawl had come to Fort Collins, big time.

The subdivision spread out north to south, covering the former farmland with building sites as far as the eye could see. Wooden stakes bloomed where crops had once been. Working farmland still bordered the subdivision on both sides. Cows grazed beside the fence line, overlooking the empty tractors. I knew the modest-sized lots would bloom yet again with enormous estate homes, nestled cheek-by-jowl with each other.

Since it was Sunday, I expected the builder's sales agent on site to be fairly busy. Ackerman had said a couple of models were already up. Following the arrows around the newly-paved empty streets, I spied only one car at the model home office and it wasn't Ackerman's sporty red number. Then I took a closer look at the model. It was a huge walkout ranch. Ackerman said a two-story. Must be another model. I wheeled around and circled through the subdivision's maze, heading for the south end. Sure enough, there was an enormous two-story rising in lonely splendor. And a shiny red car was parked beside it.

I'd had my office set the showing and call me with the lock box code. I'd assumed the model was another of the developer's. Consequently, I was surprised to see an unfamiliar real estate sign stuck in the dirt of the soon-to-be front yard with just the company name and a Denver phone number. *Great,* I thought as I parked my car and got out. Probably some one man/woman shop with an answering machine. Henry Ackerman was already out of his sporty little car and headed my way, smile in place. I braced myself.

"Thanks for coming, Kate," he said in greeting.

"Sorry I'm a little late, Henry. I headed toward the other site at first." I glanced around for his wife. "Is Ruth out in the back?"

"No. Her plans changed at the last minute. Her mother's in a nursing home and suddenly took a turn for the worse. I'll have to tour the property for both of us, I guess." He flashed a bright smile.

"Okay," I said, trying not to show my disappointment. "Let's go in, then." And I led the way up the winding walkway leading to the expansive front porch.

Unfortunately, all my anxieties came along with me, dogging my heels like panting hounds. I had convinced myself Henry Ackerman was Suspect Number One, with Cheryl Krane right behind him. However, now that I'd learned Cheryl sent Stanley to retrieve an incriminating book she'd given Mark, I was toying with rearranging my Order of Suspects.

In any case, the last place I wanted to be was alone with either of them—especially in a deserted house, way out in the middle of nowhere. Jake Chekov's warnings came back to haunt me. So much so that I fumbled the tiny numbers on the lock box, taking three tries to open it. Ackerman stood quietly, watching me.

Finally the little box sprang with its metallic sigh of release, and I retrieved the key and opened the inlaid-glass door. "Wow," was all I could say as I gazed at the expanse of light and space.

"Wow is right," Ackerman said, as he walked around the huge great room. "Wait'll I tell Ruth. I knew I should have brought my digital. Do you have one in your car, Kate?"

"Sorry, I don't, Henry. That's next on my wish list."

Watching Ackerman act like any interested buyer did more to reduce my fears than anything. He circled the great room and the exquisite open kitchen with its cherry wood cabinetry. The house was luscious, no doubt about it. I followed after him, answering questions about the builder, deadlines, contracts. We admired master suites, guest suites, mother-in-law suites, and ordinary bedrooms. Sitting rooms, sun rooms, exercise rooms, computer rooms—you name it, this house had it.

Ackerman returned to the downstairs study and leaned against the French doors for a minute, staring inside. I hoped he was imagining his home office.

"How do you think Amanda's holding up?" he asked.

His question surprised me. Obviously his mind wasn't where I thought it was. "Pretty well, considering."

He shot me a penetrating look. "Considering she's Murder Suspect Number One?"

I stared back, amazed he'd say such a thing. Unable to keep the annoyance from my voice, I said, "Henry, you of all people should know Amanda's innocent. She couldn't kill Mark."

"Anyone's capable of murder, Kate. Given the right circumstances," he said in a low voice.

His words sent a chill up my spine and awoke all those fears that had been snoozing peacefully at my feet. They snapped awake.

"Has your brother-in-law let anything slip?" he asked, checking a closet.

The smooth lawyerly tone had returned, and I recoiled at its oily sound. "I'm just as clueless as everyone else, Henry. Bill always keeps police business secret."

Ackerman headed down a side hallway. "Word has it Amanda's on the top of Bill's list," he said.

"You shouldn't believe everything you hear, Henry," I shot back as I followed him.

He paused, hand on the knob of what I assumed was another closet. Turning to me with a nasty grin, he said, "And you shouldn't be so trusting, Kate. It'll get you into trouble some day." With that, he opened the door. It was no closet. I spied stairs leading down into the dark. "Shall we?"

I stared at the open doorway for several seconds. "Shall we what?"

"Check out the basement, of course." His grin spread. "Have you been out in the sun, Kate? You look all flushed."

Every horrible image Jake Chekov had planted in my brain shimmered before my eyes now. Me, downstairs in the basement of a deserted house in the far end of a deserted subdivision with a killer.

Ackerman peered at me. "Kate? You coming?" He reached inside the doorway and flipped on the light.

No! No! No! I wanted to say, but knew I couldn't. Instead, I took a deep breath and forced myself forward. "Sure. You first." I gestured. There was no way I was going down those stairs with him behind me.

I watched him hesitate for a second, staring at me. My heart was pounding so hard, I'd have sworn he could hear it.

"As you wish, Kate." To my immense relief, he started down the stairs.

I paused at the top of the stairs and waited until he reached the bottom before starting down—slowly, very slowly. He glanced at me quizzically, then began to wander the enormous and empty basement. The lower I descended, the chillier I felt. All those concrete walls, sealing off all sound, cold as a tomb.

That did it. I grabbed my cell phone from my pocket and frantically punched in the office number, desperate to avoid becoming one of Chekov's statistics. The sound of Lisa's voice on the other end was a lifeline. "Hello, Lisa!" I yelped. "How . . . how're . . . things going?"

"Kate? Is that you?"

"Yeah! Hey, did, uh, did that guy . . . uh, you know, did he leave a message?" I floundered for a moment while I searched for something plausible. Ackerman was just a few feet away, staring up at the floor joists.

"What guy?" Lisa's bewildered voice asked. "Kate are you all right?"

"Not really," I admitted, hoping she'd remember that cogent comment if I turned up dead. "I'm over here in Devonshire Estates right now with *Henry Ackerman*." My voice must have shrilled because Ackerman turned and gave me an odd look. I no longer cared. I was determined to get out of that basement alive. "We're down in the *basement* right now. It's 2573 King's Court. Remember that, will you?"

"Kate? Is there something wrong? You sound really weird."

"I'm just busy showing this gorgeous *new* home. I'll—"

"Kate, could you come over here for a moment and tell me if this is plumbed for another bath or not?" Ackerman called over his shoulder.

If he thought I was going into that dark corner with him, he was crazy. "I'll be right there, Henry," I said loudly.

"What? *Where* are you going?" Lisa said.

"I'm going over to check the sewer drains with Henry Ackerman," I announced, as I drew close enough to scan the area in question. "Yep, Henry. Looks like it to me." I spun about and headed for the safety of the stairs again. "This house is plumbed for bathrooms here in the basement, Lisa."

"Kate, all the new construction is plumbed for bathrooms in the basement. What is *wrong* with you?" Bewildered had changed to confused.

But that was nothing compared to the perplexed look on Ackerman's face. "Kate, you barely glanced over here," he said.

"Henry, when you've seen as many sewer drains as I have, all you need is a glance," I said and started up the steps. "I noticed it's plumbed for another over in that corner." I pointed. "Why don't you go check that out while I, uh . . . finish this call?"

"Kate, I think yesterday's open house fried your brain," Lisa said. "Hey, another call is coming in. Gotta go."

And the line went dead.

I gulped and kept the phone to my ear, pretending. Ackerman would never know. "You're right, Lisa. Yeah, call him back." I glanced over my shoulder. "Henry, take your time. I'll be upstairs finishing this call."

"I have some questions about the furnace and the plumbing," Ackerman said as he headed into the far corner.

I ventured into the basement a few paces, paused, and

scanned up, down, and sideways. Then I announced in a loud voice, "Furnace, deluxe ninety percent. Copper pipes. Sump pump installed. Custom floor joists. Expansive soil counter-measures as required by law. Looks good to me." With that, I was up the stairs like a shot. To hell with Ackerman. I was out of there.

Once upstairs, I stationed myself by the open front door. I wasn't leaving him any room to maneuver. Finally, Ackerman surfaced from the basement. He approached me with a strange smile.

"Okay, Kate. I'll talk with Ruth. We'll be in touch," he said.

"That's great, Henry," I responded with enthusiasm, and held the front door wide. "You tell Ruth I'll be happy to take her through any time she wants."

Ackerman looked at me a little funny, before he exited. I didn't care. Slamming the door hard, I practically skipped off the porch. Watching him drive away, I collapsed into my own front seat, not sure whether I had just thwarted an attempted attack or suffered an embarrassing bout of paranoia.

It didn't matter. I had survived both to live another day. I revved my engine and headed home. There was nothing that a little brie and a good Merlot couldn't cure, as I relaxed in my own back yard.

"Mom? I got your message. What's up?"

I stretched out on my back yard chaise, beneath the shade of a maple, Sunday papers scattered on my lap, Sam gnawing a bone on the grass beside me. "Hey, sweetie," I said into the phone. "I called to pick your brain."

"Not much left after that Organic Chem final, but you're welcome to try. What do you need?"

She sounded tired. Balancing engineering courses and

pre-med was no picnic. "You know anyone who could recommend a good martial arts instructor?"

"For you? Awesome."

Not the response I'd expected. "Well, I just thought it would be useful. You never know." I had not mentioned my close encounters of late. Jeannie's protective instincts would go into overdrive, and she had enough on her mind as it was.

"Yeah. Good idea. Uhhh, let's see. Well, there's that Karate place on Prospect, and then there's the Kung Fu place. And Tae Kwon Do. Gee, Mom, you're going to have to decide which one you want. There are so many styles of defense. You might want to go visit the classes and see for yourself."

Obviously, this venture would take longer than I thought. I'd better make some phone calls and get schedules and prices. Maybe I could start tomorrow. That way I would have something to show Ronnie. She'd ask me, for sure.

I thanked Jeannie for her suggestion, then let her get back to work. Meanwhile, I enjoyed what was left of the autumn afternoon. Winter would tease us soon with early snow showers, followed by brilliant sunshine. For now, the scent of fall was in the air. I stared above my head into the canopy of yellow leaves and relaxed. Sam left his bone and appeared beside me, looking for a pat on the head. He rested his chin on my lap while I patted. All those anxieties and concerns I'd carried around these last two weeks could go on hold for a while. The brie was softening on the counter and the Merlot was breathing. The worries would wait.

Chapter Fourteen

It was afternoon on Monday before I finally arrived at the office for the day. I'd spent the entire morning checking out martial arts instruction. Schools, academies, workshops, plain old classes—you name it, I was there. Starting at the ungodly hour of 5:30 a.m. for the Early Bird Kickboxing class, I fortified myself with extra strong coffee and headed to the nearby health club, the same one I frequented every morning at 6:00 for my regular workout.

It was amazing how much harder it was to crawl out of bed a half-hour earlier than usual. Pure torture, plus it was darker outside. Daylight Savings Time was still in effect, even though the seasons were naturally turning. Pretty soon, we'd all experience that abrupt jolt of "falling back" as we adjusted our clocks backward. For a few brief days, early morning sunshine would welcome those of us who needed help prying ourselves out of bed. Then winter would steal even that slice of sunlight, as we slid into the Dark Time. I always found those dark days of December and January strangely peaceful, as if we were all sleeping, like seeds, ready to sprout forth again with the spring sun.

I was astounded how many folks, men and women, were

up and quite literally "at 'em" at 5:30 in the morning. I found a quiet perch in the corner of the wall-to-wall mirrored room, so I could observe without being a distraction. I never knew there were so many workout rooms scattered down the health club's corridors.

It was a good thing. Nary a flaw could escape detection in this room. There were floor-to-ceiling mirrors everywhere just waiting to catch it. A pudgy thigh here, an ample rear there—all were on unforgiving display. I wasn't sure if I'd be able to go to work after such an assault to my self-concept every morning.

Thankfully, the folks who frequented the "cardio room" with me every morning were focused, like I was, simply on getting their workout done with enough time to shower and change and rush to the office. Consequently, multi-tasking was ever present, as we went from elliptical trainers to treadmills to the weight machines. Handy plastic trays allowed us to read the morning paper and exercise righteously, while we kept an eye on the televised news and weather. Pretty we weren't, in our old sweats, mismatched shorts, and shirts, but we got the job done. Plus, we really couldn't see each other that well because we were always surrounded by equipment. We were either resolutely working out, hurrying to the next machine, or waiting semi-patiently for others to finish their sets so we could grab a turn. Wherever we went, we were camouflaged by metal, so we really couldn't get a good look at each other. Or, we simply didn't care.

The folks in the kickboxing class, however, were positive fashion plates. Sleek, shape-defining body suits were the order of the day for most of the women. After I watched for a while, I could understand why. The various moves absolutely demanded freedom of motion. I did notice a couple of older women in the back who wore baggy sweats and tops, and they seemed to do everything that the more fashionable younger gals did. Good thing. Lessons were going to cost me, so I'd be damned if I would go shopping too.

Fortunately, I was able to slip in a quick workout of my own before I hastened across town to watch ultra-fit university students attack each other in a Karate class, complete with sound effects. It wasn't clear if the loud shouts and grunts were used to psych themselves up or to scare off an attacker. I doubted that I'd remember to yell if someone jumped out at me, knife in hand, so I put a question mark beside that class.

After watching the college kids, the combination Tai Chi and Kung Fu class for seniors seemed to be in slow motion. Of course, I had to admit I was fascinated with the Tai Chi elements and their sweeping movements. But I sensed the second part of the class was definitely aimed and modified for older participants. No scary attacks. No shouting. Sort of Kung Fu Lite.

After another coffee refill, I rushed to Old Town to catch a late-morning Tae Kwon Do class, which was filled with young mothers. Watching them bending, stretching, stomping though the movements, I had to give them credit. I remembered the effort it took to regain the figure that child-bearing steals away. Hard work, indeed.

By the time I pulled into the office parking lot at 1:00 p.m., I was mentally exhausted. And I didn't have a clue yet as to which martial arts routine I liked best. The Tai Chi came closest, but Ronnie wanted me to be able to defend myself from a "potential attacker," as she so charmingly phrased it. With or without stomping or shouting, I had to choose something.

I straggled through the back door and headed for the kitchen and coffee, hoping Ronnie didn't spy me. I wanted to call a real estate agent friend in Denver and pump her for information. See if Rupert McKenzie attended the Metro Council meeting or not. A whole morning spent observing body blows had put a serious dent in my sleuthing. McKenzie was worth checking out.

Lisa leaned around the kitchen corner as I was pouring coffee. "How'd the classes go?" she asked.

I took a sip and hid my reaction to her efforts to create caffeine. "I haven't had any classes yet. I was just observing today."

"Oh, yeah? Which ones?"

I rattled off my litany of the classes I'd witnessed that morning. Leaning against the counter, I even added a few observations of my own. Two of my colleagues entered then, and added their impressions as well. I was amazed at the variety of experiences to be had. The almost-mesmerizing Tai Chi to the hothouse atmosphere of certain Yoga studios. Whoa. This could take longer than I thought.

"Seriously, Kate, you should check out the studio on Lemay. They have all university students as instructors. Great guys. And cute, too," Brenda contributed with a sly grin.

"I'm not sure cute is what I need, Brenda. I'm looking for a class I can enter without feeling like a total klutz. And those college kids looked ruthless this morning."

"Got that right, Kate. Ruthless, that's us," Ben Babbitt teased as he checked out the plate of doughnuts.

I had my back turned to the wicked temptations. It was lunchtime, and hunger was already calling. If I looked at them sideways, one would jump right into my hand, then into my mouth. Never could figure out how doughnuts managed that. Must be magic.

"Did you ever try that stuff, Ben?" I asked, watching him

choose a chocolate-glazed number. With his spiked blond hair and quick grin, Ben still looked like a student, even though he'd graduated five years ago. Those students were his clients now.

"I did a little Karate in college, but couldn't get to all the classes, so I never did much," he said, after devouring half of the pastry. "I went back to running. Easier and quicker." He winked and the other half disappeared.

"Man after my own heart," I said. "That's another thing that bothers me. Time. I really don't have any extra blocks I can allocate to fighting off would-be attackers. I mean, business keeps me running around now. I'd have to sacrifice another night; that's all I have left." I exhaled an exasperated sigh.

Another night shot to hell. Not that my nights were all that exciting, but it was the principle of the thing. If I chose to spend an evening channel-surfing and reading with my dog at my feet or in wild debauchery, it didn't matter. Both required free evenings. Of course, I hadn't debauched in so long I wasn't sure if I remembered how, so I couldn't recall if it required one night or two, but what the hey?

"Bummer," was all Ben said as he walked away, his voice revealing a young man's incomprehension at having free evenings. Ah, youth.

Brenda and I glanced to each other and laughed softly, until another voice came around the corner.

"Did I hear you ask about martial arts lessons, Kate?" Ted said as he headed for the coffee pot, mug in hand.

"Yeah, I'm trying to find a style I can do without feeling or looking absolutely stupid," I confessed.

Ted filled his oversized mug to the brim. "Then you should definitely check out some of our Kung Fu studios in town. We've got some great instructors."

"Kung Fu, uh, is that what Jackie Chan uses in the movies?" I asked in my best impression of innocent ignorance. One of my best looks. It usually discouraged meaningful discussion, and I'd wearied of this subject already. How would it ever hold my interest for lessons? Besides, I wanted to call my real estate agent friend in Denver. Get back to what I was really good at—poking into other people's business.

"Well, yes," Ted admitted with a genial laugh. "But—"

"Oh, that's too scary!" I pretended a shudder. "He's always climbing up buildings or leaping over trucks, while he's fighting off bad guys at the same time. Not for me."

"You go to Kung Fu flicks, Kate?" Lisa said as she aimed for the doughnuts.

"Yeah, well, sure," I admitted with a grin. "What can I say? I have eclectic tastes in movies. Art films to action flicks. I like 'em all."

"Cool." Lisa nodded before she sank her teeth into the sugar.

I sensed I'd gone up in her estimation somehow. Go figure. Actually, I was trying to appear weirder than usual, hoping to eliminate the glint that appeared in Ted's eyes whenever he spoke to me. I wanted to head this off before it started.

"Well, if you like those movies, you'll love our classes, Kate. They go through the history as well as instruction." Ted enthused as only a real estate agent can, when he spots a prospect.

Damn. Outfoxed myself. Now he was even more encouraged. "That's okay, Ted. Don't bother—"

"It's no bother at all, Kate. Come on over to the studio. I'll introduce you to my Sifu."

"Your see-what?"

Ted flashed his Real Estate Agent-of-the-Year smile. "My Sifu. It means Master Teacher. It's a sign of respect, since he's attained the highest level."

I heard my exit line and grabbed it. "Sorry, Ted, but I don't think that would work for me. I'm such a rebellious wench, I cannot see myself bowing to some shriveled Yoda-like teacher."

Lisa and Brenda both giggled appreciatively. Bless them.

"He's nothing like that at all!" Ted's eyes were alight with the fire of persuasion. "He's a cowboy at heart. Young guy, too. Sometimes he even wears his boots to class."

"Wow, sexy." Brenda pushed herself away from the counter. "Sign me up."

"Who's sexy?" Melanie said as she passed us, arms filled with reports.

"This new Kung Fu teacher at Ted's class," Brenda said, heading to her office. "Sounds yummy. I may sign up."

Don't even go there, I told myself, watching Ted and my office mates laugh.

Ted wiped his eyes. "So, how about it, Kate?"

I pushed away from the counter and grabbed my briefcase. If I was lucky, I could get to my office and the phone—alone. "No, thanks, Ted. Just not my style. Sorry," I said as I headed down the hall.

"Well, if you want to check out some other places, I'll be glad to give you some tips," he offered, falling in step beside me.

Boy, he gave new meaning to tenacious. No wonder he'd made Real Estate Agent of the Year. "Thanks, Ted. I'll bear that in mind," I said as I dropped my briefcase on the desk. Scooping up the mail, I began sorting, hoping Ted would take the hint and leave. No such luck.

"Do you have a few minutes now? I can give you a quick rundown."

Now I knew how he made all those sales. His clients probably just gave up and gave in, in order to get him to quit
talking. "Actually, Ted, I don't have a few minutes," I said. "I
have to make a call to another real estate agent in Denver."

"Got a hot deal cooking?"

I took a deep breath and prayed for patience. Maybe medi-
tation would help. This business was beginning to get to me.
"No, Ted, I honestly wish I did. It's just some questions I've
got about . . . about the Metro Council meeting last month.
She always attends those, so I call her whenever I need info."

Ted's smile spread from ear to ear. "I was there, too. What
do you want to know?" And without waiting for my reply,
Ted plopped into the adjacent client chair.

With an effort, I kept my mouth from dropping open.
Well, alrighty, then. I'd make use of Ted's need to dispense
information. Now, what to ask first? "Really? That's real nice
of you, Ted. Let me get my notebook."

Digging into my briefcase, I pulled out my auto mileage
notepad and paged through it while I sank into my desk chair.
The numbers blurred as I formulated what I hoped were
some reasonable questions.

"First, I wanted to know if we had a good number of
Northern Colorado Real Estate Agents attending. I've always
believed we need to network with the Denver brokers. For
long-term planning and all, you know."

"Absolutely. You're preaching to the choir on that, Kate,"
Ted said, sipping his coffee.

"So, who else attended that you know? I imagine you
know just about everyone working in real estate in this area."

Ted almost wiggled with my praise and began reciting
names. I pretended to write down one or two, all the while
waiting for McKenzie's name to sound. It didn't. After a moment, Ted paused and sipped his coffee, so I prodded.

"Is that all? No one else that you remember?"

"That's it, and like you said, I do know almost everyone."

Tapping pen to pad, I pondered out loud. "That's strange. I heard that Rupert McKenzie was supposed to give one of the presentations. I was particularly interested in what he had to say. He's got such a . . . a unique business model, shall we say?"

Ted chortled. "Yeah, we can definitely say that. Rupert's unique, all right. And you're right, he was scheduled to talk, but apparently something came up at the last minute. His secretary left me a message that he wouldn't be coming to the meeting."

My heart quickened its pace. *Ah-ha. A change of plans. Now, that was suspicious.* Wondering if McKenzie's change of plans had anything to do with Mark Schuster, I asked Ted for a brief summary of the main talk. Ted cheerfully complied while I sorted through one strategy after another, all designed to find ways to grill Rupert McKenzie without being too obvious. Given my tendency for transparency lately, I decided I'd have to hide behind a client to do it. A plan formed just as Ted was sucking in wind.

"Hey, Ted, that was great, thank you so much," I said as I sprang from my chair. Shoving pad and pen back into my briefcase, I scooted around my desk, talking all the way. Hopefully, I could escape in a cloud of words. "I appreciate that so much. Now I've got to run, see a client. Take care. Talk to you later." And I was down the hall before Ted cleared the chair.

As I drove along the lunchtime-crowded streets, I punched in another number. My first call had been to Rupert McKenzie's office to see if he was there or out at one of his building sites. I was prepared to track him down. Turned out,

Rupert was prowling around his newest development. And lucky for me, all the model homes were open for showings. Perfect cover for questioning.

The next number beeped and allowed me to access information stored in our electronic lock boxes. I wanted to check the Schuster listing. Any showings would be recorded by real estate agent ID number. There were none. Not a one. Darn. My elation at the large open house turnout was fading as each day passed and no offers came in. Not even a second showing was scheduled.

I tabbed through the directory to a familiar number and called. I needed some cheering up, and a cover for the visit to Rupert's development. Marilyn could deliver both. At the sound of her voice, I tossed out the bait.

"Marilyn, I'm only a few blocks from your place. If you agree to come with me for a couple of hours, I'll tell you all about this great new guy we've got in the office. Plus, he knows about Kung Fu. And his teacher wears cowboy boots. So, how about it? I'm turning into your neighborhood right now." My tactic was total bombardment: tease, but no details until she was in the car.

"What? Kate? Where are you? Who's this guy?"

"I'm driving up your street right now. No details until you're in the car. Do we have a deal?"

"I don't know, Kate. I've got a bunch of stuff to sort through this afternoon. My desk is a mess."

"Desks are supposed to be messy. Clean ones are scary. C'mon. I'll even stop for one of those Greasy Burgers. I haven't had lunch yet."

A long pause. I knew I had her. When in doubt, Greasy Burger always works.

"Okay, okay, you know I can't resist those. Let me grab my purse. And this new guy better be good. Where are you?"

"Pulling up in front of your house right now."

Marilyn licked the dripping sauce from her pinkie before she took another bite of her burger. Although swathed in napkins from neck to lap, she still took daintier-than-usual nibbles, lest the delicious sauce spill on her new outfit. It was the only way she would agree to "eat as we drive." Meanwhile, the clock was ticking inside my head. Who knew how long Rupert would remain at the building site?

"I don't know, Kate. Ted's done exceptionally well, from what I've heard. You might not want to discourage him," she said after swallowing.

"Yes, I do."

A dramatic sigh. "Why don't you at least give him a try?"

"You mean a test drive?" I laughed. "Forget it. This guy is a born salesman. I'd never get out of the car."

"Think how convenient it would be. You're always rushing around with real estate, and now Ronnie wants you to take self-defense classes too. This could be super-efficient. You could talk real estate and learn Karate moves at the same time. Or, Kung Fooey. Whatever."

"I don't think those are the moves Ted's interested in," I said with a chuckle. "And the last thing I want to do is encourage him. He's got that look."

Marilyn gave her cola a loud slurp. "Do not get me started on that, Kate," she said, and I could hear the disgust in her voice. "I just had a wonderfully wicked calorie-filled burger, and I don't want to have to fuss at you. It'll give me indigestion."

"Don't worry. We're about to engage in one of our favorite pastimes. Looking at new houses. Plenty of time to digest in peace." I turned my Explorer off the north-south artery and into the entrance of Rupert McKenzie's newest development.

147

Perched on the far southeastern edge of Fort Collins, only a cornfield away from the interstate, sat Jefferson Village. I'd been anxious to tour these homes, because the price range was wide enough to allow some first-time buyers into the market. I was curious to see what they looked like up close. Rupert was a savvy enough builder to balance proximity and price to best advantage.

"These look nice. All clean and neat," Marilyn said as we drove through newly-paved streets, bordered on both sides by colorful new townhomes. Muted colors were the rule, but I noticed some different shades that I hadn't seen before.

"Very attractive," I said. "Perfect for some of my young buyers. Let's hope they're as pretty inside as they are outside."

"Oh, I'll bet they are. Ginny Simpson does a lot of the interior design for builders here, and she has great style."

"You check the decorator's touch while I check the walls and windows," I said.

"Oh, dear. Does that mean you'll be prowling in every basement, like last time?"

"Oh, yeah. Basements tell tales."

"Such dreary work. I'm glad you have to do it."

Turning the corner, we headed down another block with larger homes. The same muted colors were used here, but I also noticed something else. Like the townhomes, every one of these houses had a front porch. And the architecture was reminiscent of the older neighborhoods Back East, as I lovingly referred to it. Certain construction details harkened back to that earlier era with the use of more gables and dormer windows. The entire effect was quite charming, as well as welcoming. Some were calling it New Urbanism. Whatever it was, Rupert had done a good job.

"Aren't those the model homes over there?" Marilyn pointed to the right.

Sure enough, colorful banners plus an enormous American flag marked the sales office. "Yep. We'll head over there in just a second. I want to swing by the construction office and see if Rupert's around."

"Rupert McKenzie? Why on earth do you want to talk to him? He's loud and obnoxious and—"

"And a brilliant businessman. He's managed to resurrect himself from near financial ruin at least three times that I recall."

"Four," she corrected, shoving the empty drink cup in the trash. "That's not the point. He can be a loud-mouthed boor, and I cannot abide to be around him when he starts shouting." She gave a shiver of obvious disgust.

"Oh, he's simply flamboyant. Just like you," I tweaked, driving through the streets of unfinished houses, heading toward the empty lots ahead.

"Don't be ridiculous. *I* am flamboyant," she said with an aggrieved sniff. "Rupert's just plain rude."

Spying a dingy white mobile home up ahead, I aimed for it. "That's got to be the construction office. Let me check to see if Rupert's free." I pulled to the curb and hopped out. "I'll just be a minute," I promised.

"Please."

I started to cross the vacant dirt lot when the door of the construction office opened and out bounded Rupert McKenzie. Three other men traipsed down the steps after him. Even from this distance, I could hear the conversation. Marilyn was right. Quiet, Rupert wasn't. I stood and watched Rupert march the men across the dirt and straight for a newly-dug site adjacent to this one.

It looked as if I'd have time to tour with Marilyn, after all.

Clearly, Rupert was deep in discussion. I was about to turn, when the big yellow Caterpillar caught my attention. It was fascinating to watch the operators maneuver their machines. They made it look precise, somehow.

The Cat's big jaw dropped as it slowly moved forward, scooping up an enormous mouthful of dirt. Then, like a ballerina pirouetting, the machine spun around and dumped the dirt neatly onto a nearby mound. Scooping, dumping, backing down into the excavated hole, and climbing out again, the machine scraped the site, ready for the foundation to be poured.

As I headed back to my car, I spotted a couple of trucks from the largest concrete and cement company in town. I remembered how fascinated I'd been when I once watched them pour a foundation. Clearly, I hadn't played with enough trucks when I was a child.

"It looks like Rupert's busy for a while," I said as I climbed into my car. "We'll go take our tour."

"Thank you. And when you feel the need to seek out Rupert again, don't worry about me. I'll amuse myself in the model homes."

Returning through the streets to the sales office, I parked, and we began our tour. The on-site sales agent was a young woman who was clearly in the last trimester of her pregnancy. Real estate was an attractive part-time career choice for some women, especially when they were starting their families and had little ones at home. I admired their determination to combine the two careers. Motherhood is demanding enough. Add to that the constant demands of real estate with caring for clients, looking for listings, and managing the paperwork—I didn't know how they did it.

I scooped up a packet of information on all the models, as Marilyn and I set out on the little trail that led through the sales site. Usually the models were all situated next to each other and connected by an easy-to-follow pathway. That way, potential buyers could traipse through one model after another and decide which one was right for them. If they were serious, that is. Some folks simply liked to amuse themselves by looking at new houses and the pretty decors within. Getting ideas for their own homes, no doubt.

It was hard to tell the "bona fides" from the browsers. One of the toughest lessons to learn in real estate was trying to distinguish between the two. So much of a real estate agent's time and energy could be lavished on someone who was not ready, willing, or able to purchase a home, no matter how much they wanted to. Alas, wishful thinking did not a sale make—for buyers or real estate agents.

We entered a charming townhouse, complete with its small front porch. I was surprised at the spacious look to the living and dining area. Vaulted ceilings helped. So did the beautiful kitchen, complete with stylish black fridge and blacktop range. Tile counters and island opened to an inviting family room. Rupert had done a very good job, indeed.

I was beginning to regret that I was there to probe Rupert about Mark. But lovely and tasteful homes to the contrary, I needed to gauge the depth of his dislike for Mark Schuster. I was fishing and I knew it, but someone hated Mark enough to kill him.

"Ginny's had her hand in here. I can tell," said Marilyn as we strolled through the bedrooms upstairs.

The second bedroom was smaller than I liked, but big enough if a couple wanted to start a family. Also, there was a nifty loft at the top of the stairs, which could easily be used as a kid's playroom. Or a TV room. Of course, I hadn't even seen the basement yet, but I could tell from the townhouse's footprint there would be plenty of room to create a whole new recreation area down below. Concrete walls sealed off lots of noise.

A remembered shiver from Sunday's house tour with Henry Ackerman rippled through me. I hadn't heard another word from him or his wife about this house they were so captivated with. Maybe I'd eliminated him from my suspect list too soon. Maybe . . .

"Whoa!" Marilyn exclaimed. "Nice jetted tub, but the neighbors can see everything. What if you weren't alone in the tub?"

"Doesn't look big enough for two, Marilyn. Besides, haven't you heard of blinds?"

"Bothersome details," she said airily as she wandered through the spacious master suite.

From the bedrooms I scurried down the stairs to check out the basement, leaving Marilyn to investigate all the appliances. After assuring myself there were no ugly surprises waiting below, I resurfaced.

"I'm really impressed with the quality he's got here," Marilyn said, strolling about the kitchen. "I mean for these prices, I'd expected a lot less." She waved the sales packet.

"Yeah, he's done a good job," I said. "Let's go see if the rest of the models hold up to our scrutiny."

Marilyn and I hit the trail and toured the remaining models, which carefully ascended in price. I made it a point whenever I was on the second floor of each home to gaze out the windows, peering toward the construction office, hoping Rupert's fancy silver truck was still there. I'd spied the monster when I parked near the office site and figured it had to be his. After all, the personalized license plate proclaiming RUPERT kind of gave it away.

"Boy, Kate, I've got to hand it to old Rupert," Marilyn said as we left the next-to-last model. "He's giving them a lot for the money. How did he manage that?"

"Well, one reason is his development is the farthest from town. A lot more driving. But for some folks, it's worth the tradeoff. You can really save—" I stopped mid-sentence because I had spotted a black SUV cruise past with two men I recognized. Now was my chance. "Hey, Marilyn, there go the guys that were with Rupert. If you don't mind, I'll scoot over there right now and grab a minute with him."

"Sure, Kate, go ahead. I'm enjoying myself. See you back at the sales office." She waved me away as she continued along the trail.

I raced to my car and sped off, hoping to catch Rupert before he left the site. The imposing silver truck was still parked, so I pulled up behind it and set about locating Rupert. Where to start? I scanned the vacant lots surrounding me.

Then I heard it. I needn't have worried. His voice boomed two sites away, so I honed in on his signal. Once I got closer, he was impossible to miss. Not only was his the loudest voice around, but so was his wardrobe.

Standing atop a large mound of dirt, Rupert yelled at someone in the newly-finished basement below. His royal blue shirt contrasted beautifully with a canary yellow tie and almost kept me from noticing his suit. But I could recognize expensive tailoring when I saw it, even atop a dirt mound. And then there were his boots. Expensive boots. Rupert always wore cowboy boots—on site, in the office, or at a banquet.

He was bending over one knee, so I got a good look at the sleek, patterned leather. Probably some exotic, endangered reptile, I decided as I approached the edge of the foundation walls. I peered below, curious as to what had incurred his wrath. Rupert was a stickler for details, and nothing escaped his scrutiny. At first glance, everything looked okay. The plumbing was in, the furnace and air conditioner were . . .

"Get that damn furnace outta there and don't come back until you have the model I ordered!" he shouted, pointing at the poor unfortunates installing the fixture.

I backed away from the edge, letting Rupert finish his tirade. Having witnessed one of his explosions at another site last year, I knew enough to get out of the way and let him spew. God help the carpenter who tried to hurry up and skimp when framing. Rupert was known to yell the walls down, and the carpenter with them.

Rupert spied me as he bounded down the dirt hill. "Hey, miss, you shouldn't be out here. You could get hurt on the site. There're all sorts of . . . hey, don't I know you?" He peered at me as he approached. His wavy mane of silver hair set off his suntanned face, so that even his wrinkles looked good. Over sixty and going strong, according to Ronnie.

"You probably remember me from my former life, when I used to frequent the country club," I said. "I'm a real estate agent now with Shamrock. Kate Doyle." I gave him my brightest smile, along with my hand.

"Ronnie's a great gal," he said, giving my hand a firm shake. Then he pointed behind. "If you're looking for info on the development, Kate, the sales office is over there."

"I've already been there, Rupert, and I definitely have some young buyers I'll be bringing out here," I promised. "But there were some other questions I wanted to ask. About your planned developments, I mean."

"Sure. You'll have to keep up with me, though. I'm running a little late, and I've got to check a couple more sites." He grabbed his clipboard from the dirt and strode off, with me struggling behind, trying to keep up with his long-legged stride. He headed toward a nearby site where the house was already framed. No walls yet, but the rooms were outlined.

"What kind of developments do you have coming up, Rupert? Some high-end models, maybe?" I managed, when I caught up with him. My strategy was to disguise my scrutiny behind a client. But not just any client. I chose one designed to provoke a reaction.

"Sure do, Kate." He grinned over his shoulder as he climbed the slant board that substituted for steps into the house under construction. "Next year I'm breaking ground on my new development. Washington Valley. My best one yet."

Rupert strode into the skeleton of the house-to-be, leaving me to cautiously make my way up the slanted piece of wood. The angle was steep and I wore heels, so it was slow going. I really needed to carry sneakers in my car.

I tried to stay out of the way of carpenters and electricians as they banged on two-by-fours and strung wires throughout the skeleton. Skirting the yawning black hole that opened to the basement below, I made sure I didn't go near the edge. No railing, no steps, and no lights yet, only another slanted board, leading down into the dark.

No one would notice if I fell into the pit. Rupert was talking and gesturing to a workman, and I had already become invisible. When Rupert thought I was a potential buyer, he'd been concerned for my safety. Not anymore. Now I was merely another real estate agent. There were tons of them in Fort Collins. Too many, in fact. I wouldn't even be missed.

I stayed on the small slab of tile at the doorway until Rupert finished his inspection. Checking his clipboard as he approached, he pointed to the adjacent site where the house under construction had walls up and the windows in. Maybe this one had stairs, I hoped, as I followed him out the door.

"This must be some client for you to hang around, Kate.

Who're you shopping for?" he asked as he headed out the door.

"Well, uh, yeah, it is," I said as I started my descent down the wobbly slant board. Rupert had already bounded to the ground. It was now or never, I decided, and released my trial balloon. "It's Amanda Schuster. You see, I'm selling her house now, and she's going to need—"

"What?" Rupert stopped in his tracks and spun around, faster than the Caterpillar for sure. "The *hell* you say!" His face flushed scarlet. "I'll be God—"

He erupted with a stream of curses that froze me in place. I couldn't move, but I swore the slant board swayed beneath me with the force of his fury at the mention of the Schuster name. *Just let me get to the ground,* I prayed, as the board shifted with another plume of curses spewing forth. A virtual lava flow of blasphemous, colorful phrases, and combinations of invective that brought even the construction workers to a halt. I thought I saw a carpenter cross himself, and the furnace guys nearly fell over each other trying to skulk from the site without drawing attention. Rupert paused to suck in wind, and I scooted off the board like a scolded puppy.

"Dammit, Kate! That son-of-a-bitch nearly ruined me, and you want me to find a home for his widow? I'll be God d—" Another eruption spewed forth.

I slowly crept closer to the fire, glad that I wore SPF 15 makeup, or I'd be sunburned for sure. "Rupert, please," I said, hands raised in supplication. "Don't take it out on Amanda. She had nothing to do with Mark's business. Besides, Mark's dead, and—"

"The son-of-a-bitch got what he deserved! I'd have killed the rat bastard myself, if someone else hadn't beaten me to it. I hope he burns in hell!"

Whoa. My cheeks flamed, and my trial balloon popped—

incinerated by Rupert's pure, undiluted hatred of Mark Schuster. Clearly, Rupert despised Mark enough to kill him. Was his over-the-top response merely a clever ruse to disguise his guilt?

It didn't take more than a second for me to eliminate that possibility. Rupert McKenzie was a hothead, to be sure. But up this close, I could see the fire in his eyes was banked, allowing him to release it at will. Maybe that's why he was still in such good shape. When anything or anyone bothered him, Rupert didn't worry about it. He just let it rip. I bet the man didn't have a clogged artery in his body. Surely cholesterol must dissolve at those temperatures, just like my balloon. Besides, Rupert was a savvy businessman. If he planned to eliminate Mark, he'd probably challenge him to a duel, then sell tickets. That way, he could shoot the rat bastard between the eyes and make a profit at the same time.

"I'm sorry, Rupert," I said. "I didn't mean to upset you. I'm only helping out Amanda, and I admire your work so much, I thought—"

"Schuster's widow. That's rich." Rupert mumbled his curses now.

I took that as a good sign. "I'm just trying to do my job, Rupert. And for what it's worth, I never approved of Mark's business tactics either. But I try not to speak ill of the dead. Kind of makes me uneasy."

Rupert snorted. "When the dead leave a legacy like Schuster's, they deserve it."

"Legacy?" Something about the word piqued my interest.

"Yeah, ruined businesses, ruined lives, things like that," he said in a disgusted tone as he headed across the dirt, clipboard under his arm. "I'm not the only one he nearly destroyed. Some didn't have my, uh, resilience. Some went under. Like Ken Barstow."

"The name's vaguely familiar, but—"

"He was a real estate agent turned developer. Small scale. But it was his dream to build houses. Had some good plans, too. Lined up his financing, everything, but it all hinged on getting Mark's parcel of land. I was going to sell Ken a section for his homes, but when Mark screwed me, it was all I could do to hold on. Ken, poor bastard, he just didn't have enough cushion. Lost everything. Even his wife divorced him."

Rupert paused at the edge of another site and looked me straight in the eye. It was all I could do to hold my gaze steady.

"Ask Ken Barstow if he has a kind word to say for the dead. I dare you, Kate." Rupert spun on the heel of his hand-crafted boots and strode away.

I stared after him, wondering what to say, when Rupert called over his shoulder.

"Bring Amanda over next summer, Kate. I should have some models up by then."

"I will, Rupert, and thanks." It was feeble, but it was the best I could do at the moment. My mind was already playing with Rupert's challenge while I headed toward my car.

Driving back to the model home sites, I noticed more cars than usual, so I parked down the street. Besides, I needed time to consider Ken Barstow. I tried to conjure Barstow's face but came up with nothing. Of course, this whole episode had happened right before I got into real estate, so I knew nothing of the details. But Ronnie would know. As soon as I got back to the office, I'd find a way to casually ask Ronnie about Barstow. No, that wouldn't work. She could see right through me. Darn. I'd have to find someone else to grill. Someone more trusting, or someone who didn't know me well enough to recognize when I was up to something. Someone . . .

The sound of an unfortunately familiar voice sounded behind me then. "What'd you say to Rupert to get him all riled up, Doyle? You could hear him yelling clear out to the interstate."

Remembered aggravation flooded through me. A knee-jerk reaction, I'll admit. What was it about this guy? He was deliberately annoying. I turned to see Jake Chekov grinning at me from behind the wheel of his Big Bad Ass Truck.

"Why do you assume it was me who caused Rupert's yelling? You know Rupert. He doesn't need much to set him off."

"True, but this was louder than usual. I heard it all the way in the basement of one of his new homes."

"Liar."

"I swear." He crossed himself as his grin spread. "C'mon, Doyle, what'd you say to him? He was damn near frothing at the mouth."

I had to smile at that image. "Yeah, he almost did, too."

"C'mon, 'fess up. What'd you say that annoyed him so?"

"Me? Annoying? Coming from you, that's damn near insulting," I countered, hoping to deflect him, even though I knew better. Chekov was like a laser beam.

"What'd you say, Doyle? Had to be something personal."

I decided it would be better to admit the truth than to have Chekov speculate. "I simply mentioned that I was looking for a property for Amanda Schuster and I'd always admired his work and—"

"You've got to be kidding. You actually said that to Rupert?" Chekov's eyes danced in obvious amusement.

"Yep, and I have the sunburn to prove it. Got a little too close to the fire."

Chekov chuckled as he grinned at me. "Damn, Doyle,

you're even crazier than I thought. Or braver."

"Probably both," I said.

Suddenly the laughter in Chekov's eyes changed. He peered at me. "You're up to something, Doyle. Admit it. That's why you're out here provoking old Rupert."

I gave him my haughtiest look before I turned away. "You've been down in those basements too long, Chekov."

"Be careful, Doyle," he called as I walked toward the model home sales office.

I wasn't sure if I even knew what that word meant anymore.

Chapter Fifteen

"Poor Barstow, he really did get shafted, didn't he?" I said as I stirred my coffee.

Sitting across from me was the one source left who wouldn't recognize my fishing expedition. Ted Sandowski. He didn't know me well enough. And with luck, he'd never get to. Of course, the information came with a price. Ted wanted dinner, but I pled a prior engagement, so we settled on coffee at a nearby brew house. I didn't want Ronnie to see me pumping Ted.

"Yeah, he sure did. He's never recovered. Oh, Ken still does a little real estate, but he mostly works for other brokers for a salary now. Poor guy." Ted swirled his caramel and whipped cream concoction, his gold dragon ring with its diamond solitaire catching the light.

"That's quite a comedown. Who does he work for?"

"Burton and James Properties, mostly. He told me he manages their rental office by day, then supervises one of their rental complexes by night. Brutal."

"Whoa," I said. "He works a day shift *and* a night shift?"

"A night shift supervising students, too. As if it could get any worse." Ted wagged his head. "I had to track him down for some property info one time and found him between two drunken kids, trying to break up a fight. At least I could help him with that. He looked really haggard."

"What did you do, give 'em a Kung Fu toss?" I joked.

"Naw. Let's just say I convinced them they needed to sleep it off and talk in the morning." He winked at me before he drained his coffee.

Pity was beginning to encroach on my desire to follow up Ken Barstow. "Poor guy. How does he do it all?"

Ted shrugged. "He has to, Kate. He's still paying off debts and his ex-wife."

"Which complex does he work at? I want to make sure my daughter doesn't live anywhere near the drunken students." That was a half-truth.

"Get real, Kate. This is a college town."

"I know, I know. That's not realistic. She can only afford places like that. Oh well. Just being a mom. Where does he work anyway?"

"Over at the Sunshine condos, near Campus West."

Okay, I thought as I nodded at Ted. Glancing at the wall behind the display of coffee beans from around the globe, I checked the time. Almost 6:00 p.m. If I raced home now, I could feed Sam and myself then drive out to Campus West and visit Ken Barstow.

First, I had to make a few calls for my young buyers. They were still in the midst of getting different estimates as to what needed to be done to their dream house. At least that gave me a bona fide excuse to extricate myself from Ted.

"Hey, I've got to run," I announced, consulting my watch. "I have to make some more calls and talk to my young buyers. The inspection turned up all sorts of scary surprises."

"Ouch." Ted winced in sympathy.

I scraped my chair back and grabbed my briefcase. "Take

care, Ted. See you at the office tomorrow."

"Sure, Kate. And let's do dinner sometime, okay?"

"Yeah, we'll get a group together," I said as I scurried toward the door. Safety in numbers.

Twilight shaded the foothills, as the sun's fading glow revealed their rugged contours. There was a different feel to these hours before night claimed the sky. I could never define it, but I felt it whenever I walked.

The sidewalks of the older neighborhoods near the university were narrower and cracked, but the trees were taller and thicker. There was also something reassuring and comfortable here. Perhaps the presence of all those families growing up in the surrounding houses left something of themselves lingering in the air.

Or maybe it was because the students hadn't started partying yet, my cynical side reminded me. I could still glimpse families and older couples inside some of the houses. Holdouts who tried to hang onto their comfortable homes and tree-shaded yards, despite the regular weekend mayhem that occurred with the rowdier college elements.

It was hard. I'd heard many a young couple complain that they didn't want to leave those neighborhoods, but they had small children to raise. Rowdy, drunken students and loud parties made that all but impossible sometimes.

Sam tugged at the end of the leash, clearly wanting to check out a nearby tree. As Sam had aged, I noticed he didn't pull quite so hard on the leash. He was more content to simply walk beside me, almost as if he was checking out the neighborhood too.

I had decided to take Sam, because it looked more natural for me to be walking my dog at this hour than simply taking a stroll all alone. We were approaching the Sunshine complex, where Barstow was employed. I figured we had to be close. The sound of hip-hop music was getting louder.

Rounding a corner into the parking lot, I looked for a sign indicating an office. A black painted arrow pointed toward some steps. I peered down the broken concrete stairwell and saw light shining through a window.

"Guess I'd better take a look, huh, Sam?" I said as I looped his leash around the metal railing. "You stay out here, okay? Guard the parking lot instead."

Sam woofed as if he understood, and I patted his head. He was getting skinnier as he aged, too. *Boy, that should happen to people,* I thought, as I made my way down the steps. I knocked, then pushed the door open.

The man behind the desk didn't even glance up from the papers in front of him. "Yeah, what is it?" His voice sounded hoarse and ragged.

"Hi, there," I said, my voice cheerful.

The man's head popped up and he stared, clearly surprised that I wasn't a student. From the doorway, I could see what Ted meant when he said Barstow looked haggard. That was putting it gently. His face was sallow and drawn, and his eyes were sunken. Haunted was the word I'd use.

"Can I help you? Are you looking for a rental unit? We've only got one available right now. How big a unit do you need?"

"Oh, it's not for me. It's for my daughter," I said, using Jeannie as a shield this time. "She said she talked to a Ken Barstow. I think that was the name. Is he here?"

"Yeah, that's me. What kind of unit was she looking for?" Barstow leaned back in his chair.

"She said you showed her through a rental house nearby, and she's forgotten the address. She wanted to tell her girlfriends where it was, so they could come out and take another look. Do you keep records of your showings?"

I'd searched for a plausible reason to use for probing Barstow, but I couldn't come up with anything, so I decided to simply wing it. See how he responded when I mentioned the date of Mark's death.

"Yes, we do." He reached into a drawer and pulled out a Day-Timer. "What's her name, and when did she come in?"

"Jeannie Doyle. And she said she came in about two weeks ago. On a Monday." I reached into my pocket for my grocery list and scanned it for a nonexistent date. "Monday, September twenty-seventh."

Barstow flipped through the pages and scanned the month of September. I peered over the desk, trying to decipher the upside-down jottings and notes, but couldn't.

Running his finger over the days, Barstow stopped when he came to that date. His finger tapped once, then twice. Then he spoke without looking up. "That wasn't me who showed her the property, ma'am. I wasn't here all day. I was out of the office."

My heart skipped a beat. I wasn't prepared for that response. I didn't know what to say next. With others, probing had come naturally. But with Barstow, it was different. Bone-deep fatigue radiated off this man. I doubted he'd have the strength to stab Mark Schuster in the throat.

I was about to force myself to probe anyway, when Barstow glanced up. Something resembling a smile appeared, softening his features. "My first grandchild was born September twenty-seventh. I was at the hospital all day with my daughter. She had a little boy. Ryan."

For a brief moment, joy erased the weariness from Ken Barstow's face. I joined in his celebration by giving him the biggest smile I could find inside. My heart sincerely went out to this man. "Congratulations, Mr. Barstow. You must be very proud."

"Oh, I am," he said softly.

"I'll bet you'll be a great grandfather, too," I added, backing toward the door. It was time to go. "And I'll tell my daughter she's got her places mixed up. Good night, now."

Barstow gave me a little wave, and I took the stairs two at a time. Poking around in people's lives was proving to be painful.

Sam gave me a welcoming slurp on the hand when I untied his leash. "C'mon, boy, let's head back to our car and go home. We've gotten into enough trouble for one night."

Heading across the street, Sam and I angled through the interconnecting parking lots that ran beside the string of cafes, coffeehouses, and shops that catered to students. My car was parked a couple of blocks away, and there was a shortcut behind the restaurants. Pausing beside a bush so Sam could do his doggie sniff test, I caught the sound of a familiar laugh. A musical laugh that I hadn't heard in a while.

I turned to scan the darkened sidewalks and spotted Jeannie walking toward the Mexican restaurant. But that wasn't what caught my eye. It was the guy walking beside her who caught my attention. Chester Yosarian, the computer expert. Yosh. I watched them laugh and talk to each other as they strolled along.

Well, well, well, I thought, and smiled all the way to the car.

Chapter Sixteen

The next morning, Tuesday, it was all I could do to drag myself out of bed. I deliberately overslept. Yesterday I'd been up at 5:00 a.m. to hurry to the early kickboxing class. No way today. I needed more sleep. My brain was still fogged from the day before, and all the questions I'd asked. All for nothing. No matter how suspicious McKenzie and Barstow had appeared at first, both were in the clear.

After breakfast and bolstered with strong coffee, I made a brief stop at the office. It was afternoon before I was able to return to the Schuster home and search for Cheryl Krane's book. The last few days had been so busy, Stanley's request had slipped my mind.

As I drove over, I tried calling Amanda, but settled for her voice-mail instead. I found myself not supplying as much detailed information about my activities as before. Amanda was always curious as to what I was up to. I wasn't sure why I hesitated now. Perhaps I'd become more wary of everyone lately.

As I pulled into the Schusters' driveway, I spotted the youngest one of the three skateboarders practicing all alone. My instinct nudged me to grab this opportunity away from his friends and ask him more questions. Perhaps he remembered something else about that day. I exited my car and approached the sidewalk. He was heading this way and couldn't miss me. He'd either have to stop or jump the curb.

The youngster chose to stop about ten feet away. I could tell he remembered me from his expression. I flashed him a big relax-I'm-a-Mom smile. "Hey, Greg, how's it going?"

"Uh, okay, I guess," he said, glancing nervously over his shoulder.

I figured I'd better ask fast before his intimidating older friends showed up. "Greg, I won't keep you from your practice. I just wanted to check if there was anything else you remembered from that day Mr. Schuster was killed. Anything else you didn't mention before. I kind of got the impression your friends kept you from telling all you saw. Did they give you a hard time?"

He stared at the ground as he balanced on his board with one foot. "Yeah, kinda. They called me a liar and stuff. But I wasn't lying. I really did see that guy. They were farther away, that's all."

"I believe you, Greg. I mean, how could you make up someone who looked like that?"

"For sure." Greg favored me with a brief glance.

"And he really wore regular shoes, not sneakers?"

"Yep."

"What color was his running suit?"

"Green. Dark green."

I decided to push a little. "Did you actually see him coming out of the Schuster house?"

He shook his head. "Naw. I just saw him on the path, near the sidewalk. I don't know if he went in the house or not."

"How about the car that was parked in your practice lane. The white Rabbit. Did you see who got into that car?"

"Nope. We went into Freddy's house for some drinks, and

when we came out again, it was gone."

Rats. Another disappointment. I was hoping he'd say a tall, skinny dark-haired woman came out, so I could move Cheryl to the top of my list. Ackerman had started slipping ever since yesterday's showing. The more I analyzed his actions, the more convinced I was I'd let my overactive imagination run wild.

"Darn," I said out loud. "I was hoping to get another clue." Might as well be honest with my little gold mine.

His bright blue eyes widened. "You mean about the killer?"

"Yeah. I thought maybe the Rabbit belonged to the person who committed this awful crime. I mean, whoever did it either drove here or walked here, right?"

Greg nodded his head, obviously caught up in the strategy.

Suddenly, the image of the jogger appeared in my mind, but this time there was an urgency about it. I followed the hunch. "That's why the fat jogger keeps bothering me. Who knows? Maybe the killer jogged all the way over here in disguise."

Greg blinked his blue eyes and said, "Oh, no. He didn't. He got into another car parked around the corner over there." Greg pointed down a side street.

My mouth dropped open in surprise. Whoa . . . he hadn't mentioned that before. "Really?" My heart beat faster. "What color car? Do you remember?"

He squinted his eyes shut for a second. "I think it was a gold color. Yeah, gold. It was gold. And it looked expensive, even from here."

I had to smile. *Obviously a car man, even at this early age. Wait until he gets old enough to drive. The skateboard will be under the bed.* "Gold, huh? Well, okay! That's something. In fact, that's a lot, Greg. You're great to remember so much." I let my enthusiasm pour into my voice.

Greg flushed pink and stared at his sneakers.

"Listen, I'll let you get back to your practice. Your friends will probably be out any minute." I winked at him.

He gave me a sheepish grin. "Yeah, probably."

"Thanks, Greg. Oh, and I'm sorry last Saturday's open house took all the street space. I won't do it again," I promised as I headed across the street. Greg gave me a parting wave and pushed off down the sidewalk.

I practically raced up the Schusters' path and into the house, my mind buzzing with the new information Greg had given me. The funny, fat jogger was looking more and more suspicious. Why would someone dress so strangely to go jogging in this neighborhood, if his car was parked around the corner and down the street? It had to be the killer in disguise. Why else would he/she park away from the house, except to make sure no one noticed?

As I unlocked the door leading from the kitchen to the garage, I had to admit that Cheryl Krane had slipped a notch. Cheryl drove a white Rabbit, not an expensive, gold car. Ackerman was in love with his mid-life red sports car. Then again, the killer might have rented a car as part of the disguise.

I sorted through various theories as I sorted through Mark's boxes. Fortunately, all the book boxes were stacked to the side. So, I made some coffee and went to work. It was nearly 5:00 p.m. when I found Cheryl Krane's book. A slender leather-bound volume of Edna St. Vincent Millay's poetry. The inscription inside the front cover was simple and poignant. "With all my love, Cheryl."

Closing up the boxes, I locked the garage and slipped the book into my briefcase, then stood for a long moment—considering. When I made my decision, I locked the fortress, drew up the drawbridge, and drove off. As soon as I got home, I would feed my dog, feed myself, then give Cheryl Krane a call. After I spoke with her, I'd know if I would drop the book by in person or drop it in the mail.

The sun's last rays had already disappeared behind the foothills when I finally found a chance to call Cheryl Krane. I leaned back into one of my comfortable wrought iron patio chairs and patted Sam on the head while I listened to her phone ring. After the fourth ring, she answered.

"Hello, Cheryl? This is Kate Doyle. Did I get you at a bad time?"

"No, no, not at all. What can I do for you?"

Her voice had no trace of the brash lawyer of last week's confrontation. Instead, there was an uncharacteristic nervous tremor that surprised me.

I paused, wanting to phrase my words delicately. "Cheryl, I told Stanley I'd search for your book, and I was finally able to do so. It was in one of the boxes I'd packed from the library. I didn't want to take it to your office. Do you want me to mail it to your home, or should I simply drop it by?"

I deliberately avoided using Mark's name, curious to see how she would respond.

"Oh," she said. "Oh, thank you! Thank you, Kate. I cannot thank you enough. I don't know what to say."

The sincerity of her appreciation resonated throughout her voice and all the way across the phone. I could feel it where I sat. "You're welcome, Cheryl." On a hunch I asked, "When should I drop it by? I have a few minutes now."

I heard her take in a breath, as in relief. "Oh, that would be great! I've wanted to get it back for, well, for quite a while."

"I understand. Shall I come over now, or does later work

better?" I glanced at my watch. It was 7:30 p.m. It would be dark, if not for Daylight Savings Time.

"Yes, come right over. I'm at 2513 Parkington Avenue. And Kate?"

"Yes?" I hastily scribbled the address on a napkin.

"Thank you again." Her phone clicked off.

No problem, Cheryl, I thought, and finished my coffee.

Chapter Seventeen

The graceful, winding streets of the Parkington neighborhood were always pleasant to drive through, even at night. Solid, established homes, most were over thirty years old. I always thought of thirty years as just getting settled in—for people as well as houses. The large trees, which added so much to the beauty during the day, obscured the homes at night. It was hard to decipher house numbers in the dark.

As I neared Cheryl's area, I noticed a porch light illuminating the fourth house down. Sure enough, it was hers. I pulled into the driveway and parked. Figuring I wouldn't be inside very long, I left my purse in the car, grabbed the book, and walked to the door. I gave the exterior a quick visual inspection as I rang the door chimes. Cheryl's home was a classic two-story—white with blue shutters and trim, graceful front porch pillars. I noticed lights were on in the lower and upper levels.

I waited. No answer to my first ring. I rang the chimes again, then knocked on the door for good measure. To my surprise, the door pushed open with my knocking. *It must not have been completely closed,* I thought, as I hesitated on the threshold. I pushed the door wider and stepped inside the foyer, then called out, "Cheryl? It's me, Kate Doyle." She was probably upstairs and hadn't heard my ring, I justified.

Another minute of silence passed. All I heard was the quiet tick of a gorgeous grandfather clock which stood imposingly at the edge of the living room and foyer. I saw newspapers spread out on the living room sofa beside the table lamp. The faint aroma of onions and garlic wafted through the air, re-membrances of dinner no doubt.

"Cheryl!" I called louder as I walked farther into the foyer. "Cheryl, it's me, Kate Doyle. I've brought your book." I used my loudest voice, guaranteed to reel in wandering children and dogs.

But it didn't reel in Cheryl. Convinced she was in another room and just couldn't hear me, I ventured down the hallway. As I rounded the corner into the cheerful yellow kitchen, I was about to call out again, when I heard noises. The door to the garage was open, and I thought I heard the sound of someone out there. The light was on.

That explained it. Cheryl was outside in the garage and couldn't hear me. I called out once more as I crossed the kitchen. "Cheryl? It's me, Kate Doyle. I brought your book."

Pushing open the door, I paused on the top step and looked around the large two-bay garage. The white Rabbit was parked along the far wall. It was a good thing Cheryl only had one car, because the other bay was filled with book-shelves, lined up like tall metal soldiers. Eight-foot bookcases crammed with books.

I stepped down into the garage. The same prickly sensation I'd felt in Mark's house that awful afternoon returned. The hair on the back of my neck stood on end. Something was defi-nitely wrong. Had Cheryl deliberately acted innocent and needy, hoping to lure me here alone? Was she going to pop out from behind a bookcase with a letter opener in her hand?

Swallowing down the fear that rose in my throat, I decided to call one more time. If Cheryl didn't answer, I was going to drop the book and get the hell out of here. "Cheryl?" Glancing over my shoulder, I ventured farther into the garage, then stopped.

There she was. Cheryl was seated in the Rabbit. I hadn't even looked in the car. After all, why would she tell me to come over, then leave?

"Cheryl, didn't you hear me calling?" Leaning over to look in the window, I froze.

Cheryl Krane was upright in the driver's seat. Bright red blood—her blood—dripped down her chalk-white face. She'd been shot. Blood and gore were splattered across the driver's window.

I stumbled backwards in horror, the book dropping to the floor. My breath caught in my throat. Had Cheryl killed herself in grief? Was that why she'd sounded so strange on the phone? Or, was she really the murderer and couldn't live with herself after killing her lover? If so, then why would she tell me to come over? *Why?* None of this made sense. It was madness.

Backing away from the horror, I turned to run to the kitchen. Escape. Call the police. Call Bill. Suddenly, a shadowy movement from the side caught my eye. I turned just as a heavy object crashed against the side of my head.

White lights flashed before my eyes. I felt myself collapse to the floor. Then everything went black.

Cold. Cold and hard. My cheek pressed against something cold. No, I was lying on something very cold and hard. I felt beside my cheek. Concrete. I was lying on a concrete floor. Why?

I opened my eyes and saw automobile tires close to my

head. I was lying on a concrete garage floor. Not my garage. Whose garage? My mind seemed foggy. I couldn't even answer my own questions. What was the matter—

Suddenly, I remembered. I was lying on Cheryl Krane's garage floor because someone had hit me on the head. Knocked me unconscious. Because . . . because I saw Cheryl. I sat up with a gasp. Not a smart move. A splitting pain shot right between my temples.

I staggered to my feet and grabbed hold of the car while I fearfully surveyed the garage, afraid my assailant still lurked. I saw no one. I leaned against the car and drew several deep breaths to calm down and slow the throb in my head. Steeling myself, I leaned over the Rabbit once more and peered inside at the gruesome sight.

No, it wasn't a dream. Cheryl was still there, and still just as dead. Confirming that awful reality, I knew I had to call the police immediately. Cheryl Krane did not commit suicide as I first thought, nor did she kill Mark Schuster. She'd been murdered, and only minutes before I arrived. Who else but the killer would have hidden in the garage and knocked me senseless?

That thought sent such a chill that I shuddered as I half-ran, half-stumbled up the stairs and into the kitchen. I had to call Bill. The police needed to get here now. Maybe the killer had left some clues this time. Mark Schuster's library had been wiped clean.

I grabbed a dishtowel beside the sink, soaked it with cold water, and held it to my head as I snatched the portable phone off its cradle. Collapsing into one of Cheryl's patterned kitchen chairs, I punched in the number I knew so well—Chief of Detectives, Bill Levitz.

The EMT aimed his bright light into my eyes once again.

He'd been checking for any overt signs of concussion for the last ten minutes. I sat docile as a lamb in Cheryl's living room, away from the intense activity that marked a crime scene investigation. A stream of policemen, investigators, and photographers kept traipsing through the foyer and into the kitchen. Outside, I saw uniformed officers stretch the Do-Not-Trespass yellow tape around Cheryl's neat and tidy front porch. I wanted to be as far away as possible. If it weren't for the earnest young EMT's exam and my scowling brother-in-law, who hovered in the foyer, I would have escaped the house hours ago.

"Well, Ms. Doyle, you sure were lucky," the earnest EMT declared, his young face registering concern. "When someone's sustained a blow to the head that knocks them out, we usually see signs of concussion." He snapped his light off and shoved it in the shirt pocket of his dark blue uniform. "But just to be safe, we should take you to the hospital. Have the docs check you out in the ER."

"Is that really necessary?" I said. "The headache has died down a little and—"

"She all right, Joe?" Bill called from across the room.

"She appears to be, Detective Levitz, but she'd better go in and have a scan done. Just to be sure."

At the word "scan," I started calculating expense. "Really, all I'm left with is a headache. I can take—"

"She arguing with you, Joe?" Bill said in a loud voice.

Joe grinned boyishly. "Yes, sir. She's trying to."

"Tell her it's a direct order from me. She can either go with one of my officers or arrive by ambulance, running hot, sirens and all. Her choice."

I grimaced. "Okay, okay. I'll take the officer."

While Joe packed up his medical case, Bill approached. He looked more disheveled than usual, and I knew why. He'd probably been at home, lying comfortably on the sofa in his pajamas and watching baseball on television, when he'd been called. Bill wasn't much of a fashion plate in the best of times. Hurried and worried about a family member as he must have been, I was surprised he still wasn't wearing his pajamas.

"Okay, Kate. Now that Joe has finished, you and I are gonna have a little talk." He planted both feet in front of me, crossed his arms, and scowled down. I braced myself for the severe scolding he was bound to deliver.

"Kate," he said, "I oughta arrest your ass."

"Me? I was the one assaulted. Since when do you arrest victims?"

"When they disobey direct orders to stop poking their noses into police business, that's when."

"Hey, Cheryl invited me here. I didn't just drop by for tea."

"And the reason she invited you was because you were returning a book that belonged to her. A book from Mark Schuster's library, I might add." His scowl darkened as his gray eyebrows started warring with each other.

I decided to play dumb. I had that look down pat. Plus, it usually worked. "You guys had already finished with Mark's library. I figured you'd taken everything you wanted."

"Admit it, Kate. You were poking around again, trying to find something to help Amanda, weren't you?"

"No, I wasn't. Cheryl asked me to find a book she'd given Mark. I was only helping her out, Bill. I certainly didn't plan to walk in while the murderer was still here, for Pete's sake."

"It doesn't matter, Kate. I told you to stay out of this investigation, and you deliberately disobeyed my direct order. And look what happened because of it. You could have gotten killed tonight!"

He didn't need to remind me. But, disobedient wench that

I was, I wasn't about to take this reprimand without a fight. "Bill, the truth is you ought to thank me. If I hadn't come over here, everyone would think Cheryl Krane was the murderer. It would have looked like she committed suicide after killing Mark. So, I actually helped your investigation, didn't I? Admit it."

Bill's scowl turned as black as storm clouds over the Rockies. "Kate, you'd better get your butt over to the ER right now, before I make good on my threat and throw you in jail. See how helpful you feel after sitting in a cell for twenty-four hours."

I kept my mouth shut. I didn't know if he'd actually do it, but I knew enough not to push him.

"Go on, get out of here. I mean it." Glancing at the young officer who had appeared out of nowhere, Bill said, "Gonzalez, take this troublemaker to the ER and make sure the docs check her over good. And don't leave her for a moment or she'll give you the slip. Got that?"

"Yessir, Detective Chief!" The young man snapped to.

I decided he must be recently from the military. Clean-cut and ramrod-straight, his whole bearing was a salute. All thoughts of rebellion and/or escape evaporated. Officer Gonzalez led the way and I obediently followed. He did, however, allow me to drive my own car to the hospital, while he rode behind.

"Well, Ms. Doyle, it looks okay. No sign of blood clots or concussion." The young man dressed in green scrubs and sneakers snapped my X rays onto a flat plastic wall light.

I leaned forward, fascinated by the shadowy images. That was my brain, such as it was. "So, I'm clear. I mean, I'm free to go?"

He shoved the X rays back into a large manila folder. "Yes.

Let me get you something for your headache, in case you need it."

I was too tired to feel elated. The sharp pain in my head had gradually lessened to a dull, intermittent throb. "Okay, Doc, but nothing with codeine or I'll be sicker with the medicine than the headache," I said as I followed him out of the exam room.

At 2:30 a.m., the ER was busier than I'd thought it would be. I had no idea so much was going on in the middle of the night. Car accidents, bar fights, domestic disturbances turned violent. If blood was involved, they all wound up here. Watching the various dramas parade in front of me had helped keep my mind off the uncomfortable plastic chair in the waiting room and my aching head.

"Will do," the young intern agreed as he leaned against the wall and filled in his chart.

Tall and thin, with a runner's build if ever I saw one, he looked almost as tired as I felt. I wondered how long he'd been on duty, then decided I didn't really want to know the answer to that.

"Doc, could you also tell the nice, young police officer who's chaperoning me that I'm cleared to go, please? Otherwise, he'll be standing outside my house all night." I pointed to Officer Gonzalez across the corridor and waved.

The intern glanced up and smiled. First smile I'd spied that night. "What did you do, ma'am? Back into his cruiser?"

"Nope. I just have an overly protective brother-in-law in a position of authority. He wanted to make sure I got here safely." I flashed a big grin myself. The lies were getting easier. Not a good thing.

"I'll drop your prescription at the pharmacy here, ma'am. As soon as it's ready, you can be on your way," he said, scrawling on the pad. "And, I'll tell your guard. You take it easy for the next couple of days, okay?"

"Absolutely, Doc," I said and watched him walk away. Sure enough, he spoke with Gonzalez.

Gonzalez responded with several vigorous nods. "You take care, Ms. Doyle. I'll tell the Chief you're okay," he called, before he opened the glass door and scooted outside.

Gonzalez had looked happy to be released from the boring ER nursemaid duty. There was no action here for him. It had all taken place somewhere else. That's why all these injured folks were here now. And somewhere else is where Gonzalez yearned to be, I could sense it.

Collapsing into another torturous plastic chair, I whipped out my cell phone and punched in Amanda's number. Gonzalez's close watch had kept me from checking earlier. Something had been pushing me to call her.

After five rings, her sleepy voice answered. "Hello? Who is calling at this ungodly hour?"

Good. She was waking up. "Amanda, it's me, Kate."

"Kate? What's wrong? Are you all right?"

"I'm okay." Instinct told me not to mention my injury. "I just wanted to call you before you read the morning paper. Cheryl Krane is dead."

Silence. I waited. Nothing.

"Amanda? Did you hear me?"

"I heard you, Kate, but I don't know what to say. Did she commit suicide over Mark?"

"No, Amanda. No, she didn't. She was killed. Shot in her home tonight."

A sharp intake of breath, then a tiny whisper. "Oh, no. No, Kate. That can't be."

"I'm afraid it is."

"How do you know?"

I took a deep breath and chose my words carefully. Something told me not to disclose everything this time, as I had in every other phone conversation with Amanda. I wasn't sure why. Just a feeling. Had Bill's suspicions rubbed off on me? "Because I found her. I was returning a book of hers she'd given Mark, and when I arrived at her home, she was already dead."

"My God, who could have done this?"

"I don't know, Amanda, and I'm fairly certain the police don't either. But just in case they want to ask more questions, you'd better be prepared." I hesitated, then had to ask. "Were you home tonight or out with friends?"

She paused. "I was home all night. Alone." Her voice trailed off.

Great. Once again, Amanda had no alibi and no one to verify her whereabouts. That disturbing thought about Amanda's innocence niggled again, but I shoved it to the back of my mind.

"Listen, Amanda, promise me you won't mention to anyone that I found Cheryl. Please! Bill is going to try to keep me out of the papers this time. If the police call, act shocked. And whatever you do, don't tell them I called you. Bill will arrest me for meddling." Suddenly Bill's concern about my involvement took on new meaning. Had I really helped my friend by telling her beforehand?

"I promise, Kate," Amanda said in a small voice. "Please don't get into trouble because of me." She clicked off.

I shoved my phone back into my purse and rubbed my throbbing head. Too late for that, Amanda. Way too late. Closing my eyes, I leaned my head on my arm, trying to get comfortable. When the pharmacist finished with my prescription, he'd announce it. Maybe I could sleep for a few minutes, maybe . . .

"Kate! Kate! My God, Kate, what happened?" a distraught man's voice jolted me out of my semi-peaceful state.

I looked up to see Stanley Blackstone racing toward me. How in the world did he know I was here?

He hurled himself into the chair beside me. "Kate, you have to tell me! What happened? Did you see Cheryl? Tell me, please," he begged.

Distraught hardly described Stanley. The normally neat and tidily self-contained attorney was literally falling apart. Unkempt, hair falling in his face, sport shirt flapping open to reveal a white, never-seen-the-sun chest, a sneaker on one foot, a scuffed slipper on the other. And whereas Bill Levitz might not be neat on a daily basis, at least he could remember not to wear his pajamas out of the house. Not so, Stanley. Worn flannel pajama bottoms held together by a large safety pin completed his state of disarray. Poor Stanley was a mess.

"Stanley, how did you know I was here?"

"John Sheldrake . . . in our office . . . he lives across the street from Cheryl, and he called me when he saw the police," Stanley said breathlessly. "I raced over to his house. And I saw you come out and go with that policeman." He paused to suck in air and brushed stringy, brown hair from his eyes.

"You followed me here?"

He nodded. "I've been waiting to see you. That officer wouldn't let me talk to you. I kept watching to see if he'd leave."

I pictured Stanley hiding behind the nurse's station, peering out at Officer Gonzalez, and sympathy tweaked. "Stanley, I wish I could tell you something, but the police have forbidden me from speaking to anyone. I saw the newspaper reporters talking with the detective in charge. Tomorrow they'll have the story, I'm sure."

The expression on Stanley's face was almost enough to make me change my mind. Almost. His ashen face started to redden as tears welled in his eyes. They soon spilled down his cheeks. "You found her, didn't you?" he said, his voice trembling.

I squeezed my eyes shut and debated with myself. Maybe non-verbal answers wouldn't be against orders. I nodded.

Stanley caught a wet breath. "The next door neighbor said she overheard a policeman say Cheryl was shot. Is that true?"

Closing my eyes again, I nodded. If I didn't see myself do it, maybe I could convince myself I didn't. Deciding not to push it, I said, "No more, Stanley. Don't ask any more."

There was no worry about that. Stanley buried his head in his hands and sobbed. "Why?" he wailed. "Why would some fiend kill Cheryl? Why?"

I reached out and patted his shoulder while I waved away an approaching nurse, drawn by his distress. "I don't know, Stanley," was all I could think of to say.

Stanley continued to weep, his sobs slowly growing quieter. I waited until his shoulders stopped shaking and decided to ask some questions of my own. That wouldn't be against orders.

"Stanley," I said gently. "Can you think of anyone who hated Cheryl enough to kill her?"

"No one," he replied. "She was an angel."

"How about a former client? Or someone who might have been angry because of her prosecution? Does anyone come to mind?"

Stanley slowly raised his head from his hands. Apparently my line of questioning had re-awakened the lawyer within. He turned a blotched and streaked face to mine. "I don't think so. She handled corporate clients." He wiped his face against his shirt.

I rummaged through my purse for some tissues and offered them. He accepted and blew his nose loudly. I debated my next line of questions. "Stanley, I went to Cheryl's to return the book she'd given Mark Schuster. You remember telling me about it at the open house, don't you?"

He nodded, snuffling.

"I found a key to the Schusters' house on the kitchen counter after the open house ended," I said in a quiet voice. "I was wondering if you left it there." I watched his face carefully.

Stanley lowered his head and stared at the floor. After a full minute of silence, he whispered, "Yes. Cheryl gave it to me. So I could find the book."

That confirmed my earlier suspicions. Stanley was the prowler. I didn't feel the need to question him further. Even though the prowler had frightened me, I couldn't feel animosity toward Stanley. He was too pathetic. So much so, I crossed him off my list of suspects entirely. No doubt he could kill Schuster, but not Cheryl. His grief wasn't feigned.

Just then I heard my pharmacy number being called and used that as my signal to depart. "Stanley," I said as I rose from my chair, "my prescription is ready and I have to go home now. I just want to say I'm so, so sorry." I reached out and squeezed his hand.

He squeezed back. "Thank you, Kate," he whispered.

I turned and headed for the pharmacy window. This night had been long enough. All I wanted to do was go home and curl up in bed—and hide.

Chapter Eighteen

The light morning breeze ruffled the newspaper as I stretched out on my back yard chaise. *I could get used to this,* I thought, as I lazily sipped my coffee and watched Sam snoozing in the sun. I'd forgotten how enjoyable it was to simply sit on the patio and relax. A frenetic work schedule robbed you of such simple pleasures. Actually, taking time to read the paper, rather than skimming lead paragraphs while grabbing a quick breakfast, was a luxury.

The best thing about this morning's newspaper was that I wasn't in it. There was no mention of my name in the lead story of Cheryl Krane's murder. Bill had promised he'd do his best to keep me from being mentioned. I didn't think I could stand any more unwanted publicity. Walking in on one murder victim was horrible enough. But two? People would avoid me. I let out a huge sigh of relief, when I read that a business acquaintance found the body.

I'd awakened headache-free this morning, for which I was profoundly grateful. However, my muscles were a little sore. From falling on Cheryl's concrete garage floor, no doubt. It wasn't hard to convince myself to follow the doctor's advice and take it easy. I informed my office I'd be in later that afternoon, then started relaxing.

That lasted for two hours before the antsy feeling nibbled at me again. I should be doing something. Working. Calling clients. Asking questions. And, despite Bill's advice, meddling. There were too many unanswered questions swirling inside my head.

Why would Mark's killer murder Cheryl Krane? What possible threat could she be? Had she seen something? Did the killer make a mistake that Cheryl discovered?

A familiar voice startled me out of my puzzling. "Hey, Mom, how're you doing?" Jeannie asked as she slid open the screen door to the patio.

"Hey, sweetie, I'm fine. A hard head comes in handy," I joked, and laid my paper aside.

Jeannie frowned. "That's not funny, Mom. Uncle Bill told me what happened, then swore me to secrecy." She sank her tall, slender frame into a wrought iron chair. "Promise me you won't do any more crazy stuff like that again, Mom. Please."

Her normally pretty face had screwed up in a fair imitation of a stern matriarch. It was so incongruous on her, I almost laughed, but I didn't want to hurt her feelings. She was scolding me, so I decided to let her. It would make her feel better and slide right off me. I was incorrigible.

"I promise. No more late-night deliveries of books to potential murder victims. I swear." I held my hand high.

"Mom!"

"Okay, okay. I'll be careful. Believe me, I don't ever want to walk in a house and discover a dead body again. Twice in one month is enough for a lifetime." I didn't have to fake a shudder.

"And no more working in houses late at night, either."

I peered at her. "How did you hear about that?"

She lifted her chin and fixed me with a gotcha-look. "I called Ronnie this morning. I was going to tell her what happened, but Uncle Bill had already spoken with her. We're all worried about you, Mom."

Well, damn. I was hoping to be the one to tell Ronnie, so I could edit the story. No doubt Bill gave her all the gory details. And I'm sure she told him about last week's midnight prowler. Great. Now everyone was mad at me.

"You've got to stop poking around in police business, Mom. That's not your job," Jeannie said. She was on a roll now.

"You're right, you're right," I agreed obediently.

The only way to stop her was to distract her. I watched her launch into another list of don'ts, unable to ignore how thin and pale she'd gotten these last few months. Even Jeannie's once-lustrous dark hair appeared dull, pulled back into an austere bun. Her rigorous schedule accounted for the lack of sleep and fatigue, but her newly-adopted eating habits I feared were to blame for the thinness. It was hard for a committed carnivore to watch her child waste away on fruits, veggies, and vitamins.

I'd promised not to nag, but right now I needed a diversion that would work. Jeannie was getting her second wind, and I was anxious to leave and resume my wayward ways.

"Jeannie, I promise to be careful. Honest," I vowed. Then I deliberately peered at her. "Honey, I'm sorry to say this, but you're looking really peaked. Pale and thin. Even your hair has lost its sheen. I know you like that vegan stuff, but really . . ."

Jeannie clamped her mouth shut. Her frown deepened. "Mom, don't start."

"Okay, okay, I won't. Sorry, I slipped." I rose from the chaise, ready to escape.

"Promise me you'll be careful, Mom. Don't make me call Liz."

At the mention of my older daughter—the global traveler, businesswoman, and all-around free spirit—I almost laughed. "Is that supposed to scare me?"

I couldn't help myself. That's what happened when your kids grew older. They became overly protective. The only problem is, some of us didn't want protection. However, I'd discovered there was usually a way to give them the slip. Some of us got wilier as we got older. There was no fence that could hold us.

Jeannie frowned. "Now, Mom. You know Liz would give you hell, if she found out."

Knowing my older daughter, I figured she'd actually laugh out loud, but I kept that to myself. "Well, she'll just have to get in line." I grinned. Just then, my cell phone rang. I grabbed it as Jeannie rose to leave.

"You're impossible, Mom, but I love you anyway. Be careful," she admonished before she slipped through the patio door.

"Love you, too," I called before I answered the insistent ringing. "This is Kate."

"And this is Ronnie."

Uh, oh. I could tell from her tone of voice that I was in for it. Jeannie was nothing. Ronnie would really give it to me.

"How're you feeling, Kate?"

"Oh, I'm fine, just fine," I said. "In fact, I was just about to come in. Can't take too much of this lying about."

There was a long pause. "This is no joking matter, Kate," she finally said.

"I'm not joking, Ronnie, honest. It's just that I've spent the last ten minutes being scolded by Jeannie. Bill gave it to me last night, and I'm sure you want to have at me as well. Go ahead. I deserve it." Contrition never hurt.

Another pause. "No, Kate. I don't think it does any good, because you never pay attention to any of us. So I've decided to simply give you an ultimatum. If you want to continue working for me here at Shamrock, then you'll have to take a series of lessons I'm assigning you."

That took me by surprise. "Lessons? What kind of lessons."

"I know that as your managing broker I cannot order you to do anything, since legally you are not an employee. Brokers are independent contractors. However, I do have the authority to sever your relationship with the company. You understand that, don't you, Kate?"

My stomach did an icy flip-flop. "Yes, I do," I said softly. "Are you firing me, Ronnie?"

"No, Kate, I'm not firing you. You're a good broker. I'd like to keep you around. However, since you've adopted some reckless tendencies lately, I've decided to set several conditions for you to continue with Shamrock."

My breath came a little easier. Conditions were something I could live with. There was no way I would let this murder investigation jeopardize my relationship with Ronnie or her company. I was happy there, and I wanted to remain there. I would gladly agree to any condition she set.

"You got it, Ronnie. I'll do whatever you want. You know I don't want to leave Shamrock." I hoped my sincerity would come through.

"I'll hold you to that, Kate."

"What kind of lessons were you thinking of? Martial arts? I've already visited three schools."

"Yes, I want you to enroll, and soon."

I released a huge sigh. I'd dodged a bullet for sure. "I'll do it tomorrow."

"Meanwhile, you'll start the other lessons this afternoon. The county firing range on South Taft Hill Road. Be there at three o'clock. Jake Chekov will be waiting."

I flinched and watched the bullet turn around and head straight for me. "Ronnie . . ."

"No argument, Kate. Those are my conditions. And Bill agrees with me. He's wanted you to protect yourself for years. So, there's no way you can wiggle out this time."

Damn. She had me and she knew it. I braced myself for impact. The bullet was headed right between my eyes.

"My advice is we ask for the big three and ignore the little stuff," I said to the Kerchoffs as I slowly drove south of town.

We were having a mini-conference call this afternoon— both husband, John, and wife, Susan, in their respective offices, and me on my cell phone in my office on wheels. They'd had a chance to think carefully about the inspection report and come to a decision. We had one day left before the Inspection Objection Deadline. If they wanted repairs, now was the time to ask.

"Just three?" Susan's voice piped up. "But that isn't fair!"

"I'm afraid fair has nothing to do with it," I said. "The seller has three options. He can agree to your repair request. He can pick and choose which repairs he'll make. Or he can refuse to make any at all."

It was always hard to explain the fairness issue to young buyers. As long as the furnace worked, it was legal, even if it was ancient. In this case, however, our inspection showed a crack in the heat exchanger. That was a biggie.

"Let's go with what Kate says, honey," John said. "I agree. Let's ask for the furnace, roof repair, and the leaky pipes downstairs. We can do the little stuff ourselves."

I held my breath and waited for his wife's reaction to this

eminently practical suggestion, and one which had a far better chance of being accepted than a laundry list of every single flaw. The major items tended to get lost that way. Plus, that was a technique guaranteed to annoy most sellers.

"Okay. I guess so," she said, reluctance dripping from every word.

I spied the firing range up ahead and felt some strong reluctance of my own. "I'll draw up the notice and bring it over tonight," I said before they could change their minds. "Will you be in after dinner?"

"Yeah, that'll be fine, Kate. See you then," John said, and they both clicked off.

I tossed the phone into my briefcase as I pulled onto the dirt road leading to the firing range. Choosing the closest spot to the road and farthest from the action, I parked and got out.

Talk about open space. I saw nothing but a natural stretch of the foothills in all directions. Someone unfamiliar with the West would call it barren, but I knew it teemed with wildlife and the hardy vegetation that can thrive in a semi-desert landscape.

There was other wildlife there as well, I noticed. A man stood under a simple open-roofed structure in the distance. The sound of shots echoed through the air, and I flinched. Reluctance didn't even begin to describe what I felt right now. But Ronnie had given me no choice, so I was going to follow through, no matter what.

I was secretly hoping Chekov would get so disgusted with me, he'd throw up his hands and quit. That way, I'd be off the hook with Ronnie. She'd never find anyone else crazy enough to teach me. What fool would want to be around me when I had a gun in my hand?

I headed toward Chekov's big, black pickup. As my heels sank into the sandy soil, I realized I should have brought some sneakers. Too late. Business suit, silk blouse, and heels would just have to do. After all, I imagine criminals don't wait for you to change to comfy clothes before you confront them.

Chekov turned and started on me before I even opened my mouth. "Three o'clock, real estate agent time. I figured."

I glanced at my watch as I approached: 3:05. "You know, Chekov, this whole ordeal will go a lot smoother, if you just ease up on the smart-ass comments."

He eyed me with a hint of a smile. "Ordeal? Not if you relax. Just listen to my instructions—"

"Relax! Are you kidding? You have enough munitions here to invade a small Caribbean island." My hand swept out to indicate the variety of firearms spread out on the table next to me. A rifle, some other long-barreled weapon which might be a shotgun, and four handguns. Four! What did he think I was going to do? Try them on for size?

Instead of rising to the bait, Chekov peered at me carefully. "How's your head?" he asked in what sounded amazingly like a solicitous tone.

I considered ignoring his clever change of tactics and continue my course of deliberate aggravation, then decided against it. "Much better. I haven't had a headache all afternoon. Not yet, anyway. That could change any second now. So, don't push it, Chekov."

He grinned. "You'll be fine. Trust me." When I arched a skeptical brow, he added, "I've instructed several people in your business. If they can do it, Doyle, so can you."

Ouch. That hit home, and I sensed he knew it. There was nothing I loved more than a challenge, especially if it meant proving myself. "And now these real estate agents are walking around Fort Collins, armed to the teeth. Is that what you're saying?"

"No, that's not what I'm saying at all. I simply instructed

them in marksmanship and weapons-handling. Then I sent them to the Police Department to get their licenses. I don't keep tabs on them afterwards. But I'm not here to talk about them. I'm here to teach you. Stay on task, Doyle."

Rats. He wasn't going to let me distract him. I wasn't about to give up, though. "Do you actually expect me to try all these revolvers?" My hand swept in an expansive gesture toward the table.

"Pistols. My revolvers are home on the wall."

"Whatever."

"My suggestion is you handle each one, and see which one feels best."

"You're joking. How could a gun feel good?"

"One of these will fit your hand better than the others. Stop stalling, Doyle."

I spied a distinct gleam of laughter in his eyes, but ignored it and let out a dramatic sigh of resignation instead. "All right, all right, all right," I said, feigning surrender. I'd only begun to aggravate. I selected the largest pistol of the lot and gingerly lifted it off the table, then very nearly dropped it. It was surprisingly heavy.

"Careful," he said.

"They're not loaded, are they?" I looked at him in genuine horror and quickly replaced the gun.

"Don't worry. None of them are loaded. Didn't like that one, huh?"

"Only Dirty Harry could love a gun like that. Definitely not me." I lifted the next, slightly smaller than the other one, but still heavy.

"That's a .45."

"Age?"

"Caliber."

"Will there be a quiz?"

"No, but we'll be here till nightfall, unless you quit stalling."

I didn't reply. It wouldn't work anyway, so I lifted the third, replaced it, then picked up the fourth and last pistol. Surprisingly, it wasn't heavy. The metal felt cool against my palm.

"That's a .38," Chekov said.

I was about to respond, when a man's loud voice startled me.

"Howdy, folks. Great day, isn't it?"

"Yessir. Indeed, it is." Chekov grinned.

I spun around, without thinking, the pistol still in my hand. A plump, older man dressed in hunter orange was unloading an armful of rifles on the neighboring table, just twenty feet away. He looked up, spotted me aiming at him, and blanched. Then he hit the ground, face-first. Actually, belly-first.

Chekov reached over and guided my arm downward, then addressed the cowering hunter. "Don't worry, sir. It's not loaded. We're doing some basic training here. We apologize." To me, he said, "Range Rule Number One, Doyle. Do not threaten the other marksmen. Tends to make them surly."

I fought back a smile, with little success, convinced I'd found the perfect way to thwart Chekov's plans. Just act outrageous. Not a problem. With the things I'd gotten into lately, outrageous would be a piece of cake.

"How does that one feel?" he said.

"Okay, I guess. Better than the others."

"Good. Now, this is what you're going to do—"

The loud sound of rifle fire sounded close by. I yelped and spun around. This time, Chekov grabbed the gun from my hand before I could frighten the chubby hunter next door. He was taking deadly aim at the bulls-eye in the distance.

"Is that next?" I said.

"Yep." Chekov opened a box of bullets and began to fill a cartridge. "You'll notice I've moved your target closer. You're using a handgun, not a rifle. Besides, you'd be confronting someone within close range, so we'll concentrate on that."

The image that brought to mind was an unpleasant reminder of why I was here. "So I just have to hit the target a few times, then I can go home. Is that it, Chekov?"

He grinned. "Yeah, Doyle. That's all there is to it. Hit within the target circle five times, and you can go. Now, stand over here." He pointed to the other side of the table next to him.

"How far away is the target?" I asked as I approached.

"About twenty-five feet. Do you have any other shoes in your car? Sneakers by any chance?"

"In my office. But I can always run back and get them."

"Nice try. Just be sure to sink those heels in the sand when you take your stance."

"Like Dirty Harry?"

"Picture anyone you like, Doyle. Now, this is what I want you to do." He stood facing the target, lifted both arms, and aimed. "You'll square off, feet apart, balancing your weight, shoulders facing the target. Then holding the gun with both hands, you'll sight down the barrel toward the target, then squeeze the trigger slowly." Turning to me, he said, "Now hold out your hand, palm-up."

I complied. He shoved in the cartridge, then placed the gun in my hand and gently wrapped my fingers around it.

"Keep your finger away from the trigger for now. Just hold it securely but lightly. Not in a death grip. Relax."

"Easy for you to say. This thing is loaded."

"Open your other hand, palm-up, and rest your gun hand in it. Just set your hand there and let your other hand hold on." When I did as he directed, he said, "Good, now face off and imitate what I did."

I considered being disobedient, but decided against it for some reason. Maybe the challenge was beginning to work on me, against my will. I took a stance, felt my heels sink into the sand, and made sure I was facing the target. Then I raised my arms. Sighting down the barrel toward the bulls-eye, I decided this was going to be too easy. All it took was five inside the circle. Okay, five it is. I pressed my finger against the trigger and fired.

The noise surprised me. So did the kick of the gun in my hand. I sighted down the barrel again, then fired off five more shots in rapid succession. I'd counted six bullets in that cartridge. I brought the gun back, barrel pointed up, and blew at the imaginary smoke. Just like in the movies. Harry would be proud. I grinned at Chekov. "Satisfied?"

"I will be when you hit the target."

"What?" The clatter of metal against metal caught my attention, and I turned—gun down this time. The chubby hunter, arms filled with rifles, was scurrying away to the far end of the range, orange shirttail flapping. A trail of shotgun shells marked his obviously panicked retreat. "Is he afraid of competition?" I joked.

"He's afraid of more than that, Doyle. Are you ready to get serious, now?"

"What are you talking about? I was serious. I sighted, took aim, and fired. Just like you said. Why don't you check the target?"

"You didn't hit the target. All you did was scare the wildlife. Every prairie dog in Larimer County just headed for Wyoming."

I scowled. "Don't be such a smart ass. Check the target."

"Twenty bucks says you didn't come anywhere near it."

"You're on. Check it."

He grinned and reached to take the gun from my hand, even though it was empty, then headed toward the target.

"What's the matter? Afraid I'll reload while you're out there?" I called while I watched him remove the paper bullseye from the target frame and return. He presented it to me with a flourish. It was immaculate. Untouched. I stared at it. Obviously, I had miscalculated.

"Okay, Doyle, are you ready to get to work now?" He shoved the refilled cartridge back into the pistol and offered it to me.

Chekov stood there, not looking the slightest bit annoyed. The soul of patience. I eyed the angle of the sun. True, it was still shining brightly above the foothills, but I knew how quickly it could disappear behind those peaks. Chekov's prediction of nightfall wasn't that far away. And I'd promised my clients I'd be at their house tonight with a completed Notice to Correct in my hand.

Well, damn. I guess I'd actually have to apply myself. I reached for the pistol. "Okay, tell me what I did wrong."

To my surprise Chekov said, "You didn't do anything wrong. You just did it too fast. You didn't allow yourself time to aim properly. Do everything again, but slowly this time. I'm going to be working at the next target. Tell me when you're empty, and I'll reload for you." He picked up the rifle and a long box of bullets, and headed toward the same table the chubby hunter had just evacuated.

"Any other wildlife I need worry about? Rabbits? Raccoons?"

"The rabbits are cowering in their holes. Now, get to work before they die of heart failure."

"Anything else? Hawks, owls—"

"The hawks saw you coming, Doyle. They're in Boulder by now. Stop stalling and start shooting," he said as he took aim and fired.

The rifle's loud retort made me jump. His target was so far away, it might as well be in Boulder. I glanced back at mine. Checking the angle of the sun, I squared off, took my stance, and took aim. As I sighted down the barrel toward the bullseye, I wondered if the pizza guy would deliver out here.

Chapter Nineteen

I couldn't tell if the sound of the phone ringing or the irritating buzz of the alarm clock woke me first. Whichever it was, it was unwelcome. I jerked out of my exhausted slumber and crawled out of bed. My answering machine had come on, so I stumbled toward the alarm clock and gave it a vicious shove, then reached for the phone before I collapsed back into bed. How could it be after 8:00? I never oversleep.

"This is Kate," I mumbled into the phone.

"Don't tell me I woke you?" Marilyn's voice was filled with concern. "Are you all right, Kate? Jeannie just told me what happened the other night. I simply cannot believe you walked in on another body!"

"Believe it," I said between yawns.

"Kate, are you really okay? I called Jeannie when I couldn't get you yesterday. She said you were resting. Why didn't you answer the phone? I was worried about you. Is there something you're not telling me?"

Yes, there was, but I knew if I told Marilyn everything that happened to me these past two days, then it would be all over town. I had to distract her.

"Sorry, I had the answering machine on. Besides, I only

rested in the morning. I went back into the office in the afternoon. Then I spent two grueling hours in the foothills, shooting at paper targets. Ronnie and Bill both ganged up on me and insisted I take lessons. It was excruciating."

"Actually, I agree with both of them. You've had some scary experiences lately."

"Listen, Marilyn, you have to promise me you will resist the urge to spread the word about my finding the body. I already swore Amanda to secrecy, and you have to promise too. Bill kept my name out of the papers. I don't want my friends blowing my cover, okay?"

"I promise, Kate. I won't tell a soul. I just wish you'd be careful." She took a deep breath and started in.

I reluctantly pulled myself out of bed. If I was going to listen to someone else scold me, I had to have some coffee. I pulled on a tee-shirt and headed for the kitchen, while Marilyn continued her cautionary litany.

"You can stop fussing, Marilyn," I finally said when I could get a word in edgewise. "I *am* following orders. Ronnie left me no choice. I've signed up for martial arts instruction, and I just had my first weapons class, so ease up, okay?" I didn't stop to measure the coffee, simply dumped it into the canister. Extra strength. That way maybe my eyes would stay open.

"Were you over at that range on Taft Hill?"

"Yep. Out there in the middle of the foothills."

"You weren't out there alone, were you?" I could hear the shiver in her voice.

"No. Ronnie insisted Jake Chekov do the instruction. Apparently, he's trained several real estate agents in town. He wouldn't tell me their names, though." Pouring the water into the coffee maker, I flipped the switch and leaned on the counter. I was going to hover right over the pot until it was ready.

"Oh, really?" Marilyn's voice traveled up its little musical scale in a tune I knew well.

"Don't even go there, Marilyn," I warned.

"So it was just you and Jake Chekov out there alone?"

"Well, there was another marksman practicing for a while, but I frightened him away."

"Why? Did you shoot him?"

"No, but he thought I would. Of course, I can't imagine where he'd get that idea. Chekov had enough guns to take over a small town."

"So, what happened?"

"What do you mean, what happened? I practiced shooting at that stupid bulls-eye until I finally got five in the circle. Then he kept moving the target farther away, so I could do it again. Brother! It was after five when I left. Then I had to write up a notice for my buyers, get signatures, and deliver it to the other real estate agent. Boy, was I glad to get home." The enticing aroma of coffee wafted toward my nostrils. Any minute now, I'd be human again.

"Now that you've had some time alone, what do you think of this Chekov?"

In her own way, Marilyn was as incorrigible as I was. You had to respect that. "Oh, he's your average Marine Corps Drill Sergeant. Nothing special."

"Strict, huh?"

"And tricky. I tried every tactic I could to get out of it, from basic in-your-face aggravation to gross incompetence. Nothing worked."

"That must have annoyed you terribly."

"As a matter of fact, it did." I snatched a clean mug from the cabinet and quickly poured a dark stream into the cup, even though the coffee maker was still brewing. Water hitting the hot plate hissed into steam.

"Will you be having more classes?"

"Unfortunately, yes. But enough about that." I deliberately switched subjects. "You spoke with Amanda today? How did she sound?"

Marilyn paused. "Actually, Kate, she didn't sound good at all. Her voice was so soft I kept asking her to speak up. That's not like Amanda. I'm worried about her."

"So am I, Marilyn. And for other reasons. I called her right after the murder. And she doesn't have an alibi. Once again, she was at home alone."

"Oh, no."

"Oh, yes," I said, then took a long drink of coffee. I felt the clouds lift from my eyes at last. There was hope. "I'm worried, Marilyn. I really am. Everyone in town thinks she did it, and she has no witnesses to confirm her whereabouts for either night. Not good."

There was a long pause from Marilyn this time. "Kate, this is scaring me. What can we do? What can Amanda do?"

"All she can do now is to be extremely cooperative with the police and answer all their questions truthfully. That's all she can do. As for us, there's not much we can do." I took another swallow of the rich, deep brew, and listened to Marilyn voice her concern.

Meanwhile, a recently-awakened lobe of my brain refused to accept what it had just heard. Surely there was some way to uncover this clever killer's identity. There must be a clue somewhere. *Cheryl Krane had learned something that got her killed. What was it?*

I inhaled the rich coffee aroma and drank deeply while Marilyn drew a second wind. It was too late to question Cheryl. And Stanley was a basket case. Who else might know something? Different faces danced through my mind as the caffeine gradually ignited my brain's sleeping cells. Finally one face came and stayed. I drained my cup, eased Marilyn off the phone, and headed for the shower. Meddling or not, forbidden or not, I was determined to find something that could help my friend.

It would be hard to find a more beautiful early fall morning, I thought, as I drove the curving road leading to Fort Collins Country Club. The aspens that dotted the foothills were always the first to claim the gold. Cool nights and brilliantly sunny days had done their work.

The massive cottonwood trees were next. Those lining the lake to my left had turned glorious shades of yellow veined with green, their leaves reflecting off the lake's glassy surface. Then the maples would turn blood red or burgundy, mixed with green. Orange was found elsewhere—low-lying scrub bushes that hugged rocks and steep crevices burst into flame and burnt umber.

For those of us who'd grown up in the East, where hardwood forests surround even the most modest neighborhood, fall was a riot of color. A much showier display. Every color in autumn's palette was splashed with abandon. It was different in the West. We could enjoy all the same colors. We just had to look for them in different places.

Sharon Bassett's housekeeper had said Sharon usually stayed for lunch after her Wednesday morning tennis match. *What better time,* I thought, *to catch her relaxed.* Maybe she'd be willing to answer some questions. I hoped her luncheon with Cheryl had yielded some useful information. It definitely had appeared to be an intense conversation between the two of them. Maybe Cheryl had shared a confidence with Sharon—from one jilted lover to another. That idea didn't sound too plausible, even to me, but it was all I had. If I could just start Sharon talking, maybe something useful would come out.

I wheeled my Explorer into the parking area and drove near the front, then parked and walked the lovely, sloping path to the graceful white-columned entrance. Nodding to one of the staff, I headed toward the side where the patios were located. If Sharon was relaxing after the match, it would be there.

Sure enough, I spied her at a table with friends, a red- and white-striped umbrella shading them from the sun. Sharon's summer-perfect tan was still intact and showed nicely against her short, white tennis dress. She was seated with two sleek blondes I vaguely recalled from my former life. Once again, I cursed my poor memory for names, hoping Sharon would handle introductions.

Fixing a bright smile on my face, I approached the threesome. "Hi there, Sharon," I greeted her. "Your housekeeper said I would find you here."

Sharon turned to me with a look of surprise. "Hello, Kate." She gestured to her friends. "You know Mary Flynn and Chris Honeycutt, don't you?"

Bless you, Sharon. "Oh, yes, but it's been ages," I said and grinned at the two women. Both nodded and murmured politely. I could tell they didn't have the foggiest recollection of who I was. Amazing how quickly divorce sweeps you right off the social radar screen. That was okay with me. I'd never liked being scrutinized anyway.

"My goodness, Kate, it must be something important for you to drive all the way to the north of town to find me." Sharon smiled her trademark enigmatic smile.

"Yes, it is," I said, readying the lie on my tongue. It was terrible how good I'd gotten at lying. "It's a legal matter that involves a client and, well, I promised her I'd find the best attorney for her to speak with. And I couldn't think of a better person to ask than you, Sharon. I hope you don't mind. I won't take more than a minute or two." I cocked my head slightly and fixed her with my most sincere wide-eyed innocent look.

Sharon blinked in surprise. "Of course, Kate. I'd be happy to help." Turning to her friends as she rose from the table, she said, "Mary, I'll see you tonight, and Chris, call me tomorrow, okay?" Both women nodded as Sharon grabbed her tennis racket and joined me.

"Thanks so much, Sharon. She'll really appreciate your help," I said, and headed toward one of the curving pathways that edged the rolling expanse of golf course.

"What sort of legal situation does your friend face, Kate? That way I can tell which attorney would be best."

Now that we were alone, I took a deep breath and threw all caution onto the nearby ninth green. I was banking on total honesty. "Actually, Sharon, she faces the gravest situation there is. She may be accused of her husband's murder."

Sharon stopped in mid-stride. "Kate, what are you talking about? Who is this?" She peered at me intently, as if answers were written on my face.

I resumed a leisurely stroll, so we wouldn't draw attention. Golfers were wandering the greens, and an occasional wayward golf cart puttered along. "I'm talking about Amanda. I'm worried about her, Sharon. She has no alibi for either murder. She was home alone both times. You know as well as I do, Amanda couldn't commit murder."

"Kate, I don't understand. Why are you coming to me?" she asked, the inscrutable mask discarded. Sharon looked genuinely perplexed. "Amanda already has the best criminal lawyer in town, Bob Carruthers. Did you want me to recommend someone else? Is she not satisfied?"

"No, that's not why I came, Sharon. I'm here without

Amanda's knowledge. I'm hoping you can shed some light on why Cheryl Krane was killed."

Once again, Sharon stopped in her tracks. This time I noticed she'd paled slightly beneath her tan. "How on earth could I help? I don't even know Cheryl Krane. Not really."

I turned and looked her straight in the eye. "Sharon, Marilyn and I were at the Old Town café the same day you met Cheryl Krane for lunch. We saw you having what appeared to be a very intense conversation. Forgive me for being blunt, but I was struck by Cheryl's expression at the time. She appeared disturbed by what you were saying. When I mentioned that to Marilyn, she told me that both you and Cheryl had a relationship with Mark."

Sharon's cheeks began to regain their color, and I sensed my comments were a shock to her well-preserved privacy. I knew I was treading very close to insult, with a woman who would not forgive easily, but I didn't care. I was going to help Amanda any way I could. And if shaking the unflappable Sharon Bassett would yield a clue to help my friend, then I'd shake away.

"I was hoping Cheryl might have told you something during lunch, something that might help us find Mark's killer. Something, anything." I let my own intensity show through.

Sharon swayed just a bit on her feet, then stared off at a foursome in the distance. The insistent cry of a mountain jay caught my attention as he swooped from a maple tree to a nearby evergreen. With the Rocky Mountains as a backdrop, the golf course view was spectacular.

I didn't say another word. It was Sharon's turn. Either she'd respond as the friend Amanda assumed she was, or she'd ice up and tell me to remove my nose from her private business. Clearly, there was a struggle going on inside. At last, she turned to meet my gaze again. No ice to be seen. I felt my insides relax.

"I think Cheryl was upset by what I told her," she said softly. "She had no idea of our relationship. So I suppose it was a shock to her. That's probably what you saw."

"I'm curious, Sharon. Why did you tell Cheryl Krane about your relationship with Mark? Especially after he was killed?"

She studied the cement path for a moment, then started walking slowly. I matched my pace to hers. "I wanted to know if Mark had revealed any personal information. Information about me. As soon as I saw her reaction, I knew the answer. Clearly, it was news to Cheryl."

"Did she say anything about Mark, or anyone else for that matter?"

Sharon shook her head. "Actually, Cheryl didn't say much at all. She was definitely the quiet type. Plus, I did most of the talking. I wanted to know if Cheryl had been interviewed by the police. I needed to prepare myself, if she had."

"Had she been interviewed?"

"No. In fact, she looked petrified at the very thought. Of course, I was relieved to hear that the police had not, well . . . hadn't felt the need to dig into Mark's romantic past, so to speak. I was continuing with my plans to move to Denver, and I was scared of what might happen if the police started digging into Mark's relationships." She exhaled a long sigh. "I wanted to start a whole new life, Kate. This tragedy forced me to reexamine everything."

We were tracing the pathway leading to the front of the country club now. Sharon started across the parking lot, and I followed. Disappointment rose within me. I had so hoped Sharon could remember some comment from Cheryl that might lead the police away from Amanda and toward the real killer.

"Damn," I said softly, unable to hide my disappointment.

Sharon headed toward the closest row of parked cars. "I'm sorry, Kate. I wish I'd heard something that could help. Personally, I don't think Cheryl knew anything."

"Well, she must have learned something after you talked to her. Something that got her killed."

Sharon paused and stared at me, fear in her pale blue eyes, but she didn't say a word. Instead, she reached inside the small leather pouch that was attached to her racket case and withdrew a car key. "Do you really believe that, Kate?" she asked as she leaned over to unlock her car.

"Yes . . . yes . . . I do," I stammered. Whatever words had been on my tongue disappeared at the sight of Sharon Bassett's car. A sleek, gold Lexus. I stared without speaking as Sharon opened the door and tossed her racket inside. These parking lot revelations were getting spooky.

According to Greg, the observant little neighborhood skater, the "funny, fat jogger" had driven off in a gold car that was parked down the street from the Schuster house. An expensive, gold car. Watching stylishly-slim Sharon climb into her car, I wondered if she could have cleverly disguised herself. The detectives had mentioned that clothes were strewn all over the upstairs bedroom. I pictured her stuffing extra clothes inside a sweatsuit, choosing a close-fitting hat that concealed her hair, winter gloves to hide her delicate hands, sunglasses to obscure her face, and topped off with a pair of Mark's street shoes. A clever disguise, indeed. The jogger would appear to be a man.

My pulse began to race. Was Sharon the mystery jogger? Had *she* killed Mark? Was her shocked reaction to my questions just now merely a clever performance designed to throw off suspicion? Was all this talk about starting a new life in Denver a ruse to take her conveniently out of town and off the police radar screen? I took a deep breath to calm myself and slow my speeding thoughts.

Sharon closed her car door, then leaned out the window. "Kate, I don't know what to say. Should I call Amanda?"

"Yes, why don't you," I managed. "I'm sure she'd appreciate it."

I endeavored to keep my voice and expression calm, when inside, I was desperately searching for a way to get more information from Sharon, startle her into revealing something—anything. Suddenly, the image of the jogger appeared in my mind again. It was a gamble, especially if Sharon was the killer. I'd be making myself an even bigger target than I already was. I hesitated, then took a deep breath and followed my instinct.

"Just tell her you believe she's innocent, will you, Sharon?" I said dramatically. "She needs to hear that we all know she couldn't commit murder."

Sharon nodded, sun glinting off her frosted hair. "I will, Kate. I promise."

Pausing for just a second, I rolled the dice. "I just wish the police could find that jogger. One of the neighbors saw a suspicious-looking jogger outside the house that afternoon. I can't help thinking that might be the person responsible for this awful crime." I attempted to sound as worried as possible, which wasn't difficult.

Sharon stared up at me, her expression unreadable. "A jogger? Do you really think so, Kate?"

"Yes, I do. There's no one else who has appeared as a suspect. Except Amanda." I released a dramatic sigh.

"Are the police looking for this . . . this jogger?"

"Well, they say they are." I remembered Bill's skeptically

lifted brow when I'd recounted the young skater's story.

Sharon turned the ignition, and the engine gave a low throaty purr. "I'll call you later, Kate. After I've spoken with Amanda." She slipped on her sunglasses. "And thank you, Kate."

That surprised me. "Thanks for what?"

"For sharing what was obviously privileged information with me. I appreciate your trust." She lifted her hand in a delicate wave and backed from the parking space.

I stood and watched the stunning woman I'd socialized with for a decade drive away, wondering what had just happened. Had I shared confidences with a friend or drawn a bulls-eye on myself that would make Chekov's targets shrink in comparison?

Locating my own car, I drove back through the leafy, winding roads to town, not noticing autumn's beauty this time. My mind was too busy trying to figure out Sharon Bassett's motive for killing Mark Schuster, if indeed she was the murderer. She'd obviously loved him enough to risk an affair. Being married to a divorce lawyer, Sharon surely knew the risks involved. Messy public divorce, scandal, gossip—all the things aloof, reserved Sharon seemed to abhor. Was she too aloof for murder? What could have incited her fury enough to stab Mark in the throat?

Betrayal. Rage at being dropped for a younger woman. Perhaps so. There was no woman I knew who was more concerned with preserving her physical beauty than Sharon Bassett. And she was an expert, according to Marilyn. With her inherited wealth always at her fingertips, Sharon had indulged herself in the latest anti-aging remedies. I had to admit they worked. Sharon didn't look her fifty years. Late thirties would be closer.

Turning onto an arterial street leading back into the heart

of Fort Collins, I didn't even glance at some of my favorite views—horses grazing in the pasture, Rocky Mountains in the distance. I was lost in puzzling thought. Clearly, Sharon's image of herself was of a stunning woman used to having her own way. Had she assumed their affair would continue? Did she go to Mark's house to tell him she was moving to Denver to be near him? Did she fly into a rage when Mark rejected her? Obviously, Sharon was not used to rejection of any kind. Could it have driven her to kill?

Perhaps. But killing Mark was one thing. Why then would she kill Cheryl? What possible threat could she be? After all, Mark had rejected Cheryl too. Then I remembered that Cheryl had been to Mark's house first. The skaters said the white Rabbit was parked in their space when they returned early from school, then was gone.

Had Sharon arrived, seen Cheryl's car, then parked down the street? Was she seething within with jealous fury that Mark might be indulging in one last fling with his longtime lover? Did Cheryl see Sharon's gold Lexus and recognize it as she drove off? Did she mention it to Sharon? And if so, was that her death sentence?

At that point, all the competing theories began to jumble. No more for now. I was confusing myself. How would I ever present a cogent theory to Bill?

I needed coffee. Then I would check on Amanda. I hadn't been over to see her in a few days, phoning her instead. Something pushed me to go over there now. But first, I'd make a detour past one of my favorite haunts and fortify myself.

Chapter Twenty

As I pulled into the parking lot adjacent to Amanda's condo, I noticed another familiar and expensive car—Jonathan Bassett's silver Acura—backing out of a space. Jerking my Explorer to a stop, I jumped out and waved to catch Jonathan's attention.

His window whirred down and I bombarded him as I approached. "Jonathan, how is Amanda doing? Did the police call to interview her again?"

"Yes, they did, Kate. They were here this morning, in fact." He removed his sunglasses, and I was struck by the strange look on his face. It resembled genuine concern.

"How did it go?"

He glanced away. "Judging from what Amanda told me, it didn't go well. She's convinced the police will show up on her doorstep with handcuffs any moment now."

I winced. "Jonathan, I'm really worried about her. She has no alibi for either murder. I know Amanda can be overly dramatic at times, but this time I fear her suspicions may be right. The police have no other suspect. Right now, Amanda looks like the logical choice."

"I am aware of that, Kate," he said, his voice softer than

normal. "And I promise I will do what I can. I'm going back to the office now to speak with Carruthers. Amanda gave me her consent for Bob to update me fully with what he's doing to protect her."

"Please, Jonathan, do what you can," I pleaded as I backed away from the car.

"I will, Kate, I promise." He began to send the window up, then hesitated. "She needs to calm down, Kate. See what you can do, okay? I wasn't very successful."

I nodded and watched him drive away, not sure I would be much help either. Amanda would probably pick up on my own concern. I headed for her door and knocked, while I vainly rummaged through my brain for some encouraging thoughts.

Amanda opened the door, saw me, and practically yanked me inside. "Kate! Oh, Kate! I'm so scared," she cried. "The police came this morning. Two detectives this time! Two! And they asked me so many questions. I got so confused, I couldn't answer straight. Bob took over when he could, but it was me . . . it was me that had to answer . . ."

Her voice trailed off as she clutched and unclutched her hands, her gaze darting back and forth around the open living room, not lingering long on any object. I noticed her nail polish was chipped. Unthinkable for the Amanda of three weeks ago. She was even paler than when I saw her last, and thinner. The shadows under her eyes were deeper. I fought to push the wave of worry away, lest she read my mind and spiral further downward.

"Amanda," I said as I took her twitching hands in mine. "You've got to relax. You are not helping yourself like this. Why don't you let me take you for a drive into Poudre Canyon? You know how you love it. We'll take a hike, then come back into town and have dinner."

She jerked her hands away. "I can't, Kate. Don't ask me why. I just can't right now." She spun around and hurried toward a marble and glass sofa table, littered with coffee cups, overflowing ashtrays, and packages of cigarettes. Grabbing one, Amanda quickly lit it and took one deep drag after another.

My heart ached for her. There was real panic in her eyes, and for good reason. She was her own worst enemy. Desperate for some way to distract her from the morning's distressing interview, I grabbed at anything. "What was Jonathan doing here? I thought all the divorce proceedings were null and void, since Mark died."

She glanced distractedly at me and gestured toward the dining room table. "He was returning all the divorce papers. Said I should destroy them, since they are no longer needed."

Either the cigarette or the change of topic had brought a change in her voice, however small. At least an octave lower. Hopeful, I headed for the exotic, black marble and glass table. If it would calm Amanda, I'd go through every piece of paper in that thick portfolio with her.

"I'll be glad to help you, Amanda. I agree with Jonathan. You shouldn't have these papers lying around. Let's tear them up, okay?" I unsnapped the portfolio's flap and withdrew a two-inch-thick set of legal-sized documents, bound with a black clamp.

Amanda took another puff and began to pace the living room, her arms clasped around herself. "That's fine, Kate. Thank you. I don't want to see them."

Her voice was approaching normal. "That's okay," I said as I unclamped the lot. "I'll just read the title, and you nod if you want it destroyed. Then I'll tear each one, and send the whole pile through my office shredder tonight."

She didn't answer, just kept on pacing, but I sensed she

was glad for my help. Just looking at the documents would bring back needless pain.

"Okay, first one is the petition for divorce," I announced. "We won't be needing this." And I purposely tore the pages lengthwise, then across, in a long, slow sound of finality. I hoped that sound would help Amanda on some level. At some point, this whole ordeal would be over.

I continued announcing and tearing, placing the torn pieces back into the portfolio for disposal later. So many documents. Letters, affidavits, petitions. I paused whenever I found a letter to an international investment firm. Or financial statements. But Amanda assured me each time that Jonathan had made copies of all pertinent documents related to Mark's hidden assets.

Working my way through the pile, I was about to ask Amanda to stop her pacing, which had slowed somewhat, and make a pot of her delicious coffee. I'd spent lunchtime visiting with Sharon. Once again, I was running on empty.

Glancing at the next legal-sized document, I looked for a title. Then I recognized it as a list of personal possessions. Very special possessions, very dear to Amanda and Mark. I paused to read the entire list. What I saw surprised me.

"Well, I must confess I'm amazed that Mark agreed to let you keep all the Paris engravings, Amanda. I remember your saying he insisted on half. I wonder what changed his mind."

She stopped her circuit of the living room and turned to stare at me. "What did you say?"

"I said I was surprised Mark let you keep all the Paris engravings. Didn't you tell me he insisted on keeping half?"

She looked at me strangely. "Yes, he did. He refused to bargain, even when I gave him the Degas."

"Well, he must have changed his mind, because he signed

right here, and put his initials after every item." I waved the piece of paper.

Amanda strode over to me and grabbed the document from my hand. Her intense interest was surprising, but gratifying. Anything to keep her mind away from the police. After a moment, she glanced up, clearly puzzled.

"I don't understand. I asked Jonathan to speak with Mark one more time about these pieces. He promised me he'd go see Mark that Monday afternoon. The same day Mark was killed. But when I called Jonathan that evening to ask, he told me he never got a chance to go. Too many clients. He never got there."

I snatched the paper from her hands and scrutinized each line item. Those were Mark Schuster's initials and his signature at the bottom, all right. I recognized both from all the contract pages he'd signed when I listed their house for sale. Why would Jonathan Bassett lie about something like that?

"Amanda, are you sure Mark hadn't signed this already? There were so many documents you and Jonathan were going over, searching for missing funds, shifted assets, all that. Maybe Jonathan thought you meant another document."

She looked me directly in the eye. "Kate, I am positive. I loved this collection above all else. I was willing to trade Mark a whole wall of Impressionists for this one set." Amanda pointed at the sheet of paper. "And I gave this list to Jonathan that very morning, the same day Mark was killed. There were no initials or signature then. I know Mark's signature as well as my own, Kate. He signed that document. And yet, Jonathan said he didn't. Why would he lie?"

Why, indeed? I stared at the document again, then picked up Amanda's pacing where she had left off. Amanda grabbed another cigarette.

Why would Jonathan lie about that document? Unless he

didn't want to admit he'd been to Mark's house the afternoon he was killed. That would open him to police questions. Very nasty business, being questioned by the police. Especially if Jonathan was hiding something. Or protecting someone . . . like his wife.

All those jumbled theories from this morning when I'd spoken with Sharon started zooming through my brain again, careening and diving like tiny swallows at sundown. Was Jonathan trying to protect Sharon? Had he gone to Mark's house with the document? Had Sharon appeared? Had there been a confrontation? Or, had he seen his wife's car approach as he drove off? I pictured Jonathan sitting in his car, seething with anger at Sharon's betrayal. Did he burst into Mark's home? Did he intend to confront them, only to discover his wife holding the murder weapon? Was it clever Jonathan the lawyer who helped Sharon disguise herself while he calmly wiped up telltale fingerprints, then left the scene himself?

One of the low-flying swallows dive-bombed into a building and fell limp—just like that last theory. Greg, with his knowledge of cars, would have spotted Jonathan's sleek, silver Acura, if it had been parked anywhere near Mark's house. The Lexus registered with the little skater, and it was parked around the corner and down the street.

I circled the coffee table and started another lap. Amanda stood and smoked, glancing nervously at me from time to time. Meanwhile, the swallows zoomed through the air again, fewer of them this time.

If Jonathan wasn't at the house with Sharon, perhaps he confronted her when she returned. Maybe he'd spied her car and had done his seething at home. Maybe he had let her have it when she walked in. Perhaps that was enough to shatter Sharon's inscrutable shield.

The little birds continued their sharp cries as they

swooped, while I continued my pacing. Something wasn't right.

Then, from far above the clouds, a dark shape shot through the sky. Straight as an arrow, a hawk took out the lead bird and sent the swallows scattering—and my theories with them.

Jonathan. What if Jonathan Bassett was the killer? Clearly, his wife's affair had given him reason to hate Mark. Did he confront Mark and kill him in a vengeful rage? Was this caring, solicitous attitude toward Amanda merely a ruse? Was he actually setting Amanda up? Delaying her from speaking with a criminal attorney until after she'd blundered with the police? Discouraging the investigators who were digging into Mark's relationships?

My heart pounded harder with this thought, a sure sign that there was something to it. I halted my pacing and turned to Amanda.

"Was Jonathan planning to see you again today?" I asked. "Do you have any other appointments?"

"No. I told Jonathan to call me after he spoke with Bob Carruthers." She peered at me. The shadows beneath her brown eyes made them look huge. "Kate, I can tell you're worrying about something. You're not thinking about Jonathan, are you? Surely you can't think he killed Mark?" Her face paled.

I carefully considered what I was about to reveal and decided it was more important to protect Amanda than spare her from a painful discovery of yet another indiscretion. "Amanda, I'm sorry to tell you this. I know how much you trust Jonathan. But I do believe Jonathan could have killed Mark. And that would explain why he lied about being there on Monday afternoon. He didn't want the police questioning him."

Amanda paled even more, if that were possible, and she swayed slightly on her feet. "Kate, surely you are mistaken," she whispered. "Why would Jonathan kill Mark? What reason would he have?"

I took a deep breath and prayed for guidance. "Sharon Bassett was having an affair with Mark, and she was planning on following him to Denver. She'd already filed for divorce from Jonathan."

Amanda wavered, then collapsed on the sofa behind her, obviously stunned. "My God, Kate," was all she said.

"Amanda, I wouldn't say something like this, if it wasn't true. I know it hurts. But you need to hear it."

"Are you sure?"

"Yes. Marilyn said that Sharon admitted the affair a month ago, right after she told Marilyn she was divorcing Jonathan. And when I met Sharon coming out of the lawyer's office last week, she told me she's still going through with the divorce. Even after Mark's death, she's still planning to move to Denver. Starting a new life, as she put it."

Laying her head back on the creamy leather sofa, Amanda stared at the ceiling. "Poor Jonathan," she said after a moment. "He adores Sharon. Worships her. And her money. It was Sharon's money which enabled them to live their luxurious lifestyle. What will Jonathan do without Sharon?"

I stared at Amanda for a moment, wishing I didn't have to be the one to say these things. Unfortunately, I didn't have a choice. Amanda was missing the big picture.

"Amanda, I think your sympathies are misplaced right now. We're talking about the man who may have killed your husband."

"Oh, Kate, that's not possible," she said, sitting up straight. "I know Jonathan better than you. He's too calm and controlled to do something like that. You're mistaken. You have to be."

Watching her try to convince herself as well as me, I felt sorry for Amanda. She'd used that selective blindness with Mark for so long, it was habit. She saw only what she wanted.

"I'm not suggesting Jonathan planned to murder Mark," I said. "Maybe he went there with the document first, then confronted him about Sharon. Maybe he killed in a moment of rage."

She thought about that one for a moment, I could tell.

"I don't know, Kate."

"Neither do I, Amanda, but until we know more, I think you should find any excuse you can to avoid having Jonathan over here alone. Offer to meet him at his office. Insist on it." Watching the stricken look in her eyes, I took another tack. "It'll do you good to go out, anyway. You've been hiding in this condo too long. Get out there. Promise me, okay?"

She nodded.

I glanced at my watch. "Make sure you don't mention what I've told you to anyone. Do you hear? That's an order, Amanda. I'm going to speak with Bill tonight. First, I've got to run. Got to take care of business."

Grabbing my purse from an end table, I headed for the door, paused long enough to throw Amanda an encouraging smile, then raced out. Meddling was not only life-threatening, it was also business-threatening. It was after 3:00 p.m. I needed to get back to my office and make several calls, plus check on the progress of my young buyers' request for repairs. The seller had until 12:00 tonight to sign and approve. If not, twenty-four hours later, the contract was null and void. Dead. And my young couple and I would start all over again. As hard as that was to explain to people, sometimes it was a good thing. Sometimes there was an even better house just waiting to be found.

As I jumped into my car and sped down the congested southern arteries of Fort Collins, my stomach demanded my attention. Rummaging through my briefcase, I found enough walnuts and almonds to quiet the hunger. Coffee I could find at the office, and I prayed Lisa hadn't been allowed near the pot.

Meanwhile, I tried to decide how best to present my suspicions to Bill. What evidence did I have? None. I had nothing except a document that showed Jonathan had been to Mark's house and obtained his signature. If questioned, he could easily say that he'd been to see Mark earlier. Hence, the signature and telltale date. It would be Jonathan's word against Amanda's.

That scene sent a chill through me. Amanda was definitely still at the top of Bill Levitz's list of suspects. Sending two detectives to interview was one of Bill's tactics. If it came down to Amanda against Jonathan, Amanda would lose.

I merged onto the heavier traffic of College Avenue, only a few blocks from my office now. There was one niggling thought that still bothered me about Jonathan going to Mark's house. It was the same doubt that shot down the idea that Jonathan had helped Sharon hide the murder.

Jonathan's car. His shiny, silver Acura. If he'd been at Mark's that afternoon, the kids would have seen the car. Heck, it would have been pretty crowded on those streets, what with Cheryl's white Rabbit, then Jonathan's Acura, blocking the skaters' fun. That definitely would have drawn their attention. And no one had mentioned a silver Acura.

Puzzling for a minute, I glumly admitted to myself that Jonathan could have easily met Mark somewhere else.

Hence, no Acura in the neighborhood. And once more, I was back at square one. And Amanda was nowhere. I turned toward my office parking lot and pulled into a space, the cold spot in my stomach growing much larger than my earlier hunger.

Chapter Twenty-One

"You want some?" Heather held up the coffee pot.

"Oh, please, yes." I eagerly thrust my mug across the desk. Bless her. She'd seen how I looked when I came into the office an hour ago and did the only thing she could, and it was good enough. Heather grinned as she headed down the hall, empty pot in hand.

I drank deep and wished Heather's strong coffee could take away the gnawing anxiety that still chewed at me inside. Even finding the seller's faxed acceptance of my buyer's repair request could not dispel it. Nor could the email from my out-of-town buyers that they were coming to town next weekend to search for their dream home.

This was bad. Real estate sales could usually cure any down mood. It was such a roller-coaster business that the ups and downs became addictive. You survived the lows just so you could experience the highs once more.

Unfortunately, this anxiety had nothing to do with business or with me. It was Amanda I worried about. I sensed Bill's net drawing closer and closer, and there was nothing any of us could do to help. Lord knows, I'd mucked around and meddled until I was up to my neck and beyond. Still, nothing I'd uncovered was conclusive enough to deflect Bill from his target.

I leaned back in my chair and glanced out the window at the sun, kissing the tops of the foothills. It would be sunset soon. Maybe I should just go home, curl up with Sam, and channel-surf. Listen to the CNN and CFN analysts debate world events and financial turmoil. And hide. Closing my eyes, I pictured just that—for about a minute. Then Amanda's face came back into view. So did an idea.

Reaching for my Day-Timer, I searched for Sharon Bassett's number and dialed. I was acting purely on instinct now. When she answered, I took a deep breath and plunged in.

"Sharon, this is Kate. How are you? Did I get you at a bad time?"

"Why, Kate," her surprised voice said. "I'm fine, thanks. And no, you didn't interrupt me. Is there anything I can help you with?"

Obviously, my occasional transparency had become aural as well as visual. "Well, uh, actually, there is, Sharon," I said, ad-libbing. "Marilyn, uh, just called me from the interstate. She's on her way to Denver for a new car. And she was thinking of buying a car like yours and wants to know how you like it. Said she saw you a couple of weeks ago driving out of Burgundy Acres and just fell in love with the car on sight. She's on her way to a dealership now and she forgot her address book; that's why I'm calling. You know Marilyn. When she wants something, she wants it now."

I shut my eyes, not wanting to picture Marilyn's frowning face when she learned of this tale. Her ears must be burning. Meanwhile, I waited for Sharon's reaction to the suggestion that she'd visited the Schusters' subdivision.

"Burgundy Acres?" Sharon said. "Why, no, Kate. It

wasn't me. I can't recall the last time I was that far south, except to head for the interstate. But, yes, I adore the Lexus."

"That's funny. Marilyn said she recognized your license plate." I winced in anticipation of the fussing I'd have to listen to for this presumption.

"Marilyn memorizes license plates?" Sharon's incredulous voice asked.

I had to admit that the image of Marilyn memorizing phone numbers was hard to swallow. License plates would be out of the question. It was a dumb suggestion, but I was desperate. "I know, it surprised me too, but you know how weird Marilyn can be," I replied in the only truthful statement I'd uttered so far.

Sharon paused. "Well, now you've made me curious. Let me think back . . . two weeks ago . . . two weeks ago. Goodness, Kate, that was the week Mark was murdered. Oh, my. That was an awful week."

I let her talk. I had no idea what might come out of this conversation. Was there still some part of me that believed Sharon was the killer? Was I hoping she'd slip and say something she shouldn't? Or was I trying one more time to connect Jonathan to the scene? Find something plausible I could take to Bill. Once again, I was rolling the dice. On the last roll, they had come up snake eyes. For Amanda's sake, I prayed Lady Luck would guide the dice this time.

"Well, yes, Kate, I do remember being in the south end of town that week, because I visited Amanda three or four times. But, I'm positive I was nowhere near Burgundy Acres."

I scooped up the dice again and gave them one last shaky roll. "Oh, well, maybe it was Jonathan she saw." I held my breath.

Sharon gave a mirthless laugh. "Not likely, Kate. I told him to stay away from my car. He's had three accidents in two years. You should see our insurance bills."

Crapped out. Damn. I rubbed my forehead and searched for some innocuous way to end this fruitless conversation. "So much for Marilyn's memory," I said. "Well, I'll call her back and—"

"Wait a minute. You know, Kate, now that I remember, Jonathan did take my car one day. It was scheduled for service, but I woke up with a headache. I was about to cancel when Jonathan volunteered to take it in. Can't remember which day. That whole week's still a jumble in my mind."

My heart skipped several beats. Breath caught in my throat, so I couldn't reply at first.

"That explains it," I said, trying to keep excitement out of my voice. "I'll call Marilyn right now and tell her you love the car. Thanks, Sharon. I, uh, I've got to go see a client. Take care now. Bye."

"Sure, Kate, anytime. Bye now."

As soon as she clicked off, I dropped the phone in its cradle. My heart was beating so hard, it resounded throughout my body. Maybe Lady Luck had finally smiled. I didn't dare entertain that hope yet. Not until I confirmed which day Jonathan Bassett used the gold Lexus. Reaching for the phone directory, I found the luxury car dealership and dialed the service number.

When they answered, I brought one more lie to my lips. "This is Sharon Bassett. I'm updating my insurance records and need to know what date our Lexus was last serviced. My husband Jonathan bought it in. Two weeks ago, I think."

"Certainly, ma'am," the man's voice replied. "What's your address and phone number?"

Checking my Day-Timer, I rattled off the information, then waited. "I usually bring it in, but I was sick that day. And of course, my husband can't remember things like that," I said in the tone wives often use.

"Looks like he brought it in Monday, September twenty-third, Mrs. Bassett. Seven-thirty in the morning. Early bird," he added.

This time my pulse raced so fast, a flush swept through me. "Thank you, thank you very much. I appreciate your help. Goodbye, now," I managed, before I clicked off.

I leaned back in my chair and stared at the foothills without seeing them, and willed myself to calm down while I sorted through my thoughts.

Jonathan Bassett was the killer. I no longer had any doubts. Picturing Jonathan's mid-life protruding belly, which even expensive tailoring could not hide, it wasn't hard to see him as Skater Greg's "funny, fat jogger." The jogger seen near the Schuster sidewalk had escaped in an expensive gold car, parked down the street. There was proof Jonathan drove the Lexus that day, and he went to see Mark. The initials on the list of collectibles proved that conclusively. And he lied about going. Why would he lie about something so insignificant, unless he had something to hide? Why, indeed?

Lastly, above all else, Jonathan Bassett had a motive to kill. Betrayed by his wife and facing financial ruin with divorce. Not to mention the public humiliation that would be his, once everyone discovered that Sharon had followed Mark to Denver, despite Mark's new marriage. Like some misguided middle-aged groupie following her favorite rock star. Jonathan's life was about to be diced and shredded in public for everyone to see, and it was all Mark Schuster's fault. Surely, Jonathan's hatred must have been white-hot.

I released a long sigh and felt muscles that had been tensed for hours give way. Finally, there was hope for Amanda. Now, all I had to do was find the best way to present this information to Bill. Pondering for a long minute, I decided to-heck-with-it, and reached for the phone. A funny, fat jogger seen near the Schuster sidewalk, who escaped in an expensive gold car parked down the street. I'd figure it out on the way over.

Chapter Twenty-Two

I maneuvered my Explorer through the familiar streets of my neighborhood. Sundown had already slipped into nightfall, and all I could think of was going home to relax. Eat real food for a change.

Bill had been unable to take my call. His pager seemed to be malfunctioning, the dispatcher said, and she had no idea when he'd return. Thankfully, she remembered me and said she'd leave him a message. That was the best I could do for now, and I was too exhausted to think anymore.

Unfortunately, as I rounded the corner toward my house, I realized my longed-for relaxation would have to wait. The notorious gold Lexus was parked in my driveway. By now, even I remembered the plates. I pulled my car beside the Lexus and got out, while Sharon Bassett did the same.

"Sharon, what a surprise," I said as she walked around her car. In the dark, it was hard to read her expression.

"Kate, can I talk to you inside?" she asked in a voice so soft I had to strain to hear it.

"Sure, Sharon, come on in. Sorry there's no light. I left so early."

I headed toward the front door, expecting Sharon to be

right behind me. Inserting my key into the lock, I turned and was surprised to see her back at her car. She leaned over the front seat of the passenger's side and withdrew a small suitcase before she closed her car and approached me. Good Lord. Did she plan to spend the night?

I opened the front door and flipped the nearby switch, illuminating the foyer, so I could scurry around and turn on lamps. Sharon followed me inside. The evening was so mild, I left the front door open. An excited bark and anxious whine sounded right outside the dining room screen door leading to my back yard. Poor Sam. He must be as hungry as I was. Hopefully, neither Sam nor I would have to wait much longer.

I gestured to the sofa. "Make yourself comfortable, Sharon."

"Kate, I can't!" she blurted, suitcase held to her chest. "I don't know what to do!"

Whatever inscrutability Sharon possessed was gone entirely. She looked genuinely terrified. "Sharon, please tell me what's the matter? You look petrified. What's happened?"

She swallowed. "Kate, could you repeat what you told me about the mysterious jogger those neighbors saw that day? The day Mark was killed."

A cold spot began to form in my stomach. "The neighbor said he saw a man jogging right outside the Schusters' house. He was dressed strangely, it seems, wearing a knit hat and gloves and sunglasses, even though it was a warm day." I deliberately left out the part about the expensive, gold car parked down the street.

Sharon sucked in her breath. "Did the neighbor say what color the jogging suit was?"

"Green. Dark green." I watched Sharon sway on her feet and almost reached out to steady her. "Sharon, what is it?

Why all these questions about the jogger?"

Instead of answering, Sharon gingerly set the suitcase on my antique walnut tea table. "A couple of weeks ago, I started going through closets, packing up clothes for Denver and taking things to the shelter for donation. I found this old suitcase in the back of the closet and tossed it in the giveaway pile in the trunk of my car. Then that afternoon Jonathan brought his mother home. She'd wandered away from the group home again, and they couldn't keep her anymore. So she had to stay with us until Jonathan could find a nursing home." Sharon paused, biting her lip. "It was chaos trying to care for her. I offered to help Jonathan, but he shoved me away. Said he could do it. Even though he had to stay awake every night with her, or she'd wander away. I don't know how he managed, because he was working nonstop at the office during the day. He was handling his firm's merger talks with a Denver group." She took a deep breath. "This morning Jonathan told me he'd found a place for his mother, then . . . then he asked me if I'd cleaned out the closets. I told him I had taken lots of things to the giveaway. He looked at me strangely for a moment, but didn't say anything. Later, when I actually delivered the clothes to the shelter, I decided I'd keep this suitcase to pack toiletries." Sharon stared at the suitcase, as if waiting for it to speak so she didn't have to.

I watched her stand silent for another few seconds, then I decided to help her finish this story. I had a bad feeling about that suitcase. "Sharon, I'm so very sorry about Jonathan's mother, but I sense that's not the reason you came over here tonight with that suitcase."

Sharon slowly unsnapped the suitcase locks. "When I opened it to start packing, I found these." Reaching inside, she withdrew a navy blue knit hat, a pair of black leather gloves, and the jacket of a forest green running suit.

232

I stared at the items, my pulse picking up speed. "Sharon, tell me again where you found this suitcase?"

"In the back of our bedroom closet, shoved way behind the other bags," she said, her voice cracking. "But there's more, Kate."

Daintily she pulled back the running suit pants to reveal more clothes beneath. A man's white shirt, red bloodstains dried and caked on the front. Sharon lightly touched what appeared to be a man's suit jacket beneath.

"That's Jonathan's. I recognize it," she whispered.

I caught my breath. Here was the proof we needed to connect Jonathan Bassett to Mark's murder. There was no way Bill Levitz could ignore this evidence. My heart pounded so hard, I thought it would leap from my chest.

"Sharon, we have to take this to the police. You know that, don't you?" I said as gently as I could.

She nodded. "I know, I know."

Suddenly, a cold voice sounded from the foyer. "Lucky I saw you getting into the car, Sharon."

Both Sharon and I jerked around, as if a master puppeteer had yanked our strings. I stared in horror at the sight of Jonathan Bassett pointing a gun right at us.

"You stupid bitch!" he snarled at Sharon. "You said you took everything to the shelter."

She sucked in her breath. "Jonathan," she squeaked. "You've never talked to me like that."

He sent his terrified wife a nasty smile. "Not out loud, I didn't. I didn't dare. But not anymore."

"Oh, Jonathan, you really did kill Mark, didn't you?" Sharon whimpered, cowering near the sofa.

"Yes, I killed your precious Mark. You disgusting little slut. I didn't plan to, dammit! I went over there and begged him to convince you it was over. He was getting married, for

God's sake! He could cut you loose, instead of letting you humiliate yourself and *me* by following after him like some bitch in heat!"

Sharon collapsed on the sofa, tears streaming down her face. Glancing toward the large living room window, Jonathan lowered his gun while he yanked the curtains closed. Damn. I'd hoped one of my neighbors might notice this lunatic waving a gun in my house.

"You know what that bastard did?" Jonathan's eyes took on a wild light. "He taunted me with your infidelity. Ridiculed me for not being able to keep you out of his bed. He said he'd grown sick of you long ago, but if you wanted to move to Denver, he wouldn't stop you. Then, he laughed. He *laughed* at me." Jonathan swayed slightly, waving the gun at his stricken wife.

"But I stopped the laughter. I grabbed the letter opener and rammed it in his throat." A cruel smile played on his mouth. "You should have seen the expression on his face when he realized he was dying. I pushed him back into his chair and held the knife until he stopped struggling. It didn't take long."

I shivered at the gruesome depiction, while Sharon sank her face in her hands and wept.

Jonathan sneered at her. "Did you really think I would let you walk off and leave me like that? Discard me like one of your unwanted dresses? After all those years of catering to your spoiled whims?" Sharon's sobs grew louder, which seemed to embolden Jonathan. "Pampering you, letting you have your way in everything, no matter what *I* wanted! Oh, no! It was always what *you* wanted. And I had to meekly go along. Even when you betrayed me with that bastard! And then you think you can just walk away? Take all your money out of our accounts, sell our properties, and leave me hanging by a financial thread?" He leaned over his sobbing wife and said in a menacing, soft voice, "I don't think so, my dear." And he tapped the gun lightly on the top of her head.

Sharon jerked up and shrank from the gun so close to her face.

Jonathan turned to me then, and the sight of his rage shook me. Whatever Jonathan had seething inside him was clearly bubbling over the edge now. Rage radiated from him. I could almost see it arcing over his head, shooting sparks. I sure as hell could feel it. And it was coming straight at me.

"And you. You meddling fool," he sneered. "If it weren't for you, the whole town would think Cheryl Krane killed Mark out of jealousy. Then killed herself. It was perfect! Everyone would have believed it. Then *you* had to stumble in!" He waved the gun at me.

I backed up. Outside the dining room screen door, I heard Sam's low growl. Obviously, the cataracts didn't obstruct Sam's view of the menacing man with a gun—in his house. I just hoped Jonathan was so enraged he didn't notice the black dog in the dark behind the screen.

"Why kill Cheryl?" I asked quietly, surprised how calm my voice sounded. Maybe if I could distract Jonathan enough, he wouldn't notice my inching closer to the patio door and my dog. "I can understand your hating Mark, but why Cheryl? What threat could she be?"

Jonathan smirked. "I'd seen her car parked in front of Mark's that afternoon, when I first arrived. I assumed she was begging Mark not to leave, pathetic little tramp. I wasn't about to interrupt that melodrama. So I parked around the corner. Besides, I was driving Sharon's car and everyone in town knew her car. And I didn't want rumors spread that *my* wife was begging Mark to stay. Cheryl was obviously used to humiliation. But not me. Gossipmongers like that cow, Marilyn, would have a field day."

"But why kill her?" I said again, and continued my re-treat—millimeter by millimeter.

"Because she was stupid enough to tell me she saw Sharon's car," he snapped. "I had mentioned casually that I'd been in the neighborhood and had seen her old wreck out-side Mark's. I admit, I couldn't resist twisting the knife." His lip curled. "She was always such a cold, aloof bitch. Always in control. I wanted to shake her, just once."

Strangely, I found Jonathan more threatening now that he'd calmed down than when he was frothing at the mouth in rage. The cruel delight he took in taunting a lonely woman was frightening. This was a side of Jonathan Bassett I never knew. Something about him had always made me keep my distance. Perhaps I sensed this ugly side. No wonder he'd gone over the edge when Mark turned the cruelty tables on him.

He continued, face darkening. "But instead of being em-barrassed, like any decent woman, the little tart snaps back that she wasn't the only one who visited Mark the day he died. She'd seen Sharon's car there as well. Once I heard that, I knew she had to die."

"Oh, Jonathan!" Sharon wailed.

Jonathan ignored her. He turned his cruel smile on me once more. "You thought you were so smart. Chasing clues all over town. But I kept track of your every move. As soon as you discovered something, Amanda would tell me all about it. Even the boy who saw me, jogging away in a disguise. Yes, she told me that too."

Searching for anything I could to distract him from what I could already see in his eyes, I probed again. "Why didn't you get rid of the bloody clothes? They're the only thing that can tie you to the murder. You were so clever. Keeping one step ahead of us all." Flattery never hurt.

He shot me a coldly condescending glare that froze my blood. "I didn't dare risk it here in Fort Collins. What if someone spied me dropping the suitcase in a dumpster, or even driving out to the landfill? All it would take would be one curious person, and those clothes would be in the lab and I'd be discovered. No, I had to wait until I could dump it in Denver." He sneered at his wife. "You can't believe how grateful I was, my dear, that you had taken everything to the donation box. I thought I was home free, until I drove home early and saw you leave the house."

"Jonathan," Sharon whined. "What are you going to do now?"

His cruel smile turned darker, if that was possible. "Well, now, Sharon, what do you think I'm going to do? Turn around and go home and let you go back to playing tennis every day, while I go to the office?"

Sharon just stared back, obviously paralyzed with fear. Meanwhile, I took the opportunity to move another two inches. I was off the carpet and on the tiled floor of the dining room, still a good six feet from the door.

"Stay where you are, Kate. Don't think I haven't noticed your movements. Did you think I'd actually let you run out that back door and escape?" He sent me an evil grin.

"What are you going to do, Jonathan?" Sharon whimpered.

"He's going to kill us, Sharon. Just like he killed Cheryl Krane." Trying to be stealthy hadn't worked. Maybe direct confrontation would. "You killed Cheryl because she knew too much. Now we know too much, so you have to kill us too. Right, Jonathan?"

"Nancy Drew figures it out at last," he sneered. "You're right. I'm going to shoot you both. The evidence points to

Sharon, not me. It will look like Kate's meddling got too close and cost her a bullet in the heart." He aimed toward my chest. "Then you, my poor, stupid, little Sharon. You will take your own life out of despair. One shot to the head should do it."

Sharon's whimpering grew louder. "Jonathan, you can't be serious! You wouldn't actually—"

"Shut up! Not another word. Get up off that sofa." He glared at me then. "I assume you have a television downstairs, since I don't see one here. Go turn on something noisy."

Jonathan turned from me just long enough to yank his cowering wife off the sofa and give her a vicious shove toward the stairs. It was only a few seconds, but I grabbed them.

I rushed toward the screen door, flung it wide, and screamed Sam's name as loud as I could. Sam bounded into the house with a ferocious snarl and lunged.

Jonathan stared in shock as a hundred pounds of enraged dog knocked him flat. The gun went flying through the air and I ducked. Sam clamped down on Jonathan's arm, and Jonathan let out an agonized shriek. Sharon fled out the screen door, into the back yard. She may have been screaming, too, but I couldn't hear her over the chaos in my living room.

Jonathan shrieked, Sam snarled, and I ran to grab the gun, grateful it hadn't discharged upon landing. Snatching it up, I aimed it at the man who was now writhing in pain on the floor, Sam spread-eagled above him. Good Lord. Sam must have bitten to the bone by now.

I knew I should try and help Jonathan, but I didn't know how. Sam had never attacked anyone in all of his twelve years.

"For God's sake, get him off me!" Blood covered Jonathan's shirt, as well as my carpet.

I grabbed the phone and punched in 911, while I held the gun steady. Surely the police would know what to do.

"Hang in there, Jonathan. Help is on the way," I said, as I heard the dispatcher come on the line.

Ronnie leaned back in her cushioned chair and smiled at me. "Has Bill talked to you since this morning? Is Jonathan still in surgery?"

I glanced over her shoulder toward the brilliant blue sky beyond. Colorado blue had never looked so good. "No, I haven't spoken to him since right before I went to lunch with Jeannie. And I haven't a clue how Jonathan's surgery went." I caught Ronnie's eye and sent her a wicked grin. "And you know what? I don't care. If you think I'm going to waste a minute of sympathy on that—" Ronnie's laughter stopped my rant before it even started. "Besides, Bill's already done the one thing I asked. To keep my name out of the newspapers."

"Goodness, Kate. I suppose regular real estate will seem tame for you now," she said, flipping open the file on her desk.

"Are you kidding?" I rose from the chair at the familiar sign that she needed to return to work. "I can't wait to deal with normal people once again."

"Normal people?" She laughed as she reached for her ringing phone. "Then you'd better get out of real estate."

I left her office and headed down the hall toward mine, grateful for the hundredth time since I'd awakened just to be alive. So far today, I'd felt the sun on my face, scratched my dog behind his ears, had lunch with my daughter, and even seen a look of sincere appreciation in my brother-in-law's eyes that very morning in his office.

My young clients were happy with the soon-to-be-theirs house. My older clients were coming into town, ready to retire. Life was good. So good, in fact, that I considered taking the afternoon off—head up into the canyon for some well-earned peace and quiet. *I couldn't find a more perfect day,* I thought. Then, I rounded the corner into my office and thought again.

Jake Chekov leaned against my desk. "Relax, Doyle. I just wanted to see how you were doing," he said with a smile. "Ronnie told me what happened."

I blinked, unable to conceal my surprise and my aggravation. Ronnie had promised not to say anything about my involvement in Jonathan's capture.

"Well, just for the record, Chekov, Ronnie did that without my permission," I said as I set my empty mug on the messy desk. "She promised she'd not tell anyone in the office, and Bill promised he'd keep my name out of the newspapers. So if I start hearing gossip, then I'll know it had to come from you. Just be warned, Chekov." I tried to scowl, but it was hard, because he'd started to laugh.

"Don't worry, Doyle. I won't blow your cover."

"You'd better not. Remember, you're the one who taught me how to shoot."

That really seemed to amuse him, and I had to admit the image of Chekov fleeing through the foothills like a frightened deer was kind of funny. To me, at least.

"I'm safe, then. Unless I get within ten feet of you, that is."

I actually managed a scowl, but he ignored it. "Don't mess with me, Chekov. I subdued a killer. With the help of my hundred-pound dog, that is."

He grinned. "Dirty Harry would be proud of you, Doyle. So am I. Listen, I was on the way up into Poudre Canyon. Ronnie suggested you might like to take a ride. You're welcome to come along. I promise I won't ask you to tell me about your adventures. Unless you want to, of course. And, yes, we can stop for coffee on the way out of town."

I stared at him, trying to figure out how we got from killer to going up into the canyon. Ronnie suggested he take me for a ride? What the heck?

"C'mon, Doyle. You look like you could use a little quiet time, sitting on a rock and staring at the Poudre River. I promise I'll have you back by dinnertime."

Okay, that did it. I had to do some serious work on this transparency thing. This guy had just read my mind. And if there was anyone I didn't want peering inside my head, it was Chekov. I was about to refuse his offer, politely of course, when I glanced over his shoulder and out my office window.

The foothills beckoned. And I needed to be there. With or without Chekov. "No questions, right?"

"Cross my heart." And he did.

"Okay, Chekov, you got a deal." I went around my desk and searched a lower drawer for the little, white sneakers I kept there. Shoving them and my purse inside my briefcase, I headed toward the door. Chekov was already waiting there.

"Ready?" he asked, his hand on the doorknob.

"Absolutely." I was halfway through the door, when I realized I wasn't quite ready to leave. I made an about-face and returned to my desk, all the while rummaging through my briefcase. Finally, my hand found what I was searching for.

I pulled out my cell phone and turned it off, then placed it on top of a stack of files in the middle of my desk. And without another word, I headed for the door and freedom.

About the Author

Maggie Sefton has worked for several years as a real estate broker in the Rocky Mountain West. As much as she enjoyed helping her clients find the perfect home, nothing has provided the continuing satisfaction and challenge of writing fiction and creating worlds on paper. Maggie lives in Colorado and is the mother of four grown daughters and the guardian of two demanding dogs. Visit Maggie's Web site at www.maggiesefton.com.